CLASH
OF
HONOUR

Other books by Robert Mendelsohn
published by Prion

Footsteps on a Drum
The Red Pagoda
The Hibiscus Trail

CLASH
OF
HONOUR
Robert Mendelsohn

PRION

Published in the United Kingdom by
PRION, an imprint of Multimedia Books Ltd
32–34 Gordon House Road, London NW5 1LP

A catalogue record for this book is available from the
British Library

ISBN 1–85375–143–X (paperback)
ISBN 1–85375–002–6 (hardback)

Typeset by Vision Typesetting, Manchester, UK
Printed in the United Kingdom by
HarperCollins*Manufacturing*, Glasgow

CONTENTS

—■—

To Rachel,

who married my father

PROLOGUE

—————■—————

BANGKOK, DECEMBER 1975

From under the mask of his smile, the driver watched her. Through his much-prized wide-angled mirror he saw every move she made. She was disturbed, and the waves of her anger flowed towards him as he kept half an eye on the road. He did not often get female passengers and usually he preferred men. Mostly they came looking for a good time and their misplaced guilt made them talkative. One could always sell them something: a steam bath or a companion and, later, some silk or even rubies for them to take home.

She was a tall woman whose hair was brown with flashes of red and her shapely, long legs seemed to fill the back of the car. Her hands kept pulling things out of her bag as her eyes shot daggers of green fire in all directions. He wanted to tell her not to take the crawling traffic too seriously, but she was a foreign woman whose posture and angry mood intimidated him. He had years of experience in driving *farang* into town and he knew what made them run. This woman had surely come to Bangkok to look for her husband in the massage parlour, to catch him out with a pretty Thai girl. He could read her like a book, but he had to watch the road for an open space.

The car moved. She could relax now, Anna thought. There was no call for any more planning; sleep a little maybe. But her hands remained shaky and her skin itched all over. She should have felt a little less agitated, she reasoned, as she dug into her handbag. She was well on her way to avenge his blood. It was only a question of time now; sit and wait for it to happen. Still she was uneasy, as if she had yet to start all over again.

1

Anna held the lighter with both hands and the flame caressed another cigarette. A shiver crawled up her spine, as she remembered the horror that started it all; the horror of Bang Saray. Now it was coming back again and images flew into her mind. Old pictures and sounds she never saw but knew so well. She coughed and she wanted to cry as resolve fought insecurity for possession of her soul. She grimaced and the driver with his sickening, perpetual smile said, 'We'll be moving soon.'

For ten years she had planned this. Fifteen, maybe more. The closer it got, the more she began to realize she was, perhaps, not hard enough; certainly not cruel enough to see it through.

She had lied to her husband. She had told him she was stopping in Bangkok one last time before leaving the Orient for good. She said she was going to stay a couple of days; do a little shopping, that's all.

She didn't tell him the truth. She didn't tell him how she would watch justice being done, where it all began; watch her enemy's screwed-up pride destroy him. Guilty? Was that the reason for her anxiety? Never. Why should she feel guilty? She was the wronged party, not him. He deserved all he was going to get and he expected it. It was the custom. His custom.

After this she would become herself, whatever that was, and she would live and learn to share and rely and trust and communicate and have no secrets ever again, nor lie. She would shed her deceptive walls and no one would ever accuse her of being detached and rejecting. She would not scream again in frustrated anger when in need of support; nor would she fake enjoyment while her soul was in hell.

She was, she now knew, well capable of love and she would prove it once the fears had dispersed. How much misery should she endure and dispense while avenging someone she hardly knew?

How dare she think that? Of course she knew him. She was his daughter.

She had come to look over the place where he had butchered her father, the coast at Bang Saray where it happened. And then she would be free.

Free? Could she ever be free of an obligation thrust on her by destiny? Not destiny. Her mother. Her mother did it all. Who else would dwell on pain forever and extend past suffering into the present?

A lifetime had passed since 1942, and the war had mellowed into an exhibit displayed in books and celluloid and public monuments in parks. It had become a thing that nagged one's conscience once a year while watching those elderly men and women passing the Cenotaph in grim salute.

Yes. But not for her such luxury. She had a duty to perform.

Bangkok's endless traffic was hacking at her patience and she was alone. It had been such a hassle to get through passport control and customs and into a taxi, and now they were planted motionless behind a million overstacked, shabby trucks. They were all – the buses and the cars and the bikes – going into town. The road had become a diesel-fumed parking lot. She was frozen because the air-conditioning worked too well and all she was wearing was this flimsy little dress exposing her limbs. Outside, layers of dust rode in the sizzling air and she did not open the window.

There were red and gold and turquoise temples on the roadside, their pagoda tops pointing at a cloudless mid-morning sky. There were palm trees and dusty banana and hibiscus plants. She looked at the half-naked children sitting in the muddy waters of the *klong* and she knew the air outside was on fire. What a place to die in, she thought, and the familiar pain came up her chest and numbed her throat. The car jerked forward and she sucked at her cigarette. The warm, sweet poison soaked into her lungs and her head felt heavy. A burning ember tore a painful hole into the polyester above her knee.

Her father was much younger than she was now when he packed up to go to war. She knew his house and his chair and his desk and his books and his old photographs. She knew his clothes, too, because her mother had kept them all. Embossed somewhere within her were those long-gone reassuring moments of his warmth and his love.

She could not possibly have remembered any of that from the age of three or four, yet between the realms of imagination and memory there was that vague scent of sweat he must have had when he came home in the evening, and she would race to him, her mother said, as soon as he had opened the gate. Later he would put her to bed, her mother said, never missing a night, his hair still dripping from his bath. He would tell her stories and sing and sing to her until she dropped off to sleep.

'Twinkle, Twinkle Little Star', her mother said, was her favourite, and Anna had willed herself to remember trying to stay awake longer to make him sing more.

She knew all the words and the smells and sounds, but how? That same soap was still in use in the house, but what about the rest? How could a toddler retain that much?

4

The whole thing was crazy. She had adopted her mother's memory, not her own.

She had adopted her mother's love, her mother's hates and obsessions. And now she had acted on her mother's impulse.

Her father's name had been Derek Pritchard and he was pale, green-eyed with auburn hair which fell carelessly about his forehead. He had long eyelashes and thin brows and bony cheeks that spread into a boyish smile every time he looked at her. She knew he had been a tall man because she had tried on his Aquascutum raincoat when she was fifteen. There were a few photographs of him in uniform and a small reel of black and white moving pictures. They had to borrow a projector from Wallace Heaton's since the gauge of the film had been out of production for years.

She had read his letters and his verses. All that she was told and what she thought she remembered had gelled and fermented inside her to become part of her.

What was missing most from her memory was the sound of his voice. She knew it had made her feel warm all over, but she could not remember it.

'Twinkle, Twinkle Little Star'. She remembered the song and the other songs, but she had forgotten his voice.

And that was all that was left of Derek Pritchard, and now she was going to see where he had died. Not to know it, because she already knew. Just to see it, and then sit back and wait.

There must have been an accident up ahead. The taxi stopped its exasperating motion and came to a halt. She should really get out and walk. She needed a shower and some sleep before meeting the other man.

The driver watched her and he wanted to calm her

down and tell her all this was part of life here. Too many cars and not enough roads. But the livid expression on her face stopped him. He wouldn't even get to suggest a dressmaker's shop or a trip to the floating market. She was too tense and did not look the type. She would, he knew, feel better once she caught up with her erring husband, and he chuckled to himself as he imagined the scene of her pouncing on him. Then a long empty slot opened in front of him and he raced into it, nearly killing an old lady who tried to cross the road.

The car moved and this time it kept moving. She thought she had slept for a bit. She was tired because the duty she had been charged with had taken a long time to complete, ever since she was told how her father had died at Bang Saray by the seaside, right here in Thailand, out of the way of the war and for nothing. Lieutenant Keichi Katsumata of the Imperial Japanese Army had killed him, and not in battle. Jimmy Hedges said he had and Jimmy Hedges was a doctor and her father's friend and much, much more. And he knew because he had been there when it happened.

Katsumata had cheated on her, but his punishment was on its way and it was going to be devastating.

'Katsumata,' she said out loud, and the driver heard and looked and thought she had smiled as she spoke. Perhaps she was at last feeling better. He was, for sure, now that the car was threading its way through the metal jungle at an uninterrupted, increasing pace. If the gods were smiling on him, he could make the trip one more time before the day was out.

Book 1

War And Honour

CHAPTER ONE

Spain was in his bones and he had vowed to go back there as soon as it became free again. There was something in its music and its soil, its hot summers and freezing winters that had seduced Derek Pritchard.

He loved Spain and had answered her call. He loved her enough to ignore the hissing shells and the piercing lead that came at him. There had been severed limbs and much blood and the dying groaned in many tongues.

The bright young men of the International Brigades were on the run. They were bleeding to death along with the budding Spanish Republic they had come to save.

They came from factories and shipyards and ports and from far-away farms.

Some came from universities in Berlin and Budapest and Paris, and they fought by day and sat by fires at night and sang and dreamed. Derek Pritchard had come from Cambridge, and while the night was alight with dynamite, he wrote letters and poems and took part in world-saving discussions. And then, in the midst of slaughter, he met Antonia Maria Aguilar de Soto and loved her.

He saw her first during a lull in the fighting. It had been a particularly cruel day which had mercifully come to an end. They were sitting about the rocks in the eerie silence sharing a scant meal, and he turned around and their eyes met. He looked at her and saw her small stature and her burning eyes and thought she looked like a gypsy. He offered his plate to her and he said:

'Have my share of the rice. I am not hungry.'

'A soldier is always hungry,' she said with a smile that

lit up her face.

'Oh no, I have eaten,' he said. 'On the way back from the village I plucked a water-melon. I had it all to myself.' He pushed his hair away from his forehead and she saw his vacant eyes. 'Go on, eat it,' he insisted, and handed the plate to her. He did not tell her about the corpse he had seen, that humiliating end of a once-living man that had made him retch and took all thought of food away from him.

Three times he had seen it, propped by the village church, its dead eyes gazing at the one remaining gargoyle on the roof. It was the body of a Fascist who was eating his lunch when the Republicans struck. The French sniper shot him right in his heart and he died looking up with a piece of bread in his mouth. The birds, ignoring the shooting, nibbled at the bread during the first day, and overnight the rats decimated his boots. He had swollen in the morning heat and looked like a bloated carnival figure when the Rebels had taken the village back in the afternoon of the second day. By the time Derek's company returned on the third, the corpse resembled an inflated Sancho Panza, its head still looking up, the boots and most of its feet gone, the waxy legs exposed to the sun. The village had changed hands many times that week and no one bothered to bury it. Gasoline was too scarce for an incineration.

Derek was pleased he could offer his food to someone because it was in short supply and he could not touch it, and he thought the woman could because she had not been to the village nor seen the dead Fascist.

It would have made no difference because she had seen death before and had hardened to it. She was new to their

9

ranks and knew no one. They were foreign and they looked different, but she took the plate because he had been friendly and his welcome made her think of the friends she knew before the High Command sent her to join this company.

The man she missed most was a working man, a plumber from Toledo. He had been born in the village of Real de San Vicente and his father had been a builder. He had joined the Republicans the same week she did and he was twenty-one years old, the same age as she. The others, mostly better educated than him, often looked down on him, yet he slept with them and starved with them and fought with them. He had his own ancient gun and packed his own ammunition. He was the best shot among them. He was good with his hands and could repair anything. He was a very small man and his gun was very long. Walking about with the killing instrument on his shoulder, he looked like a miniature Don Quixote carrying a lance.

The plumber from Toledo talked a lot and could imitate accents spoken in every province of the country. He could make speeches that sounded like Primo de Rivera and was especially good at doing the *Caudillo* himself. He was a gentle young man who did not brag or drink or swear or spit and he told clean jokes. He was especially close to her and told her things. He told her about his sick mother to whose bedside he would often go in the night. He would always be back at the crack of dawn and never complained when ordered to dig trenches or to wash the wounded. All the time his shooting improved, and they were going to promote him and make him a sniper as soon as a new gun could be found for him.

Then they found out he had been an informer. She never knew how they had found out because she did not believe it and did not listen. A spy? Not a man with his background. In the discussions that followed, she fought for him like a tigress. She was his lawyer and his sister and his priest while the others ran a mock trial to declare him guilty. Until the last moment, Antonia Maria argued and screamed and ranted, and then he told her quietly to stop. With a measure of relief and pride, he said they had been right. He was, he said, a Franco man from the start. He did not have a mother or a father. They were both killed by the Republicans at the beginning of the war and he was her enemy all along. He said the Rebels were going to win and shouted 'Arriba Franco' and pronounced he was glad to die for Spain. He called them all red swine who brought blood to the country, blood the same colour as their flag.

When the trial was over, the little plumber who could have become a sniper and a hero was condemned to death. The committee ordered her to shoot the man herself because she had defended him so passionately. She was told to do it quickly because they were moving on.

The little plumber asked her to use his own gun. He was put against a wall and refused to have his eyes covered, but asked for a priest. There was no priest among them and they laughed at the thought of it. They told Antonia to take his gun, load it and shoot him. She had seen him prime the weapon and load and aim and shoot it many times. He was so proud of his gun and it was kept clean.

He stood by the wall and looked her straight in the eye as she aimed.

'Shoot to kill, you red whore!' he screamed. It was the first time she had ever heard him raise his voice or curse. She was tired, and she had tears in her eyes and could hardly see. She knew he wanted to anger her to make it easy for her. She was sad, not angry, as she took aim and shot him between the eyes and he died instantly.

During the week that followed the execution, the group was all but decimated in a surprise attack by Moroccan regulars and she was sent to join the International Brigades. Ten days after catching up with them, she met Derek and he offered her his plate of rice. She did not tell him about the plumber. All she did when they talked was to tell him what had made her join the Republican side.

Antonia Maria Aguilar de Soto was not a run-of-the-mill revolutionary. She was barely twenty when, in mid-July 1936, the Nationalists rose against the Republic, backed by the regular army. She had been working in the family bookshop on the main street of Valencia. Hers was the comfortable life of a middle-class family in which no one was particularly involved in politics. Her father was a conservative who defended the King's faulty policies, which he put down to bad advice. When the revolt started, the city of Valencia remained on the Republican side of the conflict. The God-fearing Señor Aguilar did criticize the anti-clerical policies of the Republic and the sackings of churches by the mob, but only to his friends and family.

The war raged far from them in the early days of that summer. There were enthusiastic banner-carrying students and anarchists and workers in the streets; there were slogans and discussions, but these hardly interfered with their lives and people still bought books.

Once or twice a year, the family drove their car up the coast to Castellón de la Plana, then through the wine-growing *Priorato* of Tarragona and up the mountain road towards the Aragon hills and the town of Fraga. There, amongst the fig-strewn hills close to the town, they owned a small house and a few *cuadradas* of land on which grew olives, figs and some almonds. The house was sparsely furnished, but homely and cool. The neighbours, a farmer and his wife, kept the property clean and opened the windows in winter in exchange for the crops and for permission to grow onions and potatoes and beans between the olive trees. It was a satisfactory arrangement to all because there was always enough produce left for the Aguilars to eat once the neighbours were told they were coming.

Antonia Maria and her brothers, Manolo, eighteen at the time, and Pedro, sixteen, would go down the hill to swim in the cold stream a mile away. There was only one meal, at night, when the family said grace and dined by candlelight. It was there that Antonia learned to bake and cook and preserve, having spent hours watching the neighbour's wife at work.

As the Civil War continued, the Aguilars started feeling the pinch. The shop was still busy, but it was difficult to obtain books and Antonia's father had to dip into his savings to supplement their income. One day in September, he unexpectedly announced they were going to the country for their holiday. He had managed to secure enough petrol from a garage owner who owed him money. The postcard to the neighbours was duly sent and, at four o'clock in the morning of the appointed day, the family set off through the deserted streets. They had coffee and bread and cheese in a small café near Tortosa and arrived at the house in the late afternoon. The vegetables and fruit, two slain chickens, a jar of butter and another of marmalade on the kitchen table testified to the neighbours' prosperity. Manolo said they had thrived because of the war.

It seemed someone had stayed in the house shortly before they arrived. The oven, although out, was still warm and there was clean water in the basin. The cutlery, washed and dried, was on the table along with a packet of foreign cigarettes depicting a red-bearded sailor on the front. The ham they had hung in the loft during their last visit was cured and ready and someone had cut a bit off, carefully covering the end with a clean sheet of writing paper. Another packet of cigarettes lay there. Nothing much was said about this, and the boys were ordered to gather wood and light the oven.

After their lunch the next day, Antonia went down the hill to bathe in the stream as she always had. The sun had crossed the mid-sky mark and she luxuriated in the water as she listened to her brothers chatter in the woods above. The afternoon belonged to her and, as she dressed, she decided to pay the neighbour's wife a visit. Their house was a little way on the other side of the stream and Antonia whistled a popular song as she crossed the tatty wooden bridge.

The first shells started falling into the valley just before she reached the neighbour's fence. There were machine-gun volleys and in her father's olive groves behind the stream lumps of earth and dust flew and burning trees mushroomed into the sky.

The farmer stood by his door as the valley shattered and urgently beckoned her inside. The shells kept falling closer to her father's house and for a while it looked as if someone was protecting it from devastation. No one said a word until the neighbour's wife started screaming. Antonia hugged her to comfort her and then the woman screamed louder, pointing at the hill. Antonia turned around to see a small flame coming out of the roof of her father's house. The boys must have put too much wood in the soot-laden hold. Must be the oven, she thought, but the flames kept getting bigger and then, through the smoke, she saw the house itself. The roof had gone and there were flames coming out of the windows. She saw figures running out of the house towards the dirt road. The shelling had stopped, giving way to more machine-gun fire, and then she saw the soldiers. In determined, organized lines, they ran down the hill towards the people who came out of the burning house.

'Get into the car!' she shrieked. 'Get into the car and drive away.'

The soldiers were moving through the groves and in the tall maize fields. She could see them clearly, but the fleeing figures could not because they were heading straight for the column.

Antonia turned to run down to the stream and back up to her house, but the farmer came after her and he and his wife held her back.

'You can do nothing for them now,' he said softly. 'As soon as the soldiers realize who your family is, they will leave.'

Still she was struggling and wrestling and, being a strong young woman, she nearly managed to slip away from them when the farmer hit her head with his enormous fist. She fell to the ground, but did not faint. She just lay there holding back her tears and shivering.

On the other side of the valley, the soldiers had caught up with her family along the dirt road.

The neighbours took her in, apologized and comforted her with a potent glass of red herbal wine and burning brandy. She coughed and she cried and they gave her more, and then the farmer's wife brewed a cup of strong camomile tea to calm her down. That evening, she heard them put up the shutters and lock the doors and heard them talk about the three foreign Republicans who spent the night in Señor Aguilar's house. She could hear them, but she felt numb. They said the soldiers were sure to let Señor Aguilar go as soon as they met him. He certainly did not look like a Republican or a student or a Communist. She wanted to agree with them, but she fell asleep, and with sleep came a peace that stayed with her until morning.

She woke with the sound of the cock and the piglets and the barking of dogs at the back of the house. The farmer and his wife were already sitting at the table, and she joined them for a cup of coffee and bread dipped in olive oil.

'It is quiet,' the farmer said. 'The soldiers have left. You can go back now, if you are ready, and I shall come there with you.'

Antonia's head was as clear as the morning and they waved to the farmer's wife from the gate and started down towards the stream. The air was cool and her bare ankles felt the dew in the grass. Smoke was still filtering out of the ruin that had been her father's house.

Her brother Manolo had perished in the flames, his charred body slumped by what was left of the oven. The car had been turned over and left intact, save for the clock on the dashboard. Someone had chiselled that out. They found Pedro's body just short of the dirt road, and the farmer carried him into the olive grove and laid him down by the well. Next they found Señor Aguilar's body, his face buried in the earth. He was a big man and it took the farmer some time to carry him down to where his son lay.

Antonia found her mother's naked body in the maize field. She had been raped and her throat slit open, and her daughter fainted by her side. When she came to, she found herself by the well with the farmer and his wife and two other farmers standing over her. She rose and she looked at the bodies and she cried bitter tears, and then she stopped.

'We'll bury them here,' she said, and the farmer protested. They had to be taken down to God's little plot, he said, to be blessed by the village priest before being returned to the earth.

'No,' she said. 'They will be buried here because there is no God. Not here nor there by the cemetery.'

The farmers looked at each other, talked a little, and then they agreed.

On that September Monday in 1936, the first year of the war, Antonia left the village in search of the Republican forces. She gave the neighbour the car and told him the land was his, and he gave her all the money he had in the house, a bundle of food and some clothes and a bicycle. She rode east towards Catalonia and she did not look back.

Some time later, a seasoned fighter, an expert in explosives and a nurse, she was sent to the rocky outcrop where Derek Pritchard and his company were having their supper. Her life, she often said, was just about to begin.

CHAPTER TWO

She always maintained she saw him first. She said she could describe his back, the way it looked as he sat trying to eat. She remembered his expression as he turned round and caught her eye. He offered her the food and she sat down, took his spoon and his plate and she ate.

He spoke an educated Spanish in which his accent and the local jargon blended into classless expressions that appealed to her and made her laugh. Lorca's ideas streaming out of a pale, foreign, Jesus-faced young poet with the courage of El Cid. He was, to her, a hero because he had come from far to fight her war for her and did not expect her gratitude.

She had by now become, like the others in their ranks, free of inhibition. Life was fast and dangerous and often short. The Spanish women of the Republic had stepped out of the shadows. Along with the men, they fought and spoke their minds and listened to fiery speeches made by the leaders about progress and the future and free love.

Antonia joined the ecstasy. She and Derek walked the hills and their bodies shared grass mattresses in caves and dugouts and ruined houses. She allowed herself to float down an enchanting, passionate stream of freedom. She became permanently attached to the company and she repaired their shoes, assembled their homemade bombs and cooked and washed and dressed wounds and, when Derek was in camp and not fighting, she never, never left his side.

The memory of that September was pushed back into an uncharted part of her mind. Derek had become her present and future and had taken over her past. She watched him, always, and saw into his soul and knew what he had become, and she wanted the world to know his talents and his sensitivity and valour. She saw him inject enthusiasm and a fighting spirit into his comrades, transforming that hesitant, theory-laden flock into a superior fighting force. He led fearless attacks through minefields, and yet he cried like a child when the French sniper recited Baudelaire after the shooting was over. He always cried alone and only she saw him because she could never take her eyes off him. He taught newcomers how to read field maps and at times, while they listened to music from a Russian-made radio receiver, he talked about democracy, how it had at last come to Spain and had to be defended. She knew how timid he really was and admired his ability to conceal it. Slowly, as time went by, in bits and pieces she found out more about him.

His father had been an industrialist who owned steel and cotton mills and made railway carriages. He was a strong, autocratic man and young Derek called him 'Sir'. He and Derek's mother spent their summers in Biarritz, where he indulged in his passion for gambling. He was not a real gambler nor a good one because he hated to lose.

Derek saw little of his parents. He had been sent to a boarding school from the age of six and spent occasional weekends with the butler and his wife. When he was at home his father was always out at an office or a plant, and his mother rose late in the mornings since her evenings were laden with massive social obligations. Derek was mostly left alone. He felt his mother was not too comfortable with him while her guests were around because he did not excel at tennis or croquet, nor did he willingly converse much or laugh in the right places. He found solace in the company of books and had read most of Dickens and Wordsworth by the time he was twelve. He had a weakness for poetry. He felt a verse could say more to him than a complete volume, in that it expressed a mood or a feeling in a few words that needed no explanation or detail.

His mother's lifestyle didn't change. Not even when 1929 came. There were arguments in the house and slammed doors. That ended in 1931 when his father shot himself having been declared bankrupt.

His mother was in St Moritz at the time and did not come back for the funeral. The family home was sold, and Derek only saw his mother once after his father's death, getting into a taxicab outside the Café Royal in Regent Street. He was left a small legacy which was put in trust for him until his twenty-first birthday. He could use the income from it until then. His mother had remarried and he saw her name and face in the *Tatler* from time to time.

Derek told Antonia he had read about his mother's death while he was in Spain. The obituary never said what she had died of.

In the spring of 1937, Antonia found she was with child. They were in the city of Barcelona at the time, and Derek took her to the British Consulate where they were married. The anticipation of becoming a father and his anxiety over Antonia's health ignited a new, mature excitement in him. His main concern had now become the family he was about to have. The war, he argued, was over for them. The Republic was not using the International Brigades as effectively or as often as it should. It was time to bow to convention. There was, at that moment, a raw strength and sense of purpose to his demeanour, and Antonia accepted his decision. She accepted, too, her new role as a wife and mother-to-be. That short, fierce, mad summer of her youth was over. There was little left for her in Spain now.

They found space on a cargo ship out of Barcelona harbour. As it sneaked through Franco's scant blockade towards Marseilles, they looked at the disappearing city under a starry sky. He held her close and promised her they would be back, they would return as soon as Spain was free again.

CHAPTER THREE

He settled down to earn a living in the City of London, far from the rocky barren hills of battle. He travelled to Waterloo each day by commuter train and walked across the Thames to a grey, impersonal office. He talked to grey, impersonal voices about bonds and shares and certificates. In the late afternoons, he put his bowler hat on to join other home-bound faces across the same bridge.

He had a little piece of Spain waiting for him in the suburbs and he had a little English daughter blessed with an infectious smile. There was green tranquillity all around him, but he did not forget where he had first met his wife. The neighbours got used to her accent and took to calling her Toni. She spoke English quite well and wore tweeds and sensible shoes. To him, she was still Antonia Maria with that long, romantic, tongue-rolling surname. He would declaim it to himself. Antonia Maria Aguilar de Soto. Aguilar de Soto. De Soto. He'd say it faster and faster and it sounded like the echo of the rails being hit by the steel wheels on his way home. He would hear her name everywhere.

Later, she swore allegiance to the Crown and her loud Latin spirit simmered down. She never spoke Spanish to him, save sometimes in the cold winter nights she would rip his back and squeeze his body between her knees and call him *'querido'* and *'mi amor'*. Then, with her exploding passion and sweat, she would become Antonia Maria Aguilar de Soto again. He would watch her spent little body shake and arch one more time against his, then subside into sleep. In her sleep, she did not speak at all. She did not dream when they were safely together, his body locked into hers.

Having adopted England as her own, she settled down to house and garden and the Sunday roast. She was to bring Anna up in the Anglican faith and play English games with her. She struggled through *Country Life* and she queued patiently by the bus stop and in the shops. She never spoke of Spain and Derek knew it was because she missed it.

He gave her his pay packet every other Friday. He opened an account at the local bank for her and taught her how to write cheques. With his salary and the small legacy he had, they could live well. They could afford a car or even to go on occasional holidays to the Continent. But Toni would have none of it because Anna was destined to be sent to the best schools and they were going to need the money when they were old. In reality, she wanted him to get away from the office he hated and was saving for that.

They read books from the library and sometimes they sat in the gods to watch a play. In later years, her daughter would think her stingy, while her neighbours admired her prudence.

Sometimes they took a train to the coast on a cheap excursion ticket. They bought ice-cream cones if it was a warm day, and walked along the pier and watched the sea. It was far from the Mediterranean that washed her country's southern coast, and if she missed it, she didn't say. She baked and she cooked and she painted the fence and cut the lawn. She washed and ironed his shirts and mended his socks. She polished the silver, but rarely had occasion to use it, and she made and secretly sold herbal wines and cold remedies. And all the time, while Derek learned to be a stockbroker without much success or desire to attain it, Anna was growing up and learning to speak.

She grew into a pretty little girl who inherited his colouring and her mother's skin. She laughed when he made faces at her and was silent and stern-faced when she felt he wanted peace. She was always beautifully turned out and even agreed to wear hated itchy dresses when her mother said it was for Daddy. She'd sit by the window at the end of her afternoon nap, her long, auburn hair in place, her green eyes watching the gate for his approach. As soon as the gate opened, her face would light up and she'd run to fly into his arms and hug his neck and he would kiss her and know life was worth living. She'd ask him how his day was and tell him of hers and always mumble secrets into his ears. These were little worries she had and she said he must not tell, and he'd laugh and give her advice and promise it was all between them and no one else.

She was barely three, but he would talk to her in a grown-up fashion and he felt she understood. Soon, he'd confide, Daddy will not go to any office but stay at home with her and Mummy and he would write.

'Why not tomorrow?' she would ask, and he said because no one wanted to buy what he wrote.

'Mummy said you write so well,' she'd say.

'But other people must like what I write too,' he'd answer, and stroke her hair and tell her how people needed money to stay at home. Well, she could pay because she had a lot of money in her piggy bank.

He never laughed at her and at night, when she was asleep, he'd come into her room and look at her and feel she knew he was there.

At weekends, he told her stories and she drew pictures for him. They worked with Toni in the kitchen garden, and he taught her how to ride her little tricycle and they picked apples and strawberries when in season. He did not really want her to be sent away to school, but then, he thought, there was time enough for that.

Outside their world, time raced. New maps were being forcibly drawn across Europe, calling for new battles to be fought. The authorities did not know he had been in the Spanish War, and in mid-1940, Derek was drafted into the army. He was relieved to be out of his drab office and gratefully exchanged the documents and the figures for training.

In early 1942, Lieutenant Derek Pritchard found himself in Singapore, watching the Empire catch fire.

The politicians in London did not take the Japanese seriously. They were all seen as short-sighted dwarfs who could not fly a plane at night. Singapore was a fortress that would never fall. Yet fall it did, and the Japanese, riding through the Jungles on bicycles, proved they could shoot straight. Raffles Hotel, with its afternoon teas and gin slings, shut its doors to the Raj and waited for the new masters of Asia to come out of the smoke.

It was like Spain again, but shorter. The losing battle he was fighting this time was for his own country. No troops came from England, where they were needed closer to home. Those who could leave the island sailed off to Australia and some, whose ships were not sunk on the way, arrived. Derek Pritchard took no part in the last struggle for the city. He could not find his unit and was wandering the streets when the shooting stopped. He looked in vain for a departing ship, and people said the Japanese were going to kill everybody. He felt guilty about the Chinese and the Indians and the Malayans caught up in a battle between far-away combatants, and he walked about until he found an open bar downtown. He sat at a table outside to write one last letter to Toni back in England. With a photograph of her and little Anna and a glass of hot beer, he wrote and said he was not sure when this would reach her. He described the agony and the devastation and the aimless people in the streets. He wrote her this temporary farewell, he said, because he was not sure what would happen now. The Japanese are bound to ship us all somewhere, he wrote. There's no room for all these troops on this tiny island. The Japanese cannot feed us here. He ended the letter by saying he would try and write when he knew what was happening. '*Más tarde mi amor*, but for now it was '*adiós mi corazón*'.

CHAPTER FOUR

A heavy hand touched his shoulder and he looked up. He saw the vaguely familiar face of a medical officer smiling down at him. The man had a full head of thick red hair and a large freckled face with a smoking pipe in the middle of it. He pointed at the letter.

'You might as well stuff it into an empty bottle,' he said. 'Drop it somewhere into the South China Sea. That way it might reach England now that the post is dead.'

Derek folded the letter and placed it in his pocket. He struggled to put face and voice and uniform together.

'Do you remember me?' the jovial face asked. 'Hedges. Jimmy Hedges. You're Pritchard, aren't you?'

Then it came. 'Yes, of course,' Derek said, and motioned to Hedges to sit down. 'Cambridge, wasn't it?'

'Where else?' Hedges said. 'Why don't you join me at the bar? It's too hot here, while there the fan's still hard at work. It seems the Japs haven't cut the electricity off yet.'

Derek nodded and got up. Slowly, the past came back to him. The distant past. Long before this war and the one in Spain. A slice of that old, naive time when people thought dreams and ideas could become reality. Long before the defeats. There was something unpleasant about trying to remember Hedges, and as they reached the bar and settled down and the doctor ordered their drinks, he began to recall. He was, Derek remembered, thought of as a fascist and a prig and he did not go to Spain. They said he had actually visited Nazi Germany and had admired Franco and Mussolini.

But there was more. Another embarrassing memory was trying to enter his mind but he could not recall what it was. He had not seen anyone he knew of late, and this was a time of collapse and capitulation. Perhaps his last day as a free man. The war would be over for him now, and with the thought of captivity looming over the little bar, he elected not to examine the past too closely.

They sat facing the fan and made small talk. They did not discuss Cambridge or Spain and slowly the echoes of forgotten dislikes faded. Above the bar hung an ornamental parrot cage. The little bird jumped about and Derek addressed the barman.

'Why don't you let it fly back to the jungle?'

'I have paid a lot of money for it,' the barman said. 'Anyhow, it wouldn't find its way now.'

'A tree is a tree. The parrot will be happier out in the air.'

He bought the bird from the barman and opened the cage. The parrot hesitated for a bit then flew out towards the window and disappeared.

'You're out of your mind,' Hedges said. 'The thing's going to die for sure now. It's been locked up and fed in there for years. It could never survive out there, you know.'

'You are wrong, Hedges. Did you see how quickly it flew out? It yearns for its freedom.'

'You must be suffering from a depression.'

Derek put a few more coins on the bar.

'That I understand,' Hedges said. 'We won't have much use for money where we're going. Might as well be led out of here drunk.'

Derek's letter was still in his pocket when both he and Jimmy Hedges were pulled off their stools by a Japanese squad. The medical man insisted on finishing his drink and was beaten a little and prodded by bayonets into the street. With the absence of cars and horses, the city seemed dead. There were flames all over and they heard sporadic shots.

As they left the bar, the parrot came flying back. Only Hedges saw it.

As they were led along the sidewalks, there were glances from puzzled bystanders. The shock of watching British soldiers at the mercy of an Oriental enemy was visible.

'They are quite pleased to see us go,' Hedges said. 'They'll soon find out what their new masters are like.' He was going to say something else, but one of the soldiers hit him and another screamed something. Hedges stopped, looked down at both and then walked on in silence. They were taken into a military barracks in the centre of town. There was a Japanese sentry at the gate, under a large flag of the Rising Sun.

'They don't waste much time, do they?' Jimmy whispered. 'If we were as disciplined as these buggers, we would be locking them up now. There are more of us than them here, you know.'

Derek only listened to the night and imagined the sound of crickets. They were taken into a little room and pushed inside. The door slammed shut behind them. Outside they heard the rhythmic steps of the sentry. More shots were heard from nearby and Jimmy said people were being executed.

'We'll have to acquire some ruthlessness if we want to survive this war,' he said.

'*Querida*, I cannot tell you what my feelings are,' Derek wrote to Toni. He did not put it on paper. He stored the words in his mind that first oppressive night. 'I have never been locked up, but I recall the feeling. It almost makes me think of sitting in my office, but then there was you and Anna to come home to. There is nothing to look forward to here. I have seen despair before, but then you were there. I am locked in here with a Cambridge man whose nature is different to ours. I remember him vaguely from there. I know there is something we had once shared in those days. Could be hate – I don't remember. Something about him makes me feel ill at ease and on my guard, but that very feeling saves me from sinking into depression. I hope I never remember what it was and pray it won't drop in on me unannounced. If he knows what it is, he is not saying. He is trying to make me laugh and sometimes he succeeds. He insults the guards, and if they understood English they would surely shoot him. His vulgarity makes me shudder and keeps me sane at the same time. That spirit of his and his coarse sense of humour help me survive and forget the creeping feeling of hopelessness. I will not let despair come into my soul. I shall take all this as just another grey day in a hated office. The day may extend a bit, yet I know you are at the end of this tunnel, waiting. I shall ignore it all for now. How I wish I had someone here to share things with. Not you, my love, because I wouldn't want you to suffer this. Just someone who can feel, that's all. Sleep has eluded me for hours and the night outside is foreign.'

In the days that came life was just bearable. They were dirty and hungry and pale and Hedges found funny things to say all the while.

'It can always get worse,' he'd say, or: 'Others pay fortunes to lose weight while the Japs do it for us for nothing.'

Indeed, their food rations got smaller as time went by, but they began to recognize their guards and were allowed out to exercise and were not beaten that often. Two months and a day after the fall of Singapore, they were taken to the commandant's office. He told them to shave and gave them their kitbags back and said they would be allowed to have a bath.

'They are not going to shoot us today,' Jimmy said, and when the food came, more than usual, he added: 'They wouldn't fatten us up now, would they, or bother to scrub us up. Only the Japanese are allowed to die clean.'

Later, freshly shaven, dressed and fed, they were taken to an office and introduced to a Japanese officer. He was cordial and soft-spoken and he offered them green tea and cigarettes. He told them they had been selected to go on a trip. He asked whether they were treated well and told them another officer was on his way from Japan to meet them. He gave them thirty minutes to get ready.

The thirty minutes passed and extended into a week and another week, and then they were moved in the night. They were escorted by two squads of armed soldiers and were marched for two hours before they got to their destination.

It was a large, old colonial building with long corridors and columns and gardens, and they were put in a cell in an outbuilding. There were two beds and three chairs and a table. It was a clean cell and they both slept well that night. In the morning, a Japanese officer came to see them. He said they were going to be quartered there until the mission started. He talked a little and asked a few impersonal questions and did not expect them to answer. He then told them they must wait, and he left.

'Things are looking up,' Hedges said. 'At least they know we're here.'

CHAPTER FIVE

As a boy they called him Cho-chan, little butterfly. He liked hovering about the house, arms stretched, fingers dropping things over the wooden floors. He made people laugh and he sang songs, often falling asleep right in the middle of a recital. He was good at drawing flowers for his mother and he giggled a lot. He would watch the tea-ceremony lessons in the house and imitate the ladies afterwards. And he wanted to emigrate to Brazil like his uncle.

He was tall for his age, and had a broad, moon-shaped, pudgy face and strong muscles in his legs. He kept growing bigger and no shoes or clothes fitted him for longer than four months at a stretch. Yet he was popular with his smaller friends, who daily came to the house to enjoy his comforting, pleasing company. He knew how to cook soups and brew beer and slice raw fish into small, appetizing portions, and grind the mustard and cut up apples and radishes. He could sing and tell funny stories and pause in between for the others to laugh.

Later, at Keio University in Tokyo, they did not know about his childhood. Keichi Katsumata was not born a gentle giant. He had grown into one during his late teens. Nor did anyone dare to call him 'gentle giant' to his face. Not even the most militant. At Keio, they appreci-ated powerfully built boys. His big face, when serious, struck others with respect born of fear. When he spoke, and the clear baritone of his voice filled the room, there was silence. On rare occasions, in the final years of study, he would smile and his face would light up like a million paper lanterns and the world would become his for the taking. But not many people saw him smile in those years when he was maturing and spots of bristle appeared on his chin. There was little for him to smile about then, when the world was changing.

When Keichi arrived in the capital, it was 1931 and the current of nationalism was running strongly. Down from the political skies of his native Japan, grey clouds of war began their ugly descent onto the rice fields, starting a fire that would ultimately destroy.

The revival of old glories was just around the corner. There were marches in the streets and assassinations in high places. The trim, sleek Imperial army was polishing its armour into a shine. Across the sea, a decadent Asia was waiting to be taken and reshaped and led. Big ships and planes were rolling off assembly lines to await the call of the flag and remind the nation of Port Arthur and the victory over the white man in Russia. There was fever in the air. Keen young officers shot their moderate generals and formed parties and political pressure groups. They wanted to go to war and continue, but Keichi Katsumata wanted to go to Brazil.

He had been taking Spanish lessons for a couple of years. His knowledge of the language was such that his teacher, a half-caste Filipino guitarist from Yoshiwara, could converse with him in that language. They talked about flamenco and *corridas* and the guitarist told him he could now easily travel anywhere in South America or Spain and never be lost. Keichi did not want to go anywhere in South America or Spain. He wanted to join his mother's brother in Brazil. Nothing had been heard from him since the late twenties. Rumour had it that he had many *tsubo* of land and horses and a wife in Brazil. He had only been back to Hokkaido, where Keichi's family lived, once, and left an everlasting impression on young Keichi. He had an easy smile and talked a lot and he listened to gramophone records and danced about and whistled and hugged people. These were things Keichi's father never did, nor any other man in the family. His uncle was considered something of an eccentric and spoke of the heat, the sand on the beaches, the jungles and the music where he lived. He spoke of the future possibilities and of gold and tropical fruits and warm seas. But he never did tell the boy that they spoke Portuguese in Brazil.

And so it came about that Keichi, in his last year at Keio University, had become fluent in the wrong language. He had been contributing to the university newspaper and dreamt of a career in journalism. That way he might get an assignment over the ocean and find a way to join his uncle there. His father did not mind what subject he took as long as it was at Keio and as long as he remembered where he came from and did not bring shame on the family. The university was a necessary waste of time, as far as Keichi's father was concerned. But all male Katsumatas had been there, and they all came back afterwards and went into the family business of fish processing. As long as Keichi did the same, it did not matter what they were teaching him. Law was put forward as a good idea, and obligingly Keichi became a lawyer. He was going to look for gold in Brazil in any case, but that remained a secret.

The only other person who knew about his plans was his childhood sweetheart Misato, whom Keichi married in 1935 at the age of twenty-two. They agreed to go to Brazil together, but the plan had to be postponed when Yoshiro was born. For the moment, they packed their belongings and sailed north to Hokkaido. But only the young mother and baby Yoshiro remained there. Keichi, now a fully trained lawyer, was drafted into the military and despatched west to Manchuria, which his country had taken in 1931, to keep guard over the railways.

Secretly, very secretly, Keichi Katsumata hated the army. It was not a popular sentiment to have on the threshold of glory. He could not tell his wife about it, and years later he could not tell his son either. None of them could share the anguish Keichi went through being a lieutenant with the Imperial Expeditionary Force. Misato was a patriot and two of her brothers were to die in Burma for the Emperor.

In anticipation of an early landing in Singapore, the army called Keichi back and sent him on a crash course in English and Malay. His natural aptitude for languages helped, and with his ability to think in a foreign tongue he obtained a working knowledge of the other two, but Spanish remained his passion. He thought of it as his ticket to Brazil.

The army moved him to the intelligence corps because of his qualifications, and he was sent on a training course near Nagoya in the centre of Honshu. He was going to learn about interrogation methods, but then the army decided he was better suited to the Philippines and, in preparation for the Philippine campaign, they moved him to an artillery regiment before the course was over. With his files in Tokyo temporarily lost, Keichi was posted back to headquarters long before he mastered the art of the cannon. With no place for him to go to fight, he was ordered to Osaka. Someone at the Ministry of War had decided it was time to make him a signals officer and teach him the skills of radio communication. He ended up fully qualified, only to be posted to Bangkok. Not as a wireless man, but as a cultural attaché with the Japanese Embassy there. His task was to convert the Thai to a more aggressive, forward-looking way of thinking, and he read long memoranda that came from the Foreign Ministry in this connection. Nothing much was achieved and his time in Bangkok passed by in tranquillity.

The war was now raging and Keichi had not fired

one shot in anger. He was back in Japan on leave when a telegram arrived to interrupt it. There were new orders. He was to present himself in the newly conquered city of Singapore. He was not given any reason for the assignment, nor details of its nature. He set sail for the fallen colony.

During the early days of the conflict, the island of Hokkaido remained remote from the hostilities. There were plenty of fish in the sea and salmon in the springs and rivers; snow still fell on the mountains in winter. The sea lanes were safe under the invincible flag of the Rising Sun. Fishermen chanted songs from Hakodate and there were plenty of apples. Little Yoshiro, dressed in naval uniform, was told to be proud of his father. The Imperial army had exerted an almost total dominance over Japanese life ever since Manchuria was taken, and little Yoshiro was taught its songs, shown maps of victories, and coaxed to pray for his father's glory. Only successes were reported, and Misato became a fervent supporter of the military. But Keichi Katsumata himself was not touched by the carnival of war, nor impressed by its success. He disliked the short, curt words of command and distrusted the high-rankers whom the army had now turned into modern *shogun*. He hated the servility conscripts had to show because he was an officer. Automatic, blind obedience to man-made golden stripes. He hated the robot-like chain of command and abhorred the irrationality of war and the small minds of petty officers. Above all, Keichi despised the humourless uniformity of it all. On his way to Singapore, Keichi thought the army was going to misplace him again. He felt constricted and bored, and a pain plagued his chest as he took up smoking cigarettes. There was no one he could talk to and in a short time his natural vibrancy was lost to silence. An immensely morose outer shell had closed over his effervescence. What if this latest assignment was a wild goose chase? He paced the steamer's deck alone in the heat of the night. Barefoot, he felt the wood underneath and he wished he was going to Brazil to join the uncle of his youth.

CHAPTER SIX

It was a hot port and it was busy. Keichi Katsumata had never been to Singapore before and all he saw below the railings was the presence of the Imperial army. There were no civilians to be seen, other than a few who were clearing away the wrecks of some smouldering trucks. The red Rising Sun was flying proudly everywhere, its reflection quivering in the green waters. Uniforms swarmed about the place like obscure, obedient little ants. Somewhere, he knew, there must have been palm trees and bougainvillea and red-roofed colonial buildings, but only the simmering heat welcomed his ship to Singapore.

The island town had become a part of the newly extended Japanese Empire. Keichi knew that empires were not built by prayer alone and he was at last about to become a part of the killing machine whose uniform he had been wearing for so long. Inside of him, he felt the tang of distant shame.

The harbour was alive with activity. There was constant loading and unloading of wooden crates, large and small. There were field guns and anti-aircraft guns, soldiers and officers with swords, and there were military trucks. The colour had gone from how he imagined the port. The woven baskets, the fishing nets, the rattan and the civilians he had seen on the old canvas of his imagination were absent.

In Hokkaido, the air had been cool and the mountains echoed fishermen's songs of sunsets and love. But Hokkaido was far away, and here the cranes creaked under the weight of death-inflicting metal. His heart felt heavy as he descended the gangway.

Down below, he saw a small group of junior officers. One looked up at him and shouted his name. Katsumata. It sounded harsh and cruel, as if it had been a curse. He nodded and said, 'Yes, I am Katsumata', and the youngest of the group came to the foot of the gangway, clutching his long sword. He stopped, saluted and bowed, and lifted Keichi's luggage. There was an apologetic smile on the young man's face.

'Follow me, sir,' he barked, and with that the smile hardened and died away. 'We have a car waiting outside. You must be important.' There was some curiosity in the young man's eyes. 'It's the first car I've been near to since the fighting stopped.'

Keichi wanted to get a look at the town. The tropical smells, the trees and the flowers that survived the big guns would surely be just like those in Recife. His uncle had once sent a postcard from there, but he did not remember the picture. He only remembered his father saying it was a tropical port with ships like the ones in Hakodate, but without order. His father also said Recife looked primitive and hot and fit only for savages.

When Keichi said he would like to see the town, the others shook their heads. Impossible, they said. They had to go and see the Taisho. The Taisho had important things to discuss with Lieutenant Katsumata, and was not to be kept waiting. They sat, tight-lipped, hugging their swords as they drove through the city. The young one was at the wheel, avoiding the potholes and debris and horse carcasses on their way. The Chinese, Malay and Indians they saw looked hungry. A mother and her child ran barefooted across the street; her steps were short and fast and her face was ashen as she held the raggedly clad child in her arms. Would Misato and Yoshiro go hungry? Not Misato. She was too proud for that. She would not survive the temptation to poison herself if her beloved Japan was to lose the war.

They passed hundreds of empty shops and rickshaws. There were very few cars about, mostly burnt-out shells in dying posture left on the roadside. There were soldiers marching in groups, tree-lined avenues and more debris and the sweet stench of death. The car stopped, and amidst more salutes and more bows, Keichi was ushered towards the Taisho's office. More barking, he thought to himself, with a good chance of standing at attention for hours and listening and perhaps barking back in agreement.

The building was old and its long, dark corridors were cool. Keichi saw the decorations along the walls and admired the remaining chandeliers. This must have been a serene place before the peace was blasted. A sharp scream tore into him.

A group of soldiers was dragging a limp prisoner towards his party. There was pain in his eyes and streaks of sweat mingled with blood above his torn tunic. He was young and dark-skinned, too dark to be Chinese, and taller and rounder of face. As they passed each other, the man looked at Keichi. He walked more slowly now, like a human pet pulling at his leash. His lips were dry and cracked and there was hate in him. He tried to spit at Keichi's face, but couldn't and was pushed forward with the butt of a gun.

It was quiet for a moment. All Keichi could hear was footsteps on the marble flooring and then the silence exploded. They all halted and looked around. The man, with sudden, hidden, unexpected strength, tore away from his captors and ran. There was some shouting and then there was a shot and the man fell. He coughed out a little cry and he shook a little, then lay still. The group turned back to continue on their way. They had all seen death before, but Keichi felt the pressure of a bloating sickness rise from his stomach. He squeezed his sword and held on to it and walked on.

The corridor went on for ever and there were clear square spots on the walls. Once there were paintings there, Keichi thought. Big *gaijin* paintings of quiet English country scenes. Great houses and horses and hunting dogs. Red jackets and large, old sailing ships maybe.

They stopped in front of a door and he knew it was the Taisho's door because the faces around him stiffened. Someone gathered the courage to knock and an angry voice bellowed something through the thick oak. The door opened and Keichi marched in, bowed and saluted. The Taisho sat at his large desk signing some papers. He was in his middle years and had a good face.

'Sit down, Katsumata,' he said, without looking up. 'I'll be with you in a moment.' He had an intelligent voice and his accent was educated. He put his brush down and sat back. 'Hope you had a good trip, Katsumata.' He did not wait for an answer. 'How is your Burmese?'

The army had done it again. Wrong language, wrong place, wrong man, wrong everything.

'Spanish. I speak Spanish, sir. No Burmese,' he said, and he wanted to laugh.

'Funny,' the Taisho said, 'funny.' He consulted a file and said 'funny' again. He rang the bell and an orderly came in. He had a severe, scarred face and the Taisho said 'funny' one last time before he ordered some tea. He did not need to tell Keichi he was a Keio man too. There was something about him. A canopy of familiar buildings, mutual scenes and teachers, equal family backgrounds. The orderly came back with steaming cups and the Taisho barked: 'Wait outside. We do not wish to be disturbed.' Turning to Keichi, the Taisho continued. 'We have a problem,' he said. 'We need you, but you don't speak Burmese, and we have no time to get someone else. How is your English? You speak it, you read and write it?'

Keichi nodded. He meant to say he could just about get by in English. He had only said three words so far, but he knew the Taisho had understood.

'We'll have to use you for this one,' the Taisho said. 'There isn't much time. You'll have to go in two days. And you won't be alone. There are two British officers and two Burmese coming with you. We had three Burmese, but we lost one just before you came in. The fool tried to escape. Drink your tea, Katsumata. I'm going to tell you about your new job. You may not have Burmese, but you are the right man. You'd better be, because you are all I've got.'

Keichi sipped his tea, refused the offer of a cigarette, and settled down to listen.

The Burmese people, the Taisho said, did not appreciate Japan's role. Some did not want to be rid of the old colonial powers. There were pockets of resistance inside Burma. The British were helping the locals out and, in some cases, they had been moderately successful. Hit-and-run affairs – effective, but no more than nuisance value so far. The Taisho said little was known about this back at home and Keichi was to keep it all to himself. He was only being told about it because he was going to Burma himself and needed to know what was happening there. The Taisho said he would get a field officer with battle experience in that country to brief him further.

What a pack of lies, Keichi thought. The soldiers on the boat said there were thousands of English guerrillas in Burma.

He wouldn't have to watch the prisoners by himself. A sergeant and two soldiers were picked to accompany him. It was going to be dangerous, but the mission itself was political in nature. Top secret. He was the only one who would know what the trip was really about. The others, prisoners and guards alike, were to be kept in the dark until the last minute, though they would have to be told where they were going. A delicate mission, the Taisho said. The Burmese might try to escape just to get themselves shot if they knew. The British were officers, and were not expected to cooperate. Keichi was to lead the party to Thailand by boat, then by road and on foot to the crossing point to Burma.

'I will tell you what you are going there for,' the Taisho said. 'The enemy is holding a Japanese prisoner in the mountains. A high-ranking Japanese officer who was taken during a surprise guerrilla attack on an outpost in the mountains. He was only visiting there and was taken alive with another man. The enemy is not aware of the officer's identity yet, and no one on the Japanese side knows who he is either. He belongs to headquarters in Tokyo and recapturing him is of the highest importance.

'It will be up to you to persuade the enemy to exchange him for the two British officers or the Burmese. If our man is held by guerrillas, you may have to pay a ransom and our people in Burma will assist you.'

The Taisho admitted that all this was highly irregular, but the man had to be brought back. He had information the army was desperate for and he was carrying it in his head. That information was so critical that it could change the course of the war. Even shorten it.

'How can the army leave such heavy responsibility on one man's shoulders alone?' Keichi asked.

'There was another man who was also captured, but he committed *seppuku* as soon as they were taken. He feared he might be forced to talk. So far, we know for sure that the other man, the high-ranking officer himself, is alive and well, but he must be brought back quickly. You see, the High Command in Tokyo has not yet been informed of his capture. He must be brought back before they find out. It is a matter of honour. The army's honour. You surely understand that?'

What the Taisho meant was that heads would roll if the man wasn't brought back. Of course he understood.

'How can I travel through the countryside with two British *gaijin* officers?' Keichi asked.

'They will wear their own uniforms as far as the port of Pattaya in Thailand. They will then be given German uniforms. That should not raise any eyebrows because even the dumbest Japanese in Thailand knows the Germans are our allies. As soon as you cross into Burma, you can dress the *gaijin* in their own uniforms again.

'The two Burmese who are coming with you, Katsumata, are very important, well-known people. The idea is to use them in case the high-ranking officer is held by Burmese guerrillas. In that case, you will kill the *gaijin* as soon as the exchange is made. If the enemy wants the *gaijin*, you kill the Burmese. That is all. Whichever way it goes, I do not expect you to fail. Our man must be found and taken to Bangkok. The escort will be sent to the front as soon as you return. They will not be coming back, if you know what I mean. Noncoms have the habit of talking, and the mission is to remain a secret even after it has been accomplished.

'We have a problem, though, a big problem. The high-ranking officer does not wish to be brought back. That will be the real test of your ability. You will have to make sure you get him to leave, certainly against his will, and bring him to me at the Japanese Embassy in Bangkok. I will wait for you there two weeks from the day you arrive in Thailand. You are not to hand him over to anyone else.'

The Taisho's face hardened. 'No one, you understand. If I am not there when you arrive, you will have to execute him. This is an order. I know it all seems strange, but one day when all this is over I might explain it to you.'

At that point, the Taisho's face softened once more and he said: 'This is war, Katsumata. People die in wars. The two *gaijin* are no more than bait and are therefore expendable. They were captured right here in the city. In a bar. They were not caught while honouring their country by fighting. One is a medical officer, a man called James Hedges. The other, a Lieutenant Derek Pritchard. A man not unlike yourself, Katsumata. Gentle and educated and serious. He could have been a friend, had we not been at war with England. Not a very lucky man, Katsumata. Not a very lucky man, because the enemy will most certainly prefer to take the Burmese.'

43

'Not unlike yourself,' the Taisho had said. Did that mean he was going to be unlucky too? Like the sergeant and the soldiers? Was he going to be silenced the same way? The Taisho's face eased into a smile. It spread across his skin slowly, as if controlled.

'Let's have some more tea,' he said. 'This heat makes one thirsty. I do not need to repeat that all this is top secret. No one is going to remember this mission.'

The Taisho leaned forward and rang the bell. 'Except you and me, of course. You and me. The others will all be dead.'

Something was missing from the Taisho's project. Was he hiding something? Keichi did not expect to be told the whole truth, but something was wrong here. Things did not fit. Why should the army go to such lengths for a man who did not want to be released? Why was the operation such a secret?

They were using him, but then that was what people were put in uniform for, and he was an officer and would obey.

'That orderly is a little deaf, Katsumata,' the Taisho said. 'Go and open the door and see where the fool is.'

CHAPTER SEVEN

The next day, Keichi was taken to meet the two *gaijin* officers. They were in a building in the gardens of the house where the Taisho had his office. They were having their food, a tin plate of soup each, when he entered their cell. He ordered the guard to bring him a plate too, and he sat down with them.

'How rude,' one of them said. 'The bastard could have asked permission to crouch with us.'

Keichi did not fully understand what the red-haired officer said. He asked the man to repeat himself, but then the guard came in with the soup, and the man laughed and Keichi laughed with him. The other lieutenant, the pale one, did not say much and Keichi guessed him to be Pritchard, whom the Taisho had said was gentle and educated. He wanted to speak to him, but as they sat there together he was overcome by an inexplicable sensation of shyness. The other man, Hedges, was more talkative. He was a medical man, he said, and the war had caught up with him before he had a chance to go into practice.

The guard brought in a basket of fruit and some steaming rice and Keichi offered some to the others. By now, the red-haired officer was talking freely and the other one said a few things too. They talked about the war and why the British did not bomb Singapore. Keichi apologized for his bad English and mentioned that he was better at speaking Spanish. Lieutenant Pritchard said he spoke the language as he had fought in the Spanish Civil War. His wife was Spanish, he said. Then they began talking in Spanish. Lieutenant Pritchard translated some of the conversation for Hedges, but he fell asleep and they went on talking.

Speaking Spanish reminded Keichi of his time in Tokyo, of the half-caste Filipino musician who was his teacher, and of his desire to go to Brazil. He tried to show the *gaijin* how to make birds out of folded paper.

'We are going on a mission together,' Keichi told Pritchard in Spanish. 'That mission might mean the end of the war for you, if it succeeds. So you'd better listen to the details carefully and make sure Lieutenant Hedges does too.'

He was surprised at the tone of his voice. It was masterful and military, yet still his own. He had to tell them something about the plan because their cooperation was vital. They were going to travel many days together and they were going to be accompanied by other prisoners and a few guards. It would make no sense for them to try to escape because they were going to travel through territory friendly to Japan. He knew it was the duty of every prisoner of war to try to escape, but this mission could bring about their freedom. They might as well cooperate and help the Imperial army provide them with a free and safe passage through Thailand.

As he talked, Keichi found himself feeling that these two were his personal guests, sharing time with him in the Tokyo of his student days. He never mentioned the possibility of death to them. He knew he might have to shoot them if the high-ranking officer was held by Burmese guerrillas. That was the order his Taisho had given him, and that meant he was lying to them. Following, as he did, the ancient code of *bushido*, he was ashamed. Perhaps because his life was as vulnerable as theirs. Perhaps it was not shame, but fear.

They listened to him in doubtful silence, and a quiet, deep flow of mistrust came over their faces. Keichi noticed it. He could not blame them. He had been shown some of the local papers published before the city fell, and had read a two-month-old copy of the London *Daily Express* from cover to cover. His nation was hated, his army stained with a reputation for rape, murder and plunder. His leaders were described as liars and cheats and hypocrites and cowards. His people were called yellow slant-eyed dwarfs who aimed to conquer the world and enslave it. That was how the *gaijin* saw Japan and he was a Japanese. That was how they must have seen him too.

There was no mention anywhere of the gardens, the prints, the poems and ballads, the art his countrymen had produced. Not a word for Utamaru, Hiroshige or Satsuma potteries. He represented the captor, and could leave and see the sun outside, while they were behind bars. To them, he wasn't even human. That was the way of war.

Outside it was getting dark. The pastel green in the trees was becoming dark green and the reds in the sky had gone mauve. It was a cloudy evening and it was surely going to rain. Keichi got up.

'*Hasta mañana*,' he said, and did not smile, nor bow. He stretched his hand forward and Derek Pritchard took it. The other *gaijin* waved a mock goodbye from the window.

CHAPTER EIGHT

'This is just what I've been praying for,' said Jimmy Hedges as soon as the door slammed shut. 'That big ape and his mission will give us a chance to get away.'

'Escape?'

'Obviously. Surrounded by water as we are on this island, there is no way out, but Thailand and Burma present possibilities, my boy. Especially Burma. We may be able to get to India from there . . . and freedom.'

'But Lieutenant Katsumata said they might let us go

once this thing is over.'

'Don't be an ass, Pritchard. They have no intention of letting us go. One does not trust a Japanese officer.'

'I thought he was a decent sort of chap. Tried to do his best under the circumstances. Anyway, I haven't met all that many Japanese.'

'I've seen enough of the bastards to last me a lifetime. Treacherous, lying, scheming race.'

'You can't condemn a whole nation because its leaders are wrong. Has Mussolini stopped you from listening to Verdi?'

'Oh, stop dreaming, Pritchard. You've learned nothing from Spain, have you? All that talk of saving the world from God knows what.'

'Spain did me a lot of good, Jimmy. I would not have missed it for the world. I met my wife there. I learned about people. This Katsumata hates his job more than you hate him.'

'We are prisoners of war, Pritchard, not at a seminar. He's playing at being nice.'

'You don't understand Spanish. You got it all second-hand. You should have seen his eyes. Through the uniform and his sword, I saw his soul.'

'You must be going soft in the head. Do you think we've stumbled on an Albert Schweitzer here? What do you think this is, the Salvation Army? When this mission – whatever it involves – is over, they'll shoot us like fucking rabbits.'

'Do you have to be quite so vulgar?'

'War is vulgar. What do you think they want us for?'

'I've no idea, but he said it might mean the end of the war for us.'

'Too bloody right. The end because we'll be dead. It's all lies, I tell you, but who cares? Somewhere along the road, we'll make a run for it. He's a devious blackguard like all of them.'

'You have no trust, Hedges, in the basic honesty of man. You have no eyes for the beauty that supports the soul. Yes, even in wartime and sometimes between enemies. You must be a very lonely man.'

'Your compassion makes me sick. Don't feel sorry for me. I am a survivor. They won't sing any lullabies for me. It's a long trek he's planning for us, and he'll make mistakes. And when he does, we'll be ready. There must be people in Bangkok who are on our side. The way these bastards treat their allies, you can be sure there are. We'll find someone, a neutral embassy or a church or something. People hate them, you know. They fight dirty. Have you forgotten Pearl Harbor? Have you heard what they have done to the hospital here? Look, Pritchard, I don't want to spoil your dream, but for Christ's sake translate every word and watch him when I'm not. You'll see. He'll show his teeth soon enough. People do in war.'

'I have been in a war myself, remember, and that was a cruel war where Spaniards killed Spaniards, believers burned nuns, but wars do not last for ever and people change. With us, fighting the Fascists in Spain, was a young Basque teacher who had been caught in a town during a bombing raid. He carried his hate with him all the way to the mountains where he met up with us. He was hardly a shadow of a human being and could do nothing else except kill Rebels. That's what we called the Fascists in those days. He had become an expert with the knife. A sort of silent killer. He was very useful to our High Command, if a trifle distasteful to those of us from outside

Spain. He assassinated more *Falangistas* than anyone else. He got into their barracks unnoticed, sometimes dressed as a priest or a female flamenco dancer. He got into their homes, too, and often knifed whoever happened to be in bed with his victims. A teacher, he was, would you believe? Twenty-three years old. In the end, they had to keep the prisoners locked away from him.'

'Are you telling me you think me a murderer?'

'No, Hedges, that is not what I am trying to tell you. Alfonso – that was his name – was no more a murderer than you or I. After the war, Alfonso the Knife emigrated to England. He became a restaurateur and runs a respectable eating place in the City. He has grown a pot-belly and a big smile and he has a wife and two children. The only time he gets his hands on a knife is when he carves a roast. I'll take you there after the war, if you like. He too, Hedges, is a survivor, just like you, but there's no hate in him now, I promise you that. And one day, when Spain is free again, he'll go back to the Basque country and buy a farm or something and watch his grandchildren grow. At his home, the subject of the Civil War is taboo. I don't think he's ever told his children he had anything to do with it. Only people who have never been in a fight brag about heroics.

'Now I don't know what this Katsumata did before the war, but I can assure you he'll be out of his uniform and away from his sword once this is over. And one more thing, Hedges, just like Alfonso the Knife, he won't be telling his son how great the war was.'

'You insist on making him one of your saints. He is a Japanese officer and we are at war with Japan. Obviously it suits them to use us in this operation, but he's not telling us the whole truth. We'll wait and see, if we live that long.'

Derek wasn't getting anywhere. The tireless cynicism was depressing him. He said:

'A man with a voice and a smile like Katsumata's can't be all bad. A killer wouldn't sit and teach you how to make paper birds.'

'Bullshit.'

Could Hedges have been right? Could the Japanese lieutenant be a villain after all? Was he himself really a dreamer or, worse, a traitor to his country for being attracted to an enemy? But then, Katsumata was speaking Spanish to him. A language that brought his youth and his old ideals back – and more. It brought his wife's presence into his very cell.

She had come to him before in that way. Once before. Shortly after he had landed in Singapore.

He had spent an evening in the company of a young Scottish officer. They were watching a show at an outdoor nightclub when a trio of Filipino guitarists came on stage and started to sing. It was a strange experience, listening to a Spanish guitar pour its heart out beneath an oriental moon. They played a vigorous version of 'Granada', then came 'Malagueña' and 'Amapola' and all the other songs to which he knew the words. He sat there, enchanted, and suddenly he felt Antonia's arm upon his shoulder. He could hear her voice floating past his ear and her thigh brushing against his. He did not dare move, in case the apparition disappeared, and Antonia stayed with him as long as the three Filipinos remained on stage.

That show was the last open-air performance offered in the city before the Japanese struck, and he never saw the young Scot again. That had been the last sound of music.

As the lights went out and Hedges murmured a faint goodnight, he heard himself say *buenas noches*. The language he had been using and hearing had lingered in the room long after Lieutenant Katsumata was gone, and in his bed he could sense his wife's proximity. She was very much alive in her presence, and he knew she was missing him and he wanted her. He did not try to reason with himself or analyse her coming. There was nothing odd in her being with him in the wake of the Japanese officer's visit, nothing surprising in their silent conversation or in the feel of her small hand wiping the sweat off his brow. She just spoke to him and listened and the gentle accord they always had was there. She said he had not written to her lately and he said he had, but could not put it on paper. He asked about Anna and the house and she told him about the war and the bombs and the shortages, and assured him they would survive.

'Do you remember the week we sailed from Barcelona to Marseilles?' he heard her ask. 'We had no food, but we survived then and will now.' She said only three of his letters had arrived and how happy they had made her. She read them again and again, and read them to Anna, too. It was dark in the cell, and when the cool air finally arrived, he shivered a little with the drying sweat and pulled the sheet to cover her body and his. He heard himself ask if the bed was too small, and she laughed. 'I hardly take any room,' she said. 'Have you forgotten how ridiculously tiny your wife is?'

He had not forgotten anything about her. His arms searched for her and he thought he could feel her body arch towards his and became aroused. She said something about the last time they were together when the Filipinos sang, and he tried again to get closer to where she was and his excitement surged.

'Stop moving about, Pritchard. I'm trying to sleep,'

Jimmy Hedges grumbled. Derek apologized and said something about the heat and they both fell asleep and he was alone again. She had been with him a long time, and he could think about her now in his sleep and feel the softness of her skin.

Derek woke with the dawn and listened to the sound of the dying night. It was the wind that had woken him, shaking the old palm trees whose trunks rubbed against the wooden walls. He was hot and felt a little hungry.

In the courtyard, the soldiers marched up and down the cobblestones and he wondered whether Katsumata was awake too. He had said he was going to come and see them again in the morning. Perhaps he could ask for some writing paper and a pen. Antonia had told him that the letter from Port Said had not arrived. He remembered well what he had said in it and could easily write it again. They could compare the two after the war.

Outside, they were changing guards and he heard weapons being presented as sharp words of command pierced the air. Hedges could sleep through a thunderstorm, but Derek was a light sleeper. He thought of a poem he could write to Antonia about her coming to him in the night. Celestial dew falling gently on dry tropical leaves. Or something. But he fell asleep again until the guard outside the door yelled and Jimmy Hedges shot out a welcoming curse at the morning. The sun extended a growing beam of light into their cell. They were given a larger than usual breakfast. It was still the old soup in the tin plate, but there was more rice in it and a slice of fish.

'They are fattening us so that they can eat us,' Hedges said. 'Just like Hansel and Gretel. Have you ever had breakfast on GWR? They used to serve you smoked kippers before the war. How I'd love some bacon and eggs along with this crap. I'm famished.'

'I'm not very hungry. Have mine if you like. A spoonful will be enough for me.'

He handed the plate over and Hedges poured half its contents into his own.

'Have all of it, Jimmy,' Derek said, but the other man said he should have some himself.

'Look at you, you're skin and bones.'

CHAPTER NINE

———■———

'Have you ever seen an execution?' the Taisho asked.

They were having breakfast in the Taisho's office.

'Breakfast is the most important meal of the day,' the Taisho declared. 'The French have a very small breakfast – coffee and croissants. That is why they have lost the war. It's the English who surprise me. They have a feast. Do you know they eat bacon and eggs and sausages and grilled fish, too? I know all this because I once spent two months in Europe. There is nothing to it, you know,' he said, with a twinkle in his eye.

'Nothing to what, sir?'

'To an execution.' The Taisho was picking his teeth while his eyes were on his soup. Keichi was back in a corner of horror. He hoped the Taisho did not notice how the blood had left his face. The food in his stomach was struggling to stay inside him. He took a deep breath and a sip of tea, and hoped the subject might be miraculously dropped.

'A *gaijin* is being shot here today,' the Taisho said with a belch. 'The firing squad is made up of recruits and I hope they shoot properly. I need another officer to witness it. The *gaijin* was sent here last night, but the sentence was only telephoned in ten minutes ago. All I've got is the guards out there, since the rest of the men have gone out on a drill. There is talk of a counter-attack, but I don't believe it. We've dealt the enemy a great shameful blow from which they will not recover quickly. Still, I'd like to get this thing over with as soon as I can.' The Taisho looked at his watch and said, 'Let's go, Katsumata. It's right by the outer wall of this office.'

They made the *gaijin* stand under what must have been the Taisho's window. He was a young British *gaijin* with a red face and blond hair. His uniform was crumpled and he looked about him, not quite knowing what was going on. He could not have been a day over nineteen. He had full, pink lips and his baby face was the only clean thing about him.

'Is your firing squad ready?' the Taisho asked the sergeant.

'They will be out in a few minutes, sir.'

The *gaijin* was being tied to a pole by two prison guards, one of whom had grey hair and was slow on his feet.

'Where do they get the guards from?' the Taisho barked. 'The Russian War?'

The sergeant said most of the soldiers detailed for prison duty were old and some were Korean. They were not liked by other soldiers. They spoke bad Japanese, they drank, they ate hot peppery food and were cruel. Keichi looked at the *gaijin*, who was still dazed by the sun which fell right into his eyes. Keichi thought the *gaijin* was lucky not to be able to see. He himself saw and was aware, and he wished he could not. It was not a dream at all, and Keichi knew there was no more escape for him than there was for the *gaijin*. He looked asleep on his feet while his blue eyes were open. He had been beaten. His trousers were torn, revealing his white flesh.

'At last,' the Taisho said, grabbing his sword and pulling his shoulders back. The squad came marching out of the hut at the end of the hedge and were led into position by the sergeant. For a moment, all sound had gone from the air, and Keichi thought he was watching an old silent film of far-away events. A man was going to die here today, long before his time. This was war. A place with real soldiers and real bullets.

The sergeant moved forward, and behind him the squad saluted. The sergeant's lips moved in command, but Keichi did not hear him. Nor did he hear the Taisho read out the sentence and salute. Keichi saluted too, and everybody bowed. From the corner of his eye, he looked at the firing squad and saw nothing more than an embarrassed group of schoolchildren. In the shade of shame, Keichi saw their faces fall under the brim of their hats. They lifted their rifles and they aimed and the sergeant's lips moved again. Keichi looked at the *gaijin*, who still twitched his vacant eyes as he fell to the ground.

The Taisho, pistol in hand, marched up to the wall where the young man lay and bent over to inspect the bullet-riddled body. He shot him again in the head. The condemned man shook softly and then lay still. The sound came back to Keichi's ears and he heard the command and the shots. It was all there; it had happened and he knew he had not been dreaming.

'Should train these stupid peasants to shoot straight,'

the Taisho said as they walked away from the scene, 'otherwise they would not survive ten seconds in battle.'

He led Keichi back into the office and lit a cigarette.

'You see, Katsumata, there is nothing to it.'

'What did the *gaijin* do to get such a sentence?' Keichi asked.

'I can't tell you. I followed an order that came before breakfast, that's all. I know his name was Brown and he must have done something, otherwise they would have shipped him to a prison camp with the others. Maybe they made a mistake. He did look a little too young to be in a position from which to commit a serious crime. This world dictates the survival of the fittest, so have another cup of tea before you go to see your prisoners.'

'Thank you, sir.'

'I would hate to be a prisoner of war and live. That *gaijin* Brown is now surely back with past glories of his own country. Can you imagine being locked up like an animal, defeated and deflated and humiliated? Being told what to do by persons of a lesser class whose destiny it is to be your watch-dogs? I'd sooner finish myself off and join my ancestors' spirits.'

Keichi got to his feet, saluted and bowed, and the Taisho smiled. He rose and gave Keichi his hand.

'We must talk again before you go. Perhaps you would like to spend this evening with me. We could go out for a meal at a place I know.'

'Thank you, sir. I would like that if you can find the time.'

On his way to join the *gaijin*, Keichi thought about what the Taisho had said. He did not know how the *gaijin* treated their prisoners, nor was he sure that his soul would be damned for all eternity if he ever fell into enemy hands.

One of his father's brothers, the eldest, had been a prisoner of war in 1904 in Russia, when the ship he had served in sank off Port Arthur. He was a jovial man who had married well, and he had given his shares in the family company to his brothers. He used to sit on top of mountains in the summer and watch birds through his naval binoculars. He rented a small steamboat on the Inland Sea or Lake Hakone in the spring, and in the winter he travelled in search of warmth to Okinawa Island. Keichi remembered his visits to their home, and the rice biscuits and bean sweets he always brought.

There had never been any doom on his contented face. Only once did Keichi ever hear him talk of the prison camp he was in, but there was no horror attached to the story. He died a happy man, and Keichi thought he did not worry too much about the disgrace that should have awaited him in the other world.

He was looking forward to seeing the *gaijin* again. Their presence, in particular that of Derek Pritchard, would take him away from the grey presence of what had happened. He did not know why or how, but suddenly his spirits lifted and a warm wave of light-hearted anticipation engulfed him. He arrived at the cell and the guard opened the door for him. The man's teeth were dirty, but Keichi did not stop to scold him.

'*Buenos días, señores,*' he said as the *gaijin* came into his view. '*¿Como están Ustedes hoy?*'

Derek Pritchard got up to greet him with his attractive pale smile while the other man stood by the window watching the sun. Their days in the cell, Keichi knew, were coming to an end, while his own war was about to begin.

Book 2

Quest For Vengeance

CHAPTER TEN

TOKYO, OCTOBER 1975

The voice was polite and soft and coaxing. It had a giggly, almost disarming quality.

'Mr Katsumata is not in the office right now.'

Anna fought an urge to put the phone down. End the whole sordid thing right there and then.

'Is there anywhere we can reach you, Mrs Bellingham?' the secretary asked.

'I am not settled in yet.' It was a lie, but she did not want to leave her number. Amidst the vastness of this impersonal city the voice sounded caring.

'Can you call back in one week, please? Mr Katsumata will be pleased to speak to you then.'

Not if he knew what she was about. The voice chuckled playfully and said:

'Let me check Mr Katsumata's diary to make sure. One minute, please.'

Anna was excited because she was getting close and her nerves were on edge, but she held on. She still did not know exactly what she was going to do once she found him. A drop of cold sweat rolled irritatingly down her neck. A cigarette. No. She put another ten-yen coin in the slot.

'Thank you,' she said with someone else's voice, but no one heard. Nothing must stop her now. Steady. Was she taking things too far? Of course not. She must not lose heart now. It had been too painful and trying and she had been determined on this course for many years.

Anna remembered when her mother received the

news of her father's death. She was six years old. All the War Office would say was that he had been killed in Thailand, but after the war ended Toni had pestered and pestered and eventually they revealed that a Dr James Hedges had reported his death. Not expecting it to be that easy, Toni had looked in the London telephone directory and there had been his name. The man who had been with her husband when he died. At first, he had not been keen to talk, but Toni soon had the details out of him, and over the years he had become a family friend, often coming for Sunday lunch, advising Toni about Anna's schooling and almost being the father and husband he had seen killed in a place called Bang Saray near the port of Pattaya in Thailand.

He did not know what they had in mind for Katsumata. While he became close to them, visited and ate with them, he told them about his adventures with Derek in Singapore and Thailand and Burma, and all the while their plans were taking shape.

She must not falter, now that she was in Katsumata's city and in his street and speaking to his office.

The secretary's voice came back on the line.

'I can say Mr Katsumata will certainly be back in his office next week. You will call, Mrs Bellingham? Yes? I will leave him a note about you. Is this your first visit to Japan?'

Anna said thank you one more time and said she would call back and the voice said have a nice day and *sayonara*.

'Goodbye,' Anna said.

She stood there and looked at the cars and the shops and the wide Ginza street. She was calm now.

This was her man all right. The American detective

agency they employed had narrowed it down to three possibilities. There were three Katsumatas who could have been in Singapore in 1942. The Katsumata she was trying to reach now was their man's son, Yoshiro. The other two were now dead. One died in San Francisco during a tour with a group of Japanese butchers. Their man could not have been a butcher since, according to Jimmy Hedges, he was of good stock and well educated. The second Katsumata turned out to be a homosexual kabuki actor who had never married and had committed suicide. Jimmy Hedges always said Lieutenant Katsumata had a son. The man she was calling had to be the lieutenant's son and she knew all there was to know about him. Soon, in a week or so, she would meet him in the flesh and he would lead her to the murderer himself. Her mother was right. Revenge is sweet.

She tidied her hair and stepped onto the pavement. She was going to meet her husband Jonathan at the Italian restaurant on top of the Sony building. It was only a few blocks away along the Ginza and the sun was shining. Just like her boss had said it would at this time of the year.

She had worked for a Japanese trading company in London for four years and had taken lessons in the language. She showed interest in their culture and history and knew about the samurai. She was particularly interested in *kataki uchi*, the law of blood revenge. Her boss in London took great pains to explain that to her. In the old days, blood could only be redeemed by blood. If not that of the killer himself, then a member of his family, preferably a son. It was a matter of honour.

A very Latin rule, don't you think? her mother had said when she heard. The Katsumatas are expecting us.

Anna knew about Japanese pottery and calligraphy

and had tasted raw fish. She knew the difference between Satsuma and Kutani chinaware and her boss was sorry to see her go. She was good at public relations and always hired the right people for them. Japanese companies, they told her, had the habit of keeping their employees for a long time. For ever, mostly. Would she not care to stay? She could not, she said, but thank you all the same.

She was grateful to them because they had arranged the right introductions for her husband. Personal introductions that were more than useful to him as a merchant banker. Meeting the right people had enabled him to accept a position in Tokyo almost as soon as it became available. That was the opportunity she had been waiting for. To go to Japan. Get her husband to go there and take her with him. It was a new thing for British banks to try their luck on the vast Japanese market and Jonathan was one of the first to go. It was, however, what the Japanese called manipulation from below. It was her party. Jonathan was her vehicle.

Sometimes, especially during the first years of their marriage, Anna felt a cheat. The ritual of revenge she and her mother were plotting had often called for a dual existence. All for a cause more sacred than marriage or love for a man and, according to the ancient custom of *kataki uchi*, more important than life itself.

All she shared with Jonathan was that Hedges had been with her father when he died. She never mentioned the killer's name, nor that she was intent on meeting him. She often felt confused and tired and could not respond to him, and then he would feel neglected and sorry for himself and become aggressive. She forgave him because she knew he loved her, and she wished she could have shared more with him.

She would. Once it was all over.

He tried so hard to be understanding. He did not know what it was that tormented her, but he accepted that something did and gave her space. He did not ask too much and waited for her moods to pass.

Women's trouble, he used to say and laughed, and she would bury her anger at his condescending remarks and try to laugh too.

Sometimes, she would get scared. Especially when, bit by bit, the information she was gathering was coming in and bringing her closer. She would fret at the action itself and often stop and ponder her doubts and tell herself she was doing right. Sometimes, when her resolve weakened, she would reach for Jonathan. She would feel for his body and his warmth and search for his lips under the sheets and take him while he thought he was taking her.

Later, as he slept, she would lie awake and think of how it would all end, and then her confidence would return. Perhaps it returned because of Jonathan. She was not sure and could not show her gratitude. She would make it all up to him because he was the only man in the world who would have accepted her the way he did and support her without knowing why. Soon.

She loved her mother, but didn't like her very much. It was Jonathan who had gathered the pieces of their relationship and brought them together. Painstakingly, slowly, while he was courting Anna, he began to show her a part of her mother she did not know. He knew how to make Toni laugh, and when she laughed she would become more tolerant and less frugal. Generous almost. Her constant criticism would cease, and Jonathan was offered the world.

He was an athletic young man who resembled an American college baseball star. He was a health fanatic and ate roughage and greens. His clean-cut face grimaced at tobacco, but he never tried to force Anna to give the habit up. He was held in great esteem by his employers and was now making his way, pioneering the new market in Japan. She took a deep breath and looked up at the blue autumn sky. She chuckled because she was meeting Jonathan and would soon be confronted with his pleasing personality. His good spirits would bring hers out.

As she turned away from the public telephone, she heard the noise and saw the demonstration crawling up the road. Twenty thousand banner-waving marchers were coming towards her, and they looked menacing. Tough faces egged on by wild slogans that hit the streets from screeching loudspeakers. Bitterness on people's faces became violent. It was all like the Japan she hated and was scared of, but had never seen before. They looked awesome and strong and determined. Any minute now they would burst onto the pavement and kill. Revenge. That was what she had come here for.

Up front, hordes of policemen walked ten abreast. The traffic had come to a standstill. Alarm was spilling onto the quiet faces by her side as the screaming came closer. People moved nearer the building for cover. Some passers-by joined in on a last-minute impulse.

'It's Okinawa Day,' an American voice declared. 'They are marching on the American Embassy to deliver a note to the ambassador. Give Okinawa back to Japan. Happens every year here, but I've never seen them this aggressive. It's surprising.'

She turned to look at the man, but he was gone. She was not surprised at all by the aggressiveness. These were the cruel, angry faces of the true Japan, the old Japan. Not the quiet, gentle Japan she was nearly seduced by when she first arrived. She walked briskly past the demonstration, hoping no one would think she was American, but they shouted their slogans and ignored her.

She didn't want to keep Jonathan waiting. There would be much unexplained waiting for him to do once she met Katsumata. The marchers were almost out of earshot now, and, at the top of the street, she could see the Sony building. He was sure to have something funny to tell her. He would ask her again about a private language teacher and tell her she mustn't sit around doing nothing. She would answer back in mock anger and he would smile and take her in his arms and kiss her.

CHAPTER ELEVEN

—■—

Yoshiro had always found it difficult to imagine his father as a fighting man. The old man did not talk much about the war, not even when books and films came out about it and it became accepted and fashionable. There were a few photographs of him in uniform, but no medals. Yoshiro remembered his mother talking about his father's time in Singapore and Thailand and Hong Kong. Yoshiro had been there, too, in his travels, and it was in Hong Kong that he found out his father was dying.

He had come back to his hotel room to find the message light blinking by his telephone. The desk told him they had a telex for him which had been there since lunch. They would send it up right away. It was a strange telex.

He had been used to receiving messages from the office to do with business. Never before a personal note. There was no mistaking the six words that stared at him, in English, from the yellow paper. 'Call Mrs Katsumata in Hokkaido. Sorry.' No explanations. No details. He knew only one Mrs Katsumata in Hokkaido and that was his mother.

The old man used to come down to Tokyo four or five times a year. He never stayed in his son's tiny house. He always slept in the Dai Ichi Hotel and shared his days between Yoshiro's children and the cinema houses along Hibiya Street. Keichi stayed in the Dai Ichi Hotel because he could not sleep on a Western bed which had springs and was far from the floor. He preferred the hard, familiar feel of the *futon* on the *tatami* matting. He could touch the ground and be close to the world that way. But he liked *gaijin* films.

In the afternoon of his years, Keichi tried to get closer to understanding his old enemies by watching the Anglo-Saxon *gaijin* on the wide silver screens. He watched them walk and talk and sing and fight and love and work. He watched them build houses and fly planes and fish, and he watched them play games. Keichi knew that what he saw were not real people but actors, yet they represented a way of life he did not know in countries he had never seen. There were trees and rivers and deserts and lakes and mountains. They were eating their food and drinking their liquor and lately he had seen their biscuits and whisky selling right here in Tokyo.

They were vulgar and crude, yet possessed by old-fashioned sentimentality. They did not enjoy their children's respect, yet these same people had defeated the Emperor and his army. They gave sweets to the van-quished as soon as they entered their cities, yet they had invented the bomb that destroyed Hiroshima. They spoke fast and often without thinking and had open faces and fancy, expressive words, but they did not understand nor respect their elders. He was fascinated and puzzled and troubled by them, but he was grateful to them for winning the war and bringing a new way of life to Japan.

He understood their language, but not their poetry, and he did not understand their minds or why work was less important to them than play. In all his years, he had met only two Anglo-Saxon *gaijin*: the prisoners he had led to Burma all those years ago. The medical officer Hedges and that other one, Pritchard, who had died. Keichi thought that *gaijin* should have been allowed by his destiny to grow old like himself and enjoy grey hair and grandchildren. He went to the cinema houses to learn what the *gaijin* would have done in old age, and then respectfully do it for him and share the experience with him in his mind.

And now, Keichi Katsumata was in a hospital bed in Sapporo in the northern island of Hokkaido, and his wife had summoned his son Yoshiro from Hong Kong to watch him die. He knew because he had heard her tell Yoshiro that, and wanted to tell them they were wrong, but he could not speak. The bed sheets were white and there were flowers on the table and a jug of water. The bed was a Western bed with springs and it was far from the floor. He did not mind because mostly he slept. There was a picture of mountains on the wall and the room was quiet. Most of the time, Keichi thought he was back in the Imperial army, especially in the mornings when the doctor came in with a worried face and shook his head and said that Mr Katsumata was clinically dead. Keichi wanted to tell him he was lying, but his chest was bursting, and he heard the doctor tell his wife to bring his son back from Hong Kong. He wanted to smile because he was so happy to see his handsome boy there with him, but his lips did not obey. He could smell the flowers and hear the birds outside the open window, but he could not speak. Others were making decisions for him and his own mind was only alert to the past.

He dreamed about the war. He must have been dreaming because he saw his old barracks and old cars and the mountain artillery school near Sendai. He saw the Taisho and the harbour of Singapore. And he saw the converted pleasure boat that took them to Thailand.

He saw Derek Pritchard, the *gaijin* who could have been his friend, and the other man who could never be. Maybe the *gaijin* Pritchard did not die at all. His destiny was at the mercy of Keichi's dream. Perhaps he was still in the peaceful village of Bang Saray, waiting for him to join him and resume their conversations in Spanish. Perhaps that was what had happened, and he had known and forgotten it. Keichi heard that a man can see all of his life passing before him as in a moving picture when he is about to die. He could not really be dying because he did not see all of his life. Just the war and then only a small part of it. He must have been dreaming. He dreamt of the Taisho again and he saw him as he did in Bangkok in 1942, after the mission. His lips moved and his son Yoshiro tried to make out what he wanted to say.

The Taisho was not that much older than himself. Eight or ten years maybe. Keichi had seen him, but not at any of the reunions because Keichi never went to any. He did not like the army any better, not even years after it had been defeated. He thought Japan never had any business to go to war against the *gaijin* and he had been trying to find out about the peace-time *gaijin* by looking at their films. He could never remember the stories, but he could remember the houses the heroes lived in, their cars and their dogs and their horses and boats. He was dreaming about the Taisho again and he saw him as he was now.

The Taisho must have been eating too much meat, because he had become nearly bald. He must have been smoking too much because he coughed a lot, but he was alive and a banker in Tokyo now. He did not have to retire because of old age as his family owned most of the shares in the bank. He still repeated himself a lot as he had when he was young. It would be good for his son to talk to the Taisho. The Taisho would tell him about the war and what happened in Burma and Thailand and Bang Saray and about the prisoners. He wanted to remember to tell Yoshiro about that and he made himself wake up and raise his hand towards his son. He wanted to talk and he could not, and it frustrated him. He motioned Yoshiro to come closer. He wanted to tell him to go and see the Taisho. His face strained and his lips moved, but no one heard. There was a bright intensity in Keichi's eyes and again his son knew he was trying to say something to him.

The Taisho was not called Taisho these days. He was plain Mr Sakamoto and he was an old man and came to the bank only three times a week. Keichi had seen him there and had met him in the Ginza a few times. They had talked for hours and dropped into coffee shops to reminisce. Last time they had met was only a week before he was taken ill. Keichi could not think of the old man as the Taisho when they talked, but now that he had dreamt about him in the war, he could not call him plain Mr Sakamoto.

Keichi looked at his son's agonized eyes and he remembered that he had told the Taisho about Yoshiro.

The Taisho had asked where young Katsumata was working and Keichi remembered telling him about the company. The Taisho had said he knew it well. Then they talked about other things, but Keichi did not remember what they were. He needed to tell his son about Derek Pritchard, but the effort was beyond him, and he closed his eyes again and slept and did not dream.

Yoshiro looked at his father's big frame under the sheet. He was breathing regularly and his face was at peace. Almost like that of a sleeping child. A man-child who had been good. His skin was without blemish and smooth. Someone must have shaved him before he had arrived.

The old man's lips were moving and a groan came. He opened his eyes one more time and looked about him as if he had been searching for someone. Then his lips stretched into a smile of recognition, and he coughed. Keichi looked at his son and thought he was talking to him and then he saw his son get up and rush out of the room. He wanted to stop him and he stretched his hand towards him as a pain bolted through his chest. And then it was cold and dark.

Keichi Katsumata died alone in the vastness of solitude, but he had not been lonely. Yoshiro came back with the doctor, who looked at the large, limp body of Keichi Katsumata and said he was dead. He said it in a simple, matter-of-fact voice. This was a hospital. Other people died here. Everybody dies. Only lucky ones die in a hospital bed. Yoshiro did not quite understand. He felt detached from the man in the bed. He felt numb and cold. He did not know the large man in the bed. The body used to belong to his father, but the dead man inside it was not his father because his father used to smile gently and talk softly, and the dead man on the bed was quiet.

He had his own life to lead and he had to get back to his office. He might have grown up in Hokkaido, but now he was a Tokyo man and on his own and on his way up.

CHAPTER TWELVE

---◆---

'My name is Sakamoto,' the man said. 'Sakamoto. An old friend of your father's. From the days of the war, Mr Katsumata. I used to be his Taisho.'

Yoshiro's curiosity shook him and brought his energies back. He had been tiresomely harassed by the telephone all day. The blessed custom of silent mourning had vanished as people called to say how sorry they were about his father. How they would miss him. How he was sure to find his place in honour with his ancestors. The callers were mostly people he did not know. While Yoshiro struggled to find something to say, his colleagues kept their heads sunk in their papers and avoided his eyes. Mr Sakamoto's short, curt voice did not indicate his was going to be a condolence call.

'Thank you for calling,' Yoshiro said. 'My father would surely have appreciated your kindness. I have heard your name before. You are a banker, are you not, sir?'

'That is so, but it is not business I wish to discuss with you, nor do I mean to console. I wish to tell you of my time with your father in the war. There was a lot of misunderstanding about that.'

'There will be time for that later, Mr Sakamoto.'

'He especially asked me to look you up and meet you

and tell you. A man should know about his father. You have a lot to be proud of.'

'My father spoke little about the war,' Yoshiro said. All around him, machines were tapping away and people moved about. 'I am sorry. Maybe this is not the place to talk . . .'

'I quite understand. You must forgive my haste, but there is much to say. Much to say and not much time.' The Taisho was an old man, Yoshiro thought. He was persistent and he was impatient, but then he had been asked by his own father to call him. Possibly his father wanted to be dead and out of the way first. Maybe he had something to hide.

'The sooner we meet, the better,' Mr Sakamoto said. 'There is a lot of shame and misunderstanding about our time in the war. I want to set the record straight.'

Well, this was the new generation, Yoshiro wanted to say, but the conversation was becoming much too public. There were no secrets in the general office. Only people on the eighth floor had walls of their own.

'Call me when you are ready to meet with me, Mr Katsumata,' the man said, and hung up without the usual parting niceties.

The company Yoshiro worked for, Kenzo Sato Kaisha, was run by descendants of the first Kenzo Sato, all, by the grace of destiny, sons. There were no outsiders on the board, only cousins, the odd son-in-law and some who married granddaughters. Yoshiro Katsumata was poised to break this tradition and everybody knew it. He was going to move up to the eighth floor of the sturdy pre-war Sato building and have an office of his own and an air-purifier.

They summoned him up there quite often to help make decisions, to recommend the hiring of graduates or advise on policies. He played golf with the founder's elderly grandson and the nephews, and he had the chairman's ear. He was about to become the first member of the board outside the Sato family, but they were waiting for his fortieth birthday. In itself a record, since no one ever became a director before reaching the age of fifty at least. He had come from the right background, was of independent means and profit-conscious. He played a good game of tennis, his handicap at golf was low, and he was unbeatable at mah-jong. He was an object of envy to all those who aspired to success.

Whispers predicted he was going to become president one day and make real history, but all that was far from his thoughts now. He wanted time to think of his father and he wanted peace.

He had not had a chance to see his wife yet, having stayed at the Dai Ichi Hotel since his return from Hokkaido. He did not know what to say to her about his father. She knew a man's time did not belong to him alone. A man was owned by the company, since it looked after him the way the warlords looked after their samurai before. The *kaisha* was supreme, and after that the men of the family. His wife did not call to disturb him; she knew how tired he was. The hotel was impersonal and there was room to move about. There were no children to make noises and he could be on his own and sleep. His face was grey and he was coughing more than before. The two large ashtrays in front of him were full. He sipped a cup of green tea and stared into nothing.

'Any messages?' he asked. His voice was unusually soft.

'Mrs Bellingham called,' the girl said. 'The *gaijin* woman I mentioned to you.' He did not want to speak to a foreigner. Not today. To speak English required concentration he did not have. He dialled his home number and his wife answered. She said she was sorry. The children wanted to see him. Was he coming to sleep at home tonight? His little girl barged in on the extension and asked what he had brought her from Hong Kong. She wanted an ice-cream and a drawing book and an elephant. The book was for Oji-san when he next came from Hokkaido. 'Oji-san can draw so well, can't he, papa?' His wife must have managed to get the little girl off the line because her tiny voice had disappeared. His son came on and said he had done all his homework and could he ride his bicycle now that he had finished? His son asked if it was true that Oji-san was dead. Yoshiro said he could go and ride on the pavement, but only for half an hour if his mother agreed.

He told his wife they could talk tomorrow, and said he had to go because there was another call coming through. Goodnight.

The telephonist said a Mrs Bellingham was on the line. No company name or reference. A personal call. The lady had tried before. He had just told his wife he had to go and the girl must have heard that. He had to speak to the *gaijin* woman now.

'Put her through,' he said.

'Forgive the late hour,' the English voice said. 'I suppose you're about to shut up shop.'

He had not heard the expression before, but he understood what it meant.

'I am truly sorry,' she said.

'I thought only us Japanese started every conversation with an apology.'

'Oh no. We British apologize just as much.'

'Do not worry about the time. We were not going to . . . to shut the shop yet. What can I do for you?'

'You must be very busy. I am sorry.'

They both laughed and she asked whether he preferred her to call back later. She had a clear, precise voice that indicated strength. She assumed he spoke English well and did not slow down for him, and he liked that. She did not sound like a woman at all. The women he knew did not persist the way she did.

'It's quite all right, Mrs Bellingham.' He did not pronounce her name with a double R. 'How can I be of service to you?'

'It's sort of personal, Mr Katsumata. Not a thing one can discuss on the phone. I may sound a bit forward and I would apologize, but you'd agree I have overdone the "sorry" thing. I wonder whether we could meet. I won't take much of your time. This is not a very orthodox approach, but you have done business with us foreigners before. Can we meet?'

The English *gaijin* were not usually that aggressive. She had something to sell. Something new, perhaps.

'Let me look at my diary, Mrs Bellingham. What is a convenient time for you, morning or afternoon?'

She must not push now. She had done well and her brow was wet. Calm down. Christ, how could she calm down? She was finally speaking to Lieutenant Katsumata's son. She could not let go. More small-talk, she told herself as she shivered. She had gathered all her courage for this. It was now or never.

'I am at the Ginza. I have a little shopping to do. I'm trying to find a pair of shoes, but nothing fits my *gaijin* feet.' Good. He was laughing aloud. 'I thought I'd try

Mitsukoshi. Someone could make a fortune here selling jumbo-size shoes for *gaijin* ladies. The store is not too far from you, is it? Perhaps we could meet later on?'

'You mean today?'

Easy, girl, or you'll blow it. Change the subject.

'They stay open late, don't they? Nine o'clock or something.' She should have asked him if it was convenient for him. He was a man. They were in Japan. Be polite. Something was egging her on and she was straining to will him to agree. God, don't flop now. She would go to church if he agreed now. Give up smoking. Do anything.

'Would six-thirty be too late for you, Mrs Bellingham?'

That was unexpected. It was thirty minutes away. Was he playing with her?

'That would be perfect, Mr Katsumata. Thank you so much.'

'There is a small coffee shop right next to Mitsukoshi. Would that suit you?'

'Mr Katsumata, I don't know how to thank you.'

'There are a lot of foreign women in that coffee shop at this time of the evening. How will I know you?'

'I'm wearing a grey wool suit and I have a large plastic bag marked Sony.'

'I understand,' he said, and they said goodbye. He thought he should have asked her who had put her on to him. He did not understand what the urgency was or why the mystery. Perhaps she wanted to sell him some business information. He had done nothing productive all day. This was different. Fresh. Making polite conversation with well-wishing condolence callers was hard. One could meet with *gaijin* for business without creating an obligation. This woman must have something to offer. Yoshiro wondered what she looked like. An old lady, probably. No. Not looking for shoes at Mitsukoshi in the early evening. Why was she not at her home preparing dinner? Prosperous, then. He had never met with a *gaijin* woman on his own before. Not for business. The prospect of a blind encounter was intoxicating. It was a new page. Perhaps the coup he needed for that final thrust into the boardroom. Someone must want to make a deal without approaching him directly. As he looked at his watch to check the time, he found he was willing the golden hands to move faster.

She saw Yoshiro Katsumata come out of the main door of the Sato building. He was going to be early. He tidied his hair and checked his light raincoat in the shop window and consulted his watch. He was taller than she had expected and from across the road he looked younger. Her palpitations rose. She had never been sure what she was going to do when facing a Katsumata in the flesh. Her mother had said she would know, just as soon as she met the enemy, but the sight of him offered no clues. What should she do? Run across the road and grab his neck right there with the evening crowd looking on? Why? She had no quarrel with him. She must not confuse things, now that she had got this far. She took a deep breath and counted to ten as she watched him walk away. He sprinted across the wide street. He was elegantly agile. He looked the part: an arrogant son of a criminal warrior. He wanted to get there first. Sit in ambush like any man on a blind date. If the bastard didn't like her face, he'd just leave. No. He'd wait.

She stood there and watched him disappear into the multitudes. She had no right to hate him. He could not help being Katsumata's son. Perhaps she would light a cigarette. After all, she was going to give the habit up as soon as this was over. She took the pack and her lighter out of her handbag and, hiding the flame in the palm of her hand, she lit up. She walked slowly and pretended to look at the shops.

She had promised to call her mother as soon as contact was made, but this was not the time. All her mother would say was you have not met the father yet. Don't waste money on a nothing call. Anna did not need to be near her mother to feel her heart beat. Hot in pursuit of the enemy, thousands of miles away, years after the fall of the Republic, Antonia Aguilar de Soto was waging relentless war. She was fighting her family's killers, all the world's killers, in the shape of Katsumata who was the accumulation of them all. Approaching old age, Anna's mother did not have the usual aspirations of becoming a grandmother before seeing her husband's killer destroyed. There would be time afterwards for babies and knitting and strolls in the park. Her small frame harboured a giant that would guide her daughter into battle.

Anna had known all this and often she had resented it. Yet now, she smiled as she thought of how the frail soldier from the lost brigade was with her in the cool evening and how she was winning. It was time to go and meet Katsumata's son. A nation of smiling faces was crowding the pavements towards the railway stations, to cars and home. Inside, Anna's smile was burning a hole in her soul. Whose life was she leading? She stamped her cigarette out and stopped. Have another. Let him wait. Call the whole thing off. No, go now.

'I am sorry I'm late,' the beautiful *gaijin* woman said to him. He had been reading the financial pages and her voice blurred the columns and their figures. He had not noticed Anna standing over him. He was being impolite. Her voice sounded sweet, and Yoshiro rose to his feet.

'Don't get up,' she said. She was just a little taller than him. She was wearing high heels.

On the walls, there were posters of Paris and London and San Francisco. There were Japanese prints and French gallery notices and photographs of movie stars from Hollywood. There were silk-screens and calendars and a torn Beatles programme. Above their table, amidst the chatter, there was silence. He could not find words and he asked:

'Is this your first visit to Japan?' She nodded. He ordered English tea with milk. 'I hope you don't mind tea,' he said, and she smiled and said it was fine.

She thought he had perfectly shaped hands, the long, thin fingers of a concert pianist. He had a deep voice and blue-black thick hair. His narrow eyes were clear and he looked tired, but he did not act tired. She thought he was not an unattractive man. There was power beneath his skin and his manners were impeccable. Sitting down, he seemed taller than her.

She looked slowly, carefully scanning every inch of him. Here was the same blood that ran through Lieutenant Katsumata's veins. Mother's voice again.

Must understand the son first. Get to the father later. Hate him later. It was so much simpler to hate an idea. In front of her, quietly looking at her, was a human being. He seemed remote, lonely, confused and sad. Don't feel sorry for him. Don't trust him.

'It's really nice of you to meet me at such short notice,' she said. 'This must be the busiest city in the world.'

Yoshiro listened to her and watched her face through the smokescreen. The parcel his mother had sent him was to be taken to the temple tomorrow. The ancient custom of *bunkotsu* would bring a part of his father closer to him. A few bones in an urn placed at the temple nearby for him to visit and touch and see forever. But what of the *gaijin* woman? Why ask? She was his escape from the office and people's embarrassment at his grief. She was the good spirit who would protect him until he was himself again. Until he was ready to resist unwanted favours bestowed upon a middle-aged orphan.

He had just begun to understand his father. He had made up his mind, not long ago, to make friends with the big, soft-spoken man. In the hospital, he had imagined long-overdue conversations. All he had left now was a small bone to communicate with. A remnant put to rest in a place where the living can talk to their dead at leisure. His father had been proud of him and Yoshiro wanted to hear him say so. He would never see him again in his old form, unless in a dream. There was only today. All he could see now was the *gaijin* woman. She was the most beautiful foreign woman he had ever seen. Her long hair was a deep reddish-brown, her eyes were green. She had soft lips that curled when she smiled. He had seen her smile when she stood over him and again at the waiter when the tea came.

'*Arigato,*' she said. She looked strong, and Yoshiro knew she could laugh although she had known sorrow. He wanted to hear her laugh. What could she want of him? What did it matter?

'I have never been out with a Japanese man.'

'I have,' he said, and she laughed. She understood. She was quick-witted. He liked people enjoying his jokes.

'But I have never been out with a *gaijin* woman alone,' he lied.

'It's a first for both of us, then,' she said, and he lit her cigarette. She had good skin for a *gaijin*. In Australia, he had been taken by a supplier to a place of women last year. It was not a clean place and the girl he had slept with had a rough, spotty face. She said fuck this and fuck that and she smelt of beer and tobacco. But he must not think of that whore now. His father was dead, and across the table sat a woman of class. The wheel of fortune was trying to turn for him.

'Would you like some more tea?'

'Thank you, no.'

'Are you doing anything special tonight?'

'Not really. I have no plans.'

He wanted to invite her to dine with him, but he hesitated. He'd lose face if she refused.

She looked at him and saw what went through his mind. All he needed was one little push, but she must not overdo it. Perhaps she was wrong. They all looked friendly. Yet she knew something was weighing heavily on him. Perhaps he had had a bad day. Why should she care?

'Do you like Japanese food?' A non-committal, general question from which he could always retreat.

'Any food will do. I am quite easy to please,' she said. 'There are so many eating places in Tokyo. It's almost impossible to choose. What do you like, Mr Katsumata?'

That was it, then. They would eat together.

'I too like everything. You decide.'

'I can't,' she said. 'Sorry.'

'Sorry,' he said, and she laughed.

'I am quite fond of *tempura*.'

'There is a *tempura* shop three doors away. They fry the best shrimps in Tokyo. It is a Japanese place. I mean, not for tourists. No menu in English.'

'Will they let me in?'

He nodded and tried to smile. She was making him feel cheerful. People had been so careful with him all day.

They began a friendly discourse about the Portuguese origins of *tempura* and places at which it was best served. He was smiling more and she smiled less and then he got up and called the waiter.

'Shall we go, Mrs Bellingham?'

'Anna,' she said. 'My name is Anna.'

'We Japanese are more formal. But I'll call you Anna if you like.'

Conceited sod. If you like. Her face hardened as he paid the bill, but he did not notice. She had all the time in the world. All she needed him for was to lead her to his father. Might as well be nice to him. She could afford to be.

'It is nice of you to invite me,' she said. He'd expect her to be polite.

'I'm sure you will enjoy it,' he said. She had not told him yet who had given her his name and what it was she wanted, but with the cool Ginza air on his face and the beautiful *gaijin* woman by his side, Yoshiro did not care. They walked briskly, their rhythms matching, and he felt light-hearted. Had he been alone, he would have whistled 'It's a Long Way to Tipperary'. He was fond of whistling that tune when he was happy.

CHAPTER THIRTEEN

She did not hear him at first because he said it quietly, his voice lost in the crackling sound of frying batter. His face, lit by the paper lantern, assumed an agonized contortion. She watched the sliced fish being lowered into boiling oil, her elbows leaning on the polished wooden bar. She had been talking away about Europe and Japan and books and cars and her husband's job. He had been silent, and when he had said it, she looked at him and saw his eyes. They were open and smoky and sad.

'I have just lost my father,' he said. 'He died last week.' Perhaps he said it twice, but his voice was even.

Dead. Just like that. Out of the blue.

Impossible. Lieutenant Katsumata had to be alive. He couldn't simply have vanished into the custody of the spirits before facing his crimes here on earth. Yet the fact was staring her in the face. Yoshiro did not need to say it again. Her merry chatter made it easy for him to talk about it. He had not put it into words for anybody before, and now the void had lifted.

'I'm sorry,' Anna forced herself to say.

'Thank you,' he said, and her expression made him feel guilty about loading her with his sorrow.

Her chest felt heavy and the air failed to reach her. Her hand lay motionless on the wooden counter, gripping a cigarette end. The heat stung her finger, but she did not move. Was this her punishment for thinking him appealing? Did she not have to make friends with him to meet his father? All that meticulous planning up the spout. The lies, the pretence, the games of hide-and-seek. All those useless meetings with people, those roundabout conversations to find the right man, the stories invented to keep Jonathan in the dark. And all that fucking money.

She looked lost and grey and frightened, and his heart went out to her.

'I am sorry I told you that, Mrs Bellingham,' he said. 'It was selfish of me to talk to you of death.'

Her skin was taut and she was numb. She felt cheated and sick and she needed to think. Alone. No. Not alone. Must talk to her mother right now. What first had appeared to be a quaint little ethnic *tempura* house, simply decorated and meticulously clean, had become a dump. The odour of oil came close and her appetite was gone. There was stale beer on the counter, spent matches stuck into wet cigarette ends in loaded ashtrays. The whole place smelt of fish.

He watched what he deemed to be the agony that had seized her, and he marvelled at her.

'I must go home now, Mr Katsumata,' she said. To hell with manners.

'I am so sorry,' he said gently. 'It's all my fault.'

'You don't understand . . .'

Oh, but he was sure he did. He saw the pain in her eyes. Here was a woman who was foreign and was not like the others who had phoned him all day. She was sharing his loss with him as if she had known him all her life. She said she wanted to go home right away. Let him be on his own, save his face. Avoid forcing him to entertain her while grief ruled his heart.

She was taking the guilt of bad manners off his shoulders by breaking the evening off herself.

'Shall I call you a taxi?'

'I can get the underground train to Shibuya. It's only

a short walk from there to my apartment.' She grabbed her coat and her bag and her cigarettes. 'We'll talk tomorrow or the next day,' she said. She gave him her number and left.

Yoshiro watched her go. She had said she would talk to him again. She had been a friend when a friend was needed, and she had rescued him. He could now spend fifty minutes on the Seibu line and go to his own house and speak to his wife. He could see his sleeping children and bathe and sleep. The train would not be crowded. Or he could stay right where he was a little longer and eat and forget his troubles for now. Tomorrow he would go to the temple, then face Mr Sato at the office and have his wits about him. It was the Englishwoman he owed thanks to for saving him from self-pity.

At the station, Yoshiro bought himself the late edition of the financial paper and a golf magazine before taking the escalator down. His wife would be at home, waiting as ever, and she would offer him a cup of tea and a beer and she would run the hot water for him and soap his back. He would sink into the serene, silky silence of his kimono and think. Tomorrow, he would call his father's wartime Taisho. He would be ready to face him then.

'This doesn't change a thing. *Nada*,' Anna's mother said. 'We go after the son.'

'You don't understand. He's not . . . he's not like . . . like an enemy. He's like a child. He reminded me of myself.'

'Pull yourself together. It's the custom. You told me about that yourself. *Kataki uchi*, yes?'

'He is . . . the whole thing doesn't make sense any more.'

'*Kataki uchi*, Anna. It's his duty to expect it, as it is yours to discharge. He will expect it once he knows.'

It was an exceptionally clear line. Of course her mother was right. An eye for an eye? The Japanese invented revenge. Revenge had caused more wars there than territory. What was all this to do with her?

'So young Katsumata walks down the path of destiny into the firing line,' she said with mock pathos.

'Bravo, *querida*. Beautifully put. Now go to sleep. I'll think of something.'

You will think of something. If this is your fight, what am I doing here? Toni had replaced the receiver and Anna said an angry goodnight to no one.

Jonathan called. He'd been trying to reach her all afternoon. Who was she speaking to this late? Was everything okay?

Oh, sure. She'd been in the shops and found nothing to fit her. He'd be pleased to hear she had made contact with someone for the Japanese lessons. A businessman who wanted to improve his English.

Splendid. Well, he missed her anyway. The weather in Osaka was fine. He'd had a good afternoon. He had allowed his opponents to win a couple of games.

'It's all very well for you,' she said, 'enjoying yourself down there. When will you be back?'

'In three days. The plan has changed. They are taking me to the Arima Spa for a bit. It's in the hills above Osaka. I can't refuse. There'll be geishas and things, I expect. It's only for three days.'

'And three nights,' she said. They both laughed. There was strength in his voice and confidence when he said he loved her.

Fifteen minutes before midnight, Yoshiro Katsumata

called. From the hesitant tone of his voice, she deduced he had taken forever to gather up the courage.

'I hope you got back without problems,' he said.

'Yes, thank you.'

'Thank you for your company. You were very kind and understanding. *Oyasuminasai*. That's goodnight in Japanese.'

'*Oyasuminasai*.'

'You can call me any time you like.'

Just like his father. Cocky son-of-a-bitch. How dare he call this late?

Call him any time? He'd soon see. He'd crawl. He would . . . God, she was thinking just like her mother.

He did not apologize for calling at that hour and must have been in agony. So what? Who was she trying to hate? A pitiful sham of a man. Her mother would expect her to hate him. Yet, for that she would need to get closer. Be attractive. She would be calling the shots from now on.

She was calming down, but she needed relief.

She lay in her bed and the sheets were soft to the touch of her skin. She took a little drink and soon she was not angry with anyone. She saw Yoshiro leaving his office and then she saw him sitting helplessly in the coffee shop. Something about him reminded her of the first man she had known. Not just known. The first man who had made love to her. She did not remember his name. Perhaps she never knew it. He was a flower salesman and her mother never found out what had happened.

The train came back into her vision and the face of the man who sat there, watching her make notes. She was going to London to do some Christmas shopping. She could not think straight, and she wrote down what she was going to buy and for whom. To start with, she did not notice him at all. Then he spoke.

'You are far too pretty to be that busy.'

She looked up at him. He was in his early thirties, of fair complexion, and his black-rimmed glasses made him look like an intellectual. He was wearing a grey chequered suit and on his lap rested a motor magazine. His shoes were brown and polished. He had a London grammar-school accent and an unlit pipe in his mouth. There was a faded red carnation affixed to his lapel. He had cut himself shaving and his white shirt was crumpled.

'I beg your pardon?' she said, and he repeated it.

'I'm not really busy,' she said, and she told him what she was going to London for.

'You live in the country, then?'

'In the suburbs, but only during vacations. I have just started university.'

'I wish I had been to university. I could have gone there, but at the time it seemed a waste. I suppose I couldn't wait to start making a living. When you're young, you're stupid and in a hurry. Now I sell flowers. This one on my lapel is not very flattering, but it looked good yesterday.'

He said his flowers came by air from Holland, and he was selling them to flower shops in the home counties. He had never seen them grow, and did not really know much about them, but he was a professional salesman and flowers were a good game where one met nice people. Hell, it was a living.

Anna did not remember much more about the train. All she remembered was how he started talking to her and what he looked like and what he said. He told her he was free all day, and could go with her because he knew where to get real bargains. He had no family and no one to buy presents for, and she felt a little sorry for him. She went with him because he looked lonely, and especially because she had never done anything like that before and her mother would certainly have told her not to.

They walked up and down Oxford Street and Regent Street and the other little streets that led in and out and across them, and they looked at shops. The parcels she was carrying grew in number and by lunchtime they both had their hands full. He was not particularly clever, but he was quick-witted and told salesmen jokes that made her laugh. It was an easy morning and it was new and thoughtless and all hers. She was enjoying herself and did not notice when he became familiar and touched her hand or held her waist. And then, after they had an egg and tomato sandwich, he invited her for coffee at his flat. They left all the parcels at Waterloo Station and took the underground to Fulham. Things ran fast and different, and not once during the time with the flower salesman did she think of Lieutenant Katsumata or what they would do with him.

She lay on his bed and looked at the ceiling and he lay next to her. She was fully dressed and he was wearing a housecoat because he did not want his suit to crease. It was his lucky road suit, he said, his money-spinner. He kissed her arms and her forehead and he stroked her hair. Somehow, her jacket came off and was neatly laid on the back of a chair. Later, her skirt and her stockings and her shoes were removed, and she found herself lying naked under the sheets. It was all a new experience and no words passed as she waited. He touched her legs and his limbs were all over her and then she felt his hardness press against her side. She knew what it was and what it would do, and waited. But the warm proximity of it did nothing for her and she lay still, as if another girl were lying with the flower salesman while Anna looked on from the corner of the room.

He was touching her breasts and his smoker's breath came into her face. His hands hovered past her stomach and rested on her pubic mound and below. His fingers were touching her, and she put her hand on his and pressed. Her mother was far away and her own body arched towards his hand and down and up again. Suddenly, he pulled her legs apart, and she pressed them around his arm. It was strange to feel someone else's hand on that most private part, but it was not unpleasant and nature made it moist and soft. He was on top of her and she felt the smooth hardness entering her body, tearing, throbbing, paining her and she wanted to scream, but his mouth was on hers. For a split second, she felt a tang of pleasure about to descend on her, but then he shook violently and said shit and rolled off her. Then he said sorry and that was all.

He did not talk to her any more. She lay there by his side and expected something else to happen, but nothing did. Was that what the experienced girls raved about? A quick penetration by one body of another?

Then the flower salesman faded from her mind and she felt hot. Lying in her bed in Shibuya, Anna Bellingham felt the pangs of hunger. She opened her eyes, got up and went to the little kitchen. She made some toast and buttered it. She opened a can of Campbell's asparagus soup and ate an apple and she must have done it all half in her sleep because the light in the kitchen was left on all night. The next morning, she awoke late. The maid ran the bath for her. There was plenty of time, and she knew Yoshiro was expecting her to call, but she would make him wait.

The maid came into her bedroom and smiled a controlled, non-infectious smile.

'*Dozo,*' she said. 'Your bath is ready.'

Anna pulled her nightie off and faced the woman in the nude. The maid smiled again, a clear smile of fascinated embarrassment, and fled from the room. The telephone rang, but Anna ignored it. If it was Jonathan, he would phone again. Especially if his conscience was beating him for having too much of a good time. The phone persisted, its long sound following her to the bathroom. She knew the maid would never pick it up if there was someone in the apartment. The telephone gave out its last, long, whistling buzz as Anna lowered herself into the water.

It was soft and hot and wet, and the feeling of sweat coming down her brow was pleasing. She threw a bar of peach bath-salts in, and the water rapidly assumed their colour and scent. The foam spread atop the water and covered her breasts, its airy touch caressing her nipples. She lay there wanting her skin to be touched. An expectant, distant, under-the-skin passion came to her. The gentle sensation of approaching, faceless desire. It did not connect to a face or a body or a voice. She touched her pubic hair and below, and the familiar twitch of arousal came as she squeezed.

She wanted, but she wasn't sure who she wanted because it had been many years since she had found herself in this way all alone. A slow wave of frustration was approaching her body, and then she removed her hand quickly as if her mother had been watching. Guilt came in to roost along with her mother's voice. 'You must never play with yourself. It will make you blind.' She lay back and waited for the water to rinse her and cool her down, and with the fading sound of her mother's voice came Jimmy Hedges' red, bloated face. She saw it glaring at her, red-eyed and greedy, over a plate of curry at Veeraswamy's Indian Restaurant in Regent Street. The place with that giant Indian doorman who saluted as one came in.

Why would Jimmy Hedges creep into her thoughts now?

The water in the bath was cooling and she got out and walked with a towel and a shiver back into the bedroom. The telephone rang again. It was her mother. She tried to make herself comfortable, but the towel was wet.

'When are you meeting him?' Toni asked. No hello or how are you. 'You must not let him go. Find out what he knows about his father's past. Is he aware they owe our family a debt of honour? When you know all that, you can make plans. I am feeling much better now. I can come to Tokyo to help you.'

Toni's accent was ridiculously noticeable on the telephone. Anna held the receiver in one hand while trying to dry herself with the other. She was not thinking about Yoshiro Katsumata or what her mother was saying. The killer was dead, and so was the victim. Perhaps they both faced God somewhere, waiting for him to consult with all those prophets and saints before pronouncing judgement. The whole thing was out of their hands now and anyway everything had changed. Everybody was friends now; her husband was sitting with former enemies at Arima Spa, and they were toasting each other with Scotch whisky.

'I have not made any arrangements to meet him. I will tell you when I do. You can't just pounce on a

Japanese. They close up if you do. I do not want to inhibit him. Unless he feels comfortable with me, we won't find anything out.'

'There is nothing to find out. Just get him. Do not warn him, don't get involved.'

'Don't get involved? I am involved with this. I have been all my life! How can you talk like this now?'

'Jimmy Hedges was here for lunch last Sunday. He is planning a trip to the Far East. Perhaps he'll come and see you. He has become very fat and did not look well at all. He should retire and lose some weight or he'll die. Imagine, the vicar's wife had a new baby. The sixth. You would think they were Catholics.'

She hadn't been listening, as usual, Anna thought. Her mother was asking after Jonathan and Anna said he was out of town.

'Give him my love,' her mother said, and kissed her over the wire. It seemed her mother had always interrupted something. Something good. She had forgotten what it was this time because her mother's new tack confused her. But then her mother was far away and weak now, and a new sense of determination settled over Anna. She lay back and enjoyed the feel of the sheet over her skin.

Light filtered through the curtains and she pulled the covers over her head. She could stay in bed all day if she wanted. It was comfortable and she felt secure and strong, and then the darkness that ruled under the covers guided her to sleep.

CHAPTER FOURTEEN

Lost in their big leather chairs, they looked so old. They were wax figures in a life-size museum. The large boardroom table dwarfed their small frames. Some smoked, and some sipped their green tea, but all eyes were on him. Their parched faces professed interest in what he was saying and Yoshiro knew they were waiting for him to crack. How frail and spent and bored they looked. The cousins and the nephews and the two outsiders. Only Mr Sato, the chairman, seemed to listen to what Yoshiro was saying.

By the chairman's side sat an elderly man Yoshiro had never seen before. He had receding, white, short-cropped hair and a tight, wrinkled, severe face. No one had introduced him to Yoshiro when he came in to deliver his speech. That meant the man was important, and to have asked for his identity would have been rude.

The man watched his every move, while his own face remained without emotion. Not once did the man look at Mr Sato to gauge his reaction. That meant they were equals. Perhaps they had been at school together.

'With a permanent office in Hong Kong or Singapore, we could increase our sales in South-East Asia,' Yoshiro said. 'We should go into partnership with local manufacturers. We must use local labour. Both Hong Kong and Singapore are growing fast, and their development holds untold opportunities for Sato Kaisha. I urge you to consider my plans and establish a proper presence there. If we wish to obtain these people's trust, we must show them we are there to stay . . . in the commercial sense, of course. Our last, infamous visit there is well remembered by many.

'You may claim that this is what we are doing now, but that is not so. Our outlook on world trade is seen by others to be one-sided. They condemn what is called the collective selfishness of Japan. They say we do not really care to see other nations prosper more than necessary, not as long as they earn enough to pay for our cameras and watches and cars. We shall have to start paying attention to what the world is saying, gentlemen, before it is too late.

'We tell ourselves our success is the fruit of hard work. This is only partially true. We simply must give the world a chance to sell its goods to us.'

He had spoken in this vein before, and he knew he was getting nowhere. He had to get a permanent seat around this very table to achieve anything at all. To tell them once and for all it was the world, not he, who believed that Japan was playing an unfair game. Making himself unpopular by telling people the truth would not help his career. Others had tried.

Like old Mr Akashi, who wrote to the editor of the *Asahi Shimbun*. Akashi used to be Yoshiro's boss. It was Akashi who had taught him all he knew about international trade. All about the outside world and the people who lived in it. Akashi had inside knowledge of the *gaijin* way of life because he had been a prisoner of war in Australia and spoke English better than anyone in the company. He taught Yoshiro about currencies and balance of trade figures and tariffs and import licences. He taught him how to talk to *gaijin* and how to entertain them and he showed Yoshiro the faults within their own society. Akashi used to be in charge of the foreign trade department, but he never made it to the board. He had become a laughing-stock among the top brass of Sato Kaisha long before he was made to leave.

He wrote letters to the press under an assumed name, denouncing the Ministry of Trade's unfair practices. Why do we train our salesmen to roam the world selling our products without giving the world the chance to do the same here? Why does the Ministry make life so difficult for importers, while exporters enjoy tax concessions and fat expense accounts? Those foreigners who do sell goods to Japan, wrote Akashi, are soon made to stop by a wall of archaic, suffocating regulations. Worse still, he wrote, our prices here at home are pushed sky-high to pay for cheap exports to the world.

In another letter, Akashi complained that the Japanese leaders were guilty of criminal selfishness. He cited the case of the Taiwanese who were drafted to fight alongside their Japanese masters during the Second World War. We now refuse to pay their pensions and other compensations which are so generously handed to Japanese nationals. I lament, he wrote, the coming world opinion of our trading habits, which will one day be compared to our back-door actions at Pearl Harbor. Akashi wrote a lot of letters and they were all published under his assumed name. And then he was found out; his life in the company was made a misery and he resigned.

Yoshiro did not write any letters to the press, nor preach his opinions to the world. He veiled Akashi's ideas behind thickly camouflaged speeches on international trade. Mostly, people listened to him because they enjoyed his clear voice and his good looks and his sense of humour. He pointed to the success of companies that invested overseas. He talked about hiring foreigners and joint ventures and he organized overseas visits by Japanese buyers. He was, he said, all for introducing the best in *gaijin* culture into Japanese society.

Where did Japan learn about trade in the first place? Did not the man who founded Mitsubishi go west to study his trade?

'What is so different about the *gaijin*? Why do some treat them with such suspicion? They are either idolized or despised. Either giants or dwarfs. They come here and they are entertained, no expense spared. They are wined and dined and are sold the bodies of Japanese women, but are not allowed to buy into Japanese industry. Would any one of you survive the shame of a *gaijin* son-in-law?'

That will shake them, Yoshiro thought as the faces remained vacant. He thought he saw a twitch on the chairman's face. The man he did not know rubbed his stony chin. He should have talked to his father about all this, but he had missed his chance.

There was a practical reason for him to get his point through today. He was after the board's agreement to his plans to send two members of his staff to work in the United States for a year.

'It is important for our people to learn about the *gaijin* ways at first hand. To understand his likes and dislikes, his thoughts and his needs. We in Japan have engineers and doctors and artists. We produce everything under the sun, but we do not know how to communicate. To send these two young people to live and work among the *gaijin* will help. The knowledge of a foreign language is not enough.'

Yoshiro added a few polite words about the people present and he bowed. 'Thank you for your time,' he said, and bowed again.

The chairman spoke.

'Meet an old friend of the company, Mr Katsumata.' He turned to face their guest and introduced him as one Masahiro Sakamoto, a banker and a former officer in the Imperial army.

'Mr Sakamoto called me this morning,' the chairman said, 'and when I told him you were coming up here to talk to us, he insisted on joining the meeting. I hope he enjoyed the talk as much as I did.'

The others clapped their hands and Yoshiro was invited to sit down while they prepared their questions. He looked straight into Mr Sakamoto's eyes. They were cold eyes, yet strong and wise and they did not blink.

'I am happy to meet you, young man,' Mr Sakamoto said. 'You possess much experience and knowledge for one so young. I am indebted to Mr Sato for the privilege of listening to you.'

Mr Sato beamed a contented smile that heralded another round of applause. So that was the man who could tell him about his father's war years.

The man who was his father's Taisho sat in his place like a mountain, his posture erect and proud. Not a muscle moved on his face. A hard man, Yoshiro thought. A man of self-discipline whose wrinkles had a story to tell. Old men with stories of some glorious past could be persistent. The Taisho had not waited for him to make contact. He must have something up his sleeve. A confession, perhaps. If only he could have asked him directly to come out with it, the way *gaijin* do.

Yoshiro got up.

'Can I be of further assistance to you, gentlemen?' He expected someone to come up with the usual question of cost, but Mr Sato took the floor.

'I think,' the chairman said, 'we can dispense with

any questions for today. These can be put to Mr Katsumata in written form. Our honoured guest, Mr Sakamoto, would like to invite Mr Katsumata for a private lunch. It has always been the custom of this company to comply with the wishes of a guest. The meeting is adjourned. Take as much time as Mr Sakamoto requires, Mr Katsumata.'

He was not asked whether he had the time, nor could he refuse. But there were things to do nonetheless, and the Englishwoman had not called yet.

'We will go out to lunch now, Mr Katsumata,' Mr Sakamoto said in a voice that expected no argument. It contained no hesitation, no manners, no consideration and no feeling. 'I know of a small eating place across the street. We shall go there.'

They were alone in the boardroom now, and on their way to the door. Mr Sakamoto must have commanded a lot of respect from the chairman to be given the freedom of the place that way. They walked down the stairs, all eight flights. The man refused to take the lift, having dismissed it from their presence with his stick. He wore a dark pin-striped suit and had a grey felt hat in his hand, which he offered to Yoshiro to carry. The traffic on the Ginza was light and the Taisho was waiting for the pedestrian lights to turn green. He shook his head at others who did not, with the frustrated anger of one who could no longer command. Yet when they sat down at the table facing each other, erratic curves of kindness appeared across the Taisho's face. His mouth relaxed into a smile. He ordered two green teas and the smile stayed on as his eyes came alive.

'Katsumata,' he said softly with a banker's voice, 'it was with green tea that I first greeted your father in

Singapore. It is only right that we should do the same to honour him.'

Yoshiro lit a cigarette and the old man looked at him with some compassion and said:

'I gave those up recently. There comes a time when a man must give up some of the follies of youth. When the head cannot take the ravages of alcohol and muscles refuse to obey. When I was young, no one said cigarettes were bad for you. Better throw the pack away, while your lungs are still pink.'

The cigarette tasted bitter, but Yoshiro held on.

'You look a little like your father, Yoshiro,' the Taisho said in a condescending voice. 'He was larger of frame, and much younger than you are now, when he first came into my office. He was, you know, a very brave man, freshly transplanted from home leave into the midst of fallen Singapore. There was still smoke and soot and there was hunger.

'I was sending him to die in Burma or Thailand, on a mission we both knew was almost certainly a one-way street. There were other people there, but they were all under a death sentence because they could not be allowed to return. I remember his reaction. He did not want to lead an army of future corpses into a trap, but he was an officer and a man of class, and he said nothing. He had been well trained, but had never seen battle before. It was his intelligence and spirit and his leadership Japan needed in that difficult hour, and I had to use him because there was no one else.

'Of course, your father was made of tough Hokkaido stock, and we were of the same class, although we did not talk of that. There was little time to prepare him for his mission, and he was sent into the jungle to use the intuition and inventiveness his heritage had given him. I knew he would do just that, but all the same I worried about him because he did not know the whole story. He knew where he was going, and with whom, and more or less what for. He did not know why, because I could not tell him. It was a secret only a few in the command at Singapore knew.

'Did you know I saw your father after the war? We met once in the Ginza, by chance. We came to this very place and we saw each other quite a few times after that. But I never did tell him the truth. Never. I didn't get the chance, and perhaps I did not want it.'

The Taisho's face betrayed a hint of hesitation for the first time.

'Maybe I was ashamed to tell him why he had to go to Thailand and Burma, and what the real reason for all that killing was, but I will tell you. And next time you say a prayer and talk to your father's spirit, you may tell him I did. I shall never meet him again because I do not believe all souls go to the same place after death. We all belong to Japan then, just like we did when we were in Singapore. I hope you will understand. The passage of time and years sheds new light on things. Perhaps you would have acted in the same way. Perhaps not. I don't know. There is much I have to tell you, so let us order our food and then you will listen.'

The Taisho clapped his hands in the old-fashioned way to summon the waiter.

'I was never meant to become a fighting man,' Mr Sakamoto said. 'I was born into a banking family from Hiroshima who had emigrated to Tokyo at the turn of the century. They were all ruthless and hard-working and clever, and they were all successful until the time came for my own father to take the helm.

'Some fathers are better than other fathers. The man who fathered me was not interested in the bank at all. Nor in me or anyone else but himself. He was the eldest son, and by giving his rights away to my uncle, he embarked me upon a military career. Perhaps he did me a favour.

'Your father carried his doubts into his grave. He asked me to tell you of his time in the war so that you will be sure of his part in it. The last time we met, your father put an obligation upon me. He asked me again to talk to you and made me give my word to him. We were sitting right here, not far from your office.'

Yoshiro did not understand why his father never asked him to join them. There were opportunities. Perhaps he had tried. Yoshiro was a busy man, and his father did not want to interfere with his career. In the last two years, Yoshiro had had no time for friends outside business. He was being watched while his nomination to the board was waiting, and he usually felt guilty about being away from his desk. It had been his own fault.

What was he doing away from the office now? Did he really want to hear what the old soldier was going to tell him about his father?

'Your father, like you, tried to understand the *gaijin*. I think he was obsessed with that just before he died. Did he ever talk to you about that?'

'No.'

'Well, he did to me. In my youth, I spent two months in Europe, and he felt I was an expert on the *gaijin* ways. He could have talked to you better. When I was in Europe, I spent all my time with other Japanese.'

'Nothing has changed. Whenever Japanese people travel, they rely on and use other Japanese to show them around. They fly Japan Air Lines and use Japanese guides.'

'We Japanese feel more comfortable with other Japanese.'

'Do you really think that?'

'Yes. Perhaps we have been an island too long. We are a conservative people, you see.'

Yoshiro made no comment. He would have liked to have said something to the man, but Mr Sakamoto's age and position demanded his respect and his patience. Some things never changed. The food came and, while it was served and eaten, they did not speak. There was only the squeaky sounds of lips and tongues and food being swallowed in a hurry and belched over.

'Was the meal satisfactory?' the Taisho asked.

'Yes, sir,' Yoshiro said, and then, out of the silence, Mr Sakamoto began to speak, and he spoke with the voice of a Taisho.

Later, Yoshiro knew, he would ponder the story. He would remember it almost as if he had been in Singapore himself with them. A witness. A spectator. He would see the two men in front of his eyes and the figure of Keichi Katsumata would assume a new place in Yoshiro's mind. A young officer from Hokkaido who bore the same last name as he did. He had nothing to do with that man or what had happened to him. As Mr Sakamoto spoke, Yoshiro became an audience at a private screening of someone else's past.

CHAPTER FIFTEEN

—————•—————

He was in a hurry. As he left the *gaijin* in their cell, the clouds were closing in. He expected to hear the thunder momentarily and he sprinted across the courtyard to get to the Taisho's office. The orderly opened the door for him and he walked in, stood to attention then bowed and saluted. The Taisho was writing a report on the execution he had conducted earlier in the day.

'Sit down, Katsumata,' the Taisho said. 'I'll be through in a moment. This paperwork has got to be done. Give me a field command any time.'

Outside, the clouds had gathered over the city, and from a distant corner of the darkening sky, lightning came into the room.

Lieutenant Katsumata's face was pale. He looked out as the thunder rolled in like a thousand pieces of shrapnel, then the rain came pounding at the old building. The Taisho finished his report and signed it. He handed it to Keichi.

'Read what it says and sign it if you are in agreement.'

Keichi picked up the sheets and held them to the light. He was a fast reader, and he quickly put the papers on the desk and signed them.

'This is your last evening in the city, Katsumata, and Singapore is yours. I have prepared a little entertainment for us.'

'Thank you, sir.'

'There are not many pleasures available to the fighting man. Sometimes, though, there are rewards for the winner. Spoils of war, if you wish. Gentle, pretty spoils of war. You are a married man, Katsumata, and so am I, but we are both away from home and tonight we shall indulge in the brighter side of victory.'

The Taisho pulled a bottle of *gaijin* whisky out of his drawer, and took a swig from it and offered it to Keichi.

'Take it. It's from the private stock of the man who sat in this office before me.'

The smooth, golden alcohol slipped into his blood-stream and warmed his insides. The bottle was decorated with a cheerful label that glittered in the light.

'We'll take the bottle with us,' the Taisho declared, and rang the bell for the orderly, who came in and was told to get the car ready. 'We are going out in style to visit a part of town that remains intact. We shall forget our ranks tonight, and until we get back here, we will simply be men.'

Keichi did not comment. He took a second sip out of the bottle. He was not accustomed to the potent effect the liquid bore in its softness. By the time they were seated in the Taisho's car, he was bubbling inside and his excitement rose. The streets were empty and they sailed down the broad avenues all by themselves with the Taisho driving the car.

'Soon, after the debris is cleared, confidence in us will come. The people will be out in the streets again and the famous roadside kitchens will appear. Smells of drying fish and frying pork and rice and spices will fill the evening air again. There are shortages here now, but our dinner will not be affected. Our host is a Chinese merchant who has ties with Japan. He is not short of anything.'

Soon, they were upon the outskirts of the town. Entering a private road that seemed to be running through a park, they saw the house. It stood alone at the end of the winding road. There were two oil lamps on each side of the ornamental cast-iron gate, and a smiling Indian dressed all in white stood to attention and saluted as their car stopped.

'Here we are,' the Taisho said, 'close to the gates of heaven.' It was a large white house with tall columns and white shutters. The gardens had lawns and fountains and hedges. Floodlights shone on the tall walls, and when the Taisho switched his engine off, they heard faint sounds of music coming out of the night. The rain had stopped and a myriad of diamond-like raindrops sparkled on the paved path they walked on.

A well-dressed Chinese gentleman stood by the open door with a greeting grin splashed over his face.

'Welcome to my humble house,' he said.

'This is Lieutenant Katsumata,' the Taisho said. 'He is a newcomer to Singapore and is leaving again tomorrow night. This is a farewell party for him.'

Their host took their capes and their hats and then stretched his arm out for their swords, but the Taisho did not unbuckle his. The garments were heaped on the arm of another servant who stood behind the master of the house.

'I shall take you to the room,' the Chinese said. 'My personal butler awaits you there. The dinner will be prepared by my own cook, and I know you will forget the war when you sample his talents.'

They sat down, Japanese-style, around a low table. There were pillows strewn over the floor and the white tablecloth enhanced the colourful abundance of fruits on top. There were bananas and pineapples, mangoes and water-melons. There were ripe guavas and papayas, star apples, custard apples and grapes. The fruits were beautifully shaped into the long, narrow form of the islands of Japan. There was an assortment of cold meats and fish and vegetables on a silver platter. A wooden trolley boasted a selection of drinks fit for a state reception, and soft piped music filtered into the room. There were Chinese prints on the walls and screens depicting old battles with pretty women looking on.

'Nothing new about that,' the Taisho said, looking at the battle scenes. 'There's a woman behind every soldier's valour. But they will join us later. We have to talk first.'

He waited until the butler had brought in the dishes of hot food and had left. The Chinese merchant looked in to be thanked for his magnificent hospitality.

'We shall be alone for an hour,' the Taisho barked. 'Then send the girls in, all of them.'

Their host bowed and smiled and closed the door behind him. Outside, the lightning and the ensuing thunder were back in force.

'There will be a boat waiting for you and your people at the port tomorrow after dark. It is a converted pleasure boat. Used to be owned by a rich English *gaijin*, and it sleeps twelve in comfort. The Western colonials know how to live, Katsumata, but they don't know how to die. We have painted the red cross on her deck, although the Royal Navy is nowhere to be seen, nor the Royal Air Force. The boat is manned by an Imperial navy crew of three officers. They know where you are going, not what you are going for. They will be waiting for you at the port of Pattaya on your return, however long it takes.

'Once you land in Thailand, you will be met by a Captain Kato from whom you will take orders until you set off. Captain Kato will provide you with a car and will instruct you on where to go. Are you enjoying your food?'

'Yes, sir, thank you.'

'Officially, you will be in Bangkok on leave. Some of the people you knew at the embassy are still there and they do not know about the mission. Captain Kato is the only man in Thailand who knows. The two *gaijin*, who, for all intents and purposes, are German officers, will be there on leave too. You will all be staying at the Oriental Hotel on the river. I suppose you could allow them a measure of controlled freedom. Thailand is our ally and they would not get very far if they tried to run. The Burmese will also stay at the Oriental, and must be kept under guard. There is a large number of Burmese in Bangkok, and some may be on the side of the enemy. It's been a hard campaign there, and not all Asians understand liberty. They have been slaves to the *gaijin* for too long. We Japanese are fortunate to have had a continuous history on our very own soil.

'You will be told by Captain Kato when to leave Bangkok. He will provide you with the latest information regarding the prisoner. As I have told you, the prisoner does not wish to be taken back. This could make an exchange deal difficult, and you may be forced to kidnap him. If you have to use force to bring him back and there is no exchange, I leave the fate of the *gaijin* and the Burmese in your hands. Not one of them must live to tell the tale. You should not, during the trip, get too involved with them. That will make it difficult for you to remember that they are the enemy when the time comes. You have been commissioned by the Imperial army and will know how to behave with honour.'

Lieutenant Katsumata appeared to be making careful

mental notes of every word. He showed not the slightest interest or curiosity in his own future. The Taisho told him that once he had delivered the high-ranking officer to him in Bangkok, the mission would be completed. The boat would take him back to Singapore where his next orders would be waiting.

'This,' the Taisho said, 'is the plan you are to follow. There may be last-minute changes, and if there are Captain Kato will communicate those to you. Should something happen to Captain Kato, you are to proceed as planned. Remember, after the final briefing you will be on your own. That's all, Katsumata.'

The Taisho took a bottle of Kikumasamune ceremonial wine off the table.

'Warriors toast each other with this wine before battle, Katsumata. *Kampai!*' They drank.

The Taisho took his sword and his belt off and motioned to Keichi to do the same. He rang the little silver bell and the door opened. Three young girls were ushered in by the Chinese merchant and they stood by the wall facing them.

'Chinese, Malay or Indian,' the Taisho said. 'You choose any one you like, or all three.'

The music came back through the concealed loudspeaker and Keichi took a stiff drink from the *gaijin* whisky bottle.

'Don't drink too much,' the Taisho said. 'Let the girl you choose caress your body instead. You can rest your head on her bosom and the songs of love she will sing will make you forget all the songs you have ever heard.'

Outside, the storm and the rain were gone. Through the broken cloud, the bright face of a full moon slid gently in to light the sky.

Across the barrier of time and place, Yoshiro Katsumata sat mesmerized. It was not the story that hit him, but the way in which Sakamoto and his voice were nullified and replaced with clear reality. He saw his father and the Taisho as they sat looking at the girls, his father about to make his choice. How could these words, these vivid, beautiful scenes, emerge from this dull man's lips? Were they figments of his own haunted imagination?

He watched Mr Sakamoto's mouth move, but he did not hear him. Yet still, he could see the two men sitting in the Chinese merchant's house thirty-three years ago, watching the women who came to please.

'She was not pure Malay,' Mr Sakamoto said. 'Perhaps she had *gaijin* or Chinese blood because her skin was alabaster white and her eyes were round, and she had long, beautiful legs that showed through the slit in her skirt. Her hair was black and long and she had a set of perfect teeth. She smiled at Keichi and he pointed at her. He looked at me and said, "I want her". He got up to take her out, but I stopped him and said we were staying right where we were. The table was moved away and the servants spread mattresses and sheets upon the floor, and then the lights went out.'

Mr Sakamoto stopped talking. He sipped some green tea and then he asked Yoshiro to forgive him.

'I shall not tell you what happened next because he was your father.'

Yoshiro did not need Mr Sakamoto to tell him. He could smell the lavender and the scent of roses and herbs. He could hear the sound of clothes being pulled over bare, soft skin. He could feel the touch and hear the whispers of passion on the floor there, far away and long ago.

He saw the Malay girl lie on her back and smile and

111

spread her arms and her legs. Then he saw the man's boots being kicked off, then his trousers. He saw the man's bare back. The woman rolled over closer to the man and she rubbed his head and kissed his ears and bit him. The man mounted her and entered her and someone screamed a scream of release, and then he saw no more.

The space around them was smoky and no one came to disturb them. All Yoshiro could hear was Mr Sakamoto's voice.

In the morning, the two officers had breakfast around the same table as the sun was being born outside. They went for a stroll in the gardens and later they drove back through the well-to-do suburbs. The sun climbed up fast now revealing a clear blue sky. The houses, proud, white colonial islands, towered out of green, well-groomed parks. There were coconut trees and royal palms and hibiscus bushes in bloom. There were orchids and papaya trees and occasionally roses. There were blue swimming-pools and tennis courts.

'This is where the *gaijin* spent the wealth this colony made for them,' the Taisho said.

With the morning now in full command of their world, martial music came blaring out of the car's radio. They did not talk any more and sat in silence as the news came in. It was all good. Victories all over the new Empire. Asia had defeated the Europeans by force of arms, the reader said without emotion. With the imminent defeat of Western imperialism, there would soon be peace. Our glorious troops would return to these shores and from here they would build the new order they are destined to lead.

The two British officers were being walked in the

courtyard as their car came to a halt. There was an armed guard behind them, holding an unseen leash to their necks. Keichi hoped they would not be ashamed as they watched him walk free, after a night of illicit pleasure, into the building. The sight of the new blue sky and the thought of their imminent departure fired him with new optimism.

On the Taisho's table, there was a cable in code from Bangkok.

'All is well,' the Taisho announced. 'Captain Kato is ready for you and will be waiting at the port of Pattaya when you arrive. The location of the high-ranking officer has now been established.'

'May I respectfully suggest we allow the prisoners to spend the whole day in the fresh air? It is a gesture they would appreciate.'

'I do not care for that remark. What we do with them must be for the good of the mission, that's all.'

'Yes, sir. I am sorry.'

'Do not get too involved with these *gaijin*.'

Mr Sakamoto said he was feeling tired and was going to leave soon. There was, he said, much more to tell. He had given the young man the background to his father's mission. He had painted the past in the best colours his memory could select.

'I had become attached to your father,' Mr Sakamoto said. 'Even fond of him. To have to tell him lies was almost unbearable. I needed all the love I had for Japan and the Emperor to come to my aid. Friendship among men is temporary. Only Japan and the throne are eternal.'

'What happened then? Did they leave on the boat that night?'

'In the afternoon, there was a meeting. We sat in my

office with the big map on the wall. Your father talked and so did a field officer, who discussed the terrain and the guerrillas.

'I wondered who would be alive after the mission. I knew the sergeant and the two soldiers would not survive long after coming back. I did not know about the Burmese and the *gaijin* officers. It was all in the hands of destiny. Your father had to come back because he had to deliver the high-ranking officer. We had to have him before his captors found out who he was and what he stood for. By "we" I mean the army in Singapore, not the government in Tokyo.'

'I thought you soldiers blindly followed the orders of the government.'

'You are showing disrespect, but I do understand. These are different times. Anyway, we did not always see eye to eye with Tokyo. At army headquarters in Singapore, most of the people were soldiers who often saw things the bureaucrats in Tokyo did not see. The Imperial army was running its own war, but that was not treason. It was there to protect the Emperor and build an empire for him in which he and his people could be secure. Sometimes, we had to do things on our own. We were there on the spot. The army wanted that officer back at all costs. I would have preferred to have had a more experienced officer to head the mission, for your father would never have understood the division between government and army. You had to be a regular man to understand that military execution of political directives can take different forms.'

Outside, the evening was drawing near. All over the Ginza, lights were coming on. Mr Sakamoto said he was sorry to have taken Yoshiro away from his office for so long. He had so far been quite relaxed, and as soon as he apologized, his posture changed. He seemed to be agitated. He rose to his feet.

'I have to go now. I am being entertained tonight.'

The waiter was summoned to call for Mr Sakamoto's car and the bill was signed. The older man declined Yoshiro's offer of help with his coat and within minutes they stood by the door.

'I shall call you in a few days,' Mr Sakamoto said in a flat voice. 'Do not think too harshly of our generation,' he added as his car came and the chauffeur jumped out to open the door.

There was a message from Mrs Bellingham back at the office. 'Call me back when you can,' it said. His mother had called from Hokkaido and he was late for a meeting of his export department. People were still at their desks, and typewriters were clicking away. Yoshiro dispatched an assistant into the meeting-room to say he was going to be delayed. Neither his mother nor Mrs Bellingham were there to answer their phones.

Having signed a few letters and some documents, Yoshiro Katsumata went to his meeting. Everybody got up as he entered the room and he motioned to them to sit down and continue. His mind was not there. He pretended to sit and listen, just like the board members did up on the eighth floor. He was thinking of the man the Taisho had talked about. That Keichi Katsumata was different and remote and strange. Difficult to relate to, because Yoshiro was nearly forty and the other man was younger, a soldier facing a predicament so different from his own.

As his underlings read prepared financial statements and forecasts, Yoshiro closed his eyes in mock concentration. The man Mr Sakamoto had told him about was foreign. It was as if he had lived on another planet. He would have to get used to him and try to understand him before he could recognize him as the man who was once his father.

Book 3

The Wheel Of Fate

Chapter Sixteen

LONDON, OCTOBER 1975

His receptionist asked him to save the stamp for her. She said her little nephew was a collector and had never seen a Japanese stamp before.

'Certainly,' Jimmy Hedges said. 'You can soak it off yourself.'

The insignificant little design on the corner of the postcard was not particularly attractive. The postcard was from Anna. They had settled down to a routine and Jonathan seemed to be doing well. She was thinking about writing a book about modern Japan. Was there a publisher amongst his clientele? Was he coming out to see them? She sent her love and that was all.

Some of Derek's prowess with the written word must have surfaced in his daughter, Toni said when Jimmy told her about the book. Better late than never. Did she have the time to do this? What was the title of the book?

'It was only a postcard, damn it. I read the whole thing to you twice.'

'Are you really going back to the Orient?'

'I am thinking about it. Only thinking about it. I am too busy to go anywhere right now. Too busy even to talk. There's an army of people outside my door. Some are sick and some think they are sick. I'll have to go and find out, won't I?'

'We can talk about your trip this weekend. You are coming down for lunch on Sunday, aren't you?'

'Yes, I am,' he said, and put down the receiver.

Jimmy Hedges was bending the truth. The only

people in the waiting-room were his secretary and that awful Mrs Whatshername, one of his oldest patients. He had seen her married twice and widowed twice and had heard the same complaints over the years. She had a watertight insurance deal that paid his fees in full. He could not escape her today or any other day. She annoyed him just by being there, but most of all it was her voice that irked him, and that couldn't be cured. It was a tinny, thin, drawling voice, and she spoke slowly, pronouncing every word as if she was reading the Bible to a deaf and dumb foreigner. Mrs Whatshername would take an hour to tell him about her aches and pains and usually he would listen.

Today he was a little impatient and a little short-tempered. His receptionist guessed as much just before she announced Mrs Whatshername. She even volunteered a little word of advice for the widow's benefit, but the warning did not fall on willing ears. Mrs Whatshername was not going to deprive herself of sharing her current troubles with Dr Hedges. As far as she was concerned, she had been paying for his ear for years. Most of the time he was the epitome of charm and understanding and compassion.

'I can't help it if he's in a bad mood,' she squeaked to the receptionist, 'not in my condition.'

'What seems to be the trouble, my dearest?' said Dr Hedges as she was ushered in.

'Well, Dr Hedges, you remember that old pain here, below my chest. It's been troubling me for the last twenty-four hours and I can't believe indigestion can last that long. And that's not all. I seem to have lost my energy. I can't go out shopping because I get tired after a few minutes and I have no desire to eat. None. And you know what my appetite is like. On top of that, my back has been playing up and my sleeping-pills have no effect at all. They just depress me. I have not slept since I came to see you last week.'

He looked at her and listened to some of the things she said, but not to all. He could have recited the same speech himself and he often did, but today he was thinking of his possible vacation in the Orient. His face contracted in an effort to remember the names of the places and the time it would take to visit them all. Mrs Whatshername did not mind his silence in the slightest. She took it to be an expression of interest and she blabbered on and on while he took a trip to the distant past. He had heard how Singapore had changed and how Lee Kwan Yu had made it into a modern city that was the envy of the world. Some of the relics of the Empire were still there. At the old Raffles Hotel you could still get as good a gin sling as ever and cricket was being played on the green. The Indian servants had become merchants and dealt in Japanese cameras. There was a Mercedes Benz assembly plant there and Singapore was moving into new territories claimed from the sea. The port he last saw when they all left with that Lieutenant Katsumata had become the busiest port in Asia. He wondered what had become of the building he and Derek Pritchard were held in and he wondered about Lieutenant Katsumata.

The boat they had sailed on was a little beauty. She was elegant and comfortable and had classic lines. Not even the red cross the Japanese had sprayed on her could hide her proud, shapely bow. She could not have been much older than a year then. The best oak, teak and Iroko wood planks had been used to put her together and she had a strong marine engine that was as silent as it was reliable. Jimmy Hedges always had a soft spot for boats and at one time he owned a sixty-two-footer on the Hamble. He was going to cross the English Channel and go down the Canal du Midi all the way to the Mediterranean. He never made it because the party he had assembled for that purpose had fallen apart after one of the couples split up. But he did have some fun weekends on board.

That boat was pretty, too, but not a patch on the boat that took him and Derek Pritchard and Katsumata and the rest to Thailand. Nor was any weather ever as perfect, or any sea as calm and blue and warm. He was not sure how long it had taken them to get to Pattaya. He had forgotten. He remembered Katsumata and Derek Pritchard sunning themselves on the foredeck, chatting their eternal, accursed Spanish and admiring each other. He could not talk to the other Japanese and the Burmese kept to themselves.

There was plenty of food on board and Lieutenant Katsumata had brought a few bottles of Scotch whisky with him. He was quite generous with it because he was not much of a drinker and neither was Derek. Their abstinence made him feel ill at ease, and at times he thought they did it on purpose. The sergeant and the two soldiers were not allowed to sit at the table with them. The lavish dining-room was reserved for Katsumata and his prisoners. The Burmese had beautiful table manners and both spoke English well and they all talked, but only at the table. The naval officer who captained the boat was with them sometimes, but he was a quiet little man who said little and only in Japanese.

They were all allowed to walk about freely. Only once was there a call for his medical services, to cure one of the sailors of diarrhoea, but his success did not impress anyone. It was a quiet cruise. It was restful, if lonely, and he used to look forward to mealtimes and to the taste of Katsumata's Scotch.

Derek Pritchard did talk to him, but only when he needed to translate something Katsumata had said. With the passage of time, the gloomy memories had gone from Jimmy's mind and all he remembered of that voyage was the freedom, the food and the blue seas. Not once did the Royal Navy interrupt what now seemed to have been a pleasure cruise. Once they were intercepted and boarded by a Japanese frigate, but they were let go in a hurry once Lieutenant Katsumata unfolded the printed sheet of paper he kept with his collection of maps.

'One would think we were going around the world, judging by the charts that yellow bastard is carrying,' he had remarked to Derek. The silly man only heard the word 'bastard' and had spent an hour telling him off for calling Katsumata that. The two had formed a screwed-up mutual admiration society, the way they were constantly searching for each other. Perhaps the language they shared made Derek think of his wife.

There could have been more to it, but Jimmy never worked it out. The Japanese officer must have been a totally loyal Tojo man, otherwise he would never have been entrusted with the mission. Derek, on the other hand, was a left-wing liberal who would have routed all the Fascists in the world single-handedly if he could. He only spoke Spanish because he had volunteered to fight for the losing side in a war that was not his in the first place.

It was fashionable to belong to the Reds at Cambridge and Jimmy made himself very unpopular by vocally opposing those who went to Spain. Even now, whenever he encountered someone who had shared his youth on the banks of the River Cam, the old animosity surfaced. No one knew exactly why he was to be avoided. They would stop and chat and then suddenly they would remember an urgent appointment or a train and leave without exchanging telephone numbers.

Perhaps it was all in his mind.

He did not really need anyone because his father had left him thirty thousand pounds and the house in Harley Street, where he was to become prominent as a society doctor. In 1946, he was richer than most and, being a careful young man, he followed his accountant's advice. By the mid-fifties, his portfolio stood at many times his original legacy. His practice was thriving. There was only one direction to follow now and the sky was the limit. He might not have been the best doctor in the world, but he had style and panache and he had charm. Above all, he was a bachelor; he knew how to listen, and women in particular liked him. A man who did not brush away his patients' pains the way their husbands sometimes did was all most of them wanted. He was larger than life and jovial and knew his wines, and sometimes he would tell them how irresistible they were and how sorry he was they were his patients.

'Did you know,' he would occasionally lament, 'I never married because then I could never hope to have you?'

Such a confession from a dashing, understanding, impeccably dressed man of medicine was flattering. More often than not, such encouragement helped cure whatever it was they came to him for.

There was a large photograph of a younger, slimmer Jimmy Hedges after his liberation. Rumour had it he had walked hundreds of miles through jungles and mountains and minefields and rivers to get away from the Japanese prison camp. A reluctant war hero. Reluctant because he never talked about his war years, but he did not deny the rumours. Hearsay, he would mumble, claptrap, best forgotten. Why should anyone know how much fun he had had at the hands of the Japanese?

'Do you think aspirin is bad for the stomach?' the high-pitched voice asked. 'Perhaps I should change my diet.' Mrs Whatshername was intent on getting her money's worth, but Jimmy did not hear the question. Not the first time.

'Wholemeal bread is supposed to be good for you, but it's fattening, isn't it, Dr Hedges?'

You are just getting old, he wanted to say. Like all of us, your face is drawn and there are lines around your eyes and the blond dye fools no one. Your skin is dry, which makes your hands look leathery, and you take too much sun. Your breath smells foul and your breasts have shrivelled. Look at me, look at my receding hairline and my big belly and my varicose veins. You can't cheat the years any better than I can. That's the price we pay for not dying young. But why hurt people?

'No,' he said instead. 'There's a stomach bug going around. Started in an infant school in Kensington. Seems to crop up only in the best parts of London.'

Thank God for the virus. You can blame any ailment under the sun on some virus.

They did not call it the Orient any more. Nowadays, they called it the Far East, a cold geographic term to replace the Orient and its magic. The old, enchanting voyage by ship through the Suez Canal and on to the Indian Ocean was now replaced by hours locked in a jet plane. The tea-planters, French in Indo-China, British in Ceylon, were all gone, and in their stead came cheap package tours to Hong Kong for cut-price shopping. Anna's King of Siam had become a constitutional monarch while little girls in Pattaya sold their bodies for marks and dollars and pounds and yen.

Yet still Jimmy Hedges yearned to go back there, to watch the endless sea make love to the port walls and remember the little pleasure boat that took them all to Thailand with Katsumata. A free wartime excursion with a Japanese lieutenant for a tour guide. But only the first part of that trip was pleasant. He was not going to think of the end. It all happened a long time ago and it was bad and dark and depressing. He shouldn't be thinking of that.

Concentrate on something else. A non-existent remedy for Mrs Whatshername's non-existent malady. A glass of something before dinner. That was it. He would send out for dinner. Steamed sea bass in ginger sauce to start, fried rice and chow mein, paper-thin sliced beef to follow. There was a bottle of Chablis on ice since yesterday. That's it. Chinese. And a plate of lychees to end the feast. He could also ask for steamed mushrooms in oyster sauce, just in case he was still hungry. He liked them rubbery, not overcooked.

The day was saved again, as it always was. Just before he got himself involved with the agonizing side of his war and his trek across Thailand, the part he willed himself – and was mostly able – to forget. Today it sank underneath an ocean of gastronomic delight. He could make a note of the food he wanted Kung Chi to deliver and hand it to his receptionist.

That's what it was. It was the food he wanted to taste again out in the East. That was why he wanted to go back there. Not to dig out skeletons best left alone.

Mrs Whatshername was talking about her back pains again and he said he would make notes on her case. Would she excuse him while he wrote some details down?

He took his pen out and scribbled down the fish and the rice and the paper-thin sliced beef. All neatly done and underlined, along with the mushrooms and the chow mein. When he finished he dried the ink with his blotter and pressed the bell for the receptionist. She was quick, as she always was, and when he handed the note to her, he winked. She smiled an efficient smile and was gone. I must be getting old, Jimmy Hedges thought to himself. I forgot to mention my lychees. With a little luck, Kung Chi would remember, but then he might not.

Mrs Whatshername stopped talking about her back. 'You do wonders for me, Dr Hedges. I feel better already. I think I'll go home now and have some tea. I won't have any cakes or biscuits, and I promise I won't touch cheese. Some fruit perhaps?' Jimmy lifted the receiver, heard his receptionist order his food and barged in and shouted 'lychees' twice. Mrs Whatshername said that was a good idea. She had a tin of lychees in her flat and that would go nicely with the tea. 'What would I do without you, Dr Hedges?' she said. 'I'm feeling so good, my appetite is back.'

Jimmy put the receiver down. 'It's quite all right, madam,' he said, 'that's what I'm here for. That is what you're here for. That is what I'm sending you all these bills for.' Mrs Whatshername got up and told him he was worth every penny and then she left.

It was quiet in the surgery now, and through the open door Jimmy heard the receptionist cover up her typewriter. She was preparing letters for his signature and she would stay until the boy from the Chinese restaurant brought the order. The dining-room was one floor up, but he wanted to eat in his surgery. It was only six o'clock, but he had had an early lunch.

'Mrs Pritchard rang,' the receptionist said. 'She said to make sure you call her back. Shall I get her for you now, Dr Hedges, or will you remember to call after dinner?'

'Please get her now,' he said.

Toni was excited. 'Sorry to disturb you, Jimmy, but I have to talk to you about your trip.'

'I thought we were going to discuss it on Sunday. Is lunch off?'

'Oh no, of course not, but listen to this. There are flights to Bangkok for six hundred pounds return, including two weeks in a hotel.'

'Two weeks isn't enough. In any case, I want to go to Singapore too, and I don't know that I'd care for the cheap hotels these tour operators put you in.'

'It's the Siam Intercontinental, the most beautiful in Bangkok. It's a new hotel, Jimmy.'

'I much prefer the Oriental . . .'

'They say it isn't what it used to be when you and Derek stayed there. When that woman and Derek . . .' She went silent. She can't still be sore about that, he thought, not after more than thirty years. He had been a fool to have told her about it, but he had not meant to upset her. Derek had been dead for years, and the first time he told her about the Thai woman was at least ten years ago. Maybe fifteen. Why did she have to work herself up? She was no child. He only told her the story because he thought she'd feel less sorry for the chap. Hell, it was wartime.

'Come, come now,' he said in his consultant's voice. 'Forget it. What does it matter now? What was it you wanted to tell me?'

She did not answer. She was angry, but did not want to admit it. That stupid old jealousy over a dead man's loins. She was silent, but she was there because he could hear her breathing. The doorbell rang and he could hear his receptionist's footsteps, and the door opening and slamming shut again.

'He never looked at other women, Toni. You know that. For Christ's sake pull yourself together. Sometimes I regret ever having told you anything at all. I should have kept quiet, but you insisted, didn't you? You didn't give me any peace. You insisted on knowing what he said and when and how he laughed and why. You wanted to know how he was eating and what and how much. Now what was it you wanted to say about my trip?'

'We'll talk on Sunday. I have some brochures for you. I spoke to the travel agency.'

He heard his receptionist leave. His food would be getting cold.

'Okay, Toni, we'll talk on Sunday, but I don't want to hear about that other thing. Give me your word.'

'I'll see you on Sunday. Bye-bye.'

The telephone went silent and Jimmy sat there for a minute before he rose to get his hands on Kung Chi's hot little cardboard boxes. Patiently, slowly, lovingly, he set his desk out for his meal. The food was hot and the wine ice-cold, and there were twitches of hunger in his stomach. He made himself wait while he collected chopsticks, a serviette and a cut-glass wine goblet. When all was laid out, he sat for a moment surveying the delectable sight in front of him and then he poured himself a glass of Chablis. The cold dry wine was perfect and it slipped down his throat and flowed into his bloodstream. He drank two glasses before he started on the sea bass. He wanted to attack the rice while the fish was still in his mouth, and try the beef at the same time, but the evening was all his and he was determined to take his time.

When at last he had finished, he sank back into his soft leather armchair and looked at the table. He had left absolutely nothing in the containers. One solitary grain of rice stuck stubbornly to the table-mat and it took him a full two minutes to release it and suck it and swallow it. Now he was full he felt tired, but not tired enough to sleep.

It was time for some happy memories, and he summoned those while he poured the last of the wine into the glass.

The Oriental Hotel. The day that was to upset Derek Pritchard's widow for so long was a source of much pleasure to Jimmy Hedges. Now was as good a time as any to think of it and remember it and live it again.

CHAPTER SEVENTEEN

———■———

They had arrived in Bangkok only two days before. A Japanese officer who had been waiting for them at the port of Pattaya took Lieutenant Katsumata for a walk that had lasted all day. The prisoners were left on board while the two officers talked. They only came back towards evening. Derek Pritchard did not take to the other officer and was visibly perturbed when Katsumata left for the city, leaving the newcomer in charge of the boat. They stayed on board a second night and the two Englishmen were left on their own while the Burmese were inter-rogated by the officer, a Captain Kato. The sergeant was given the night off and the two soldiers kept a loose guard on deck while Derek attempted to answer Jimmy's questions about Katsumata's real intentions towards them.

Katsumata had told him a little more, he said. There was a prisoner the Japanese wanted very badly. He was held by Burmese guerrillas who were pro-British, and he, Hedges and the two Burmese were to be used as barter.

'Rubbish,' Jimmy said. 'We'll be shot. That Japanese is a smart son-of-a-bitch. He'll get his man and then have us both shot.'

'You don't know Katsumata as well as I do. I trust him to keep his word.'

The next evening, when they were all washed and clean and elegant in their German uniforms, Katsumata had invited the two Englishmen for dinner at the Oriental Hotel. They would be getting under way soon, and tonight they would have a sort of good-luck party at which they were to forget the job at hand, their nationality and the war. The lieutenant hoped they would be, Pritchard explained to Hedges, just human beings. Fellow voyagers.

What a romantic fool Derek was. But that night he was happy and likable and Jimmy remembered feeling almost close to him then. His boundless naïveté reached new heights that evening. Perhaps he had been feeling sorry for him.

They followed the sergeant into the foyer of the hotel.

'Noel Coward heard the tune for *Private Lives* in a taxi in Tokyo,' Derek said. 'He wrote the play right where we are now. Imagine that.'

The air was warm and the white plantation shutters looked down on them as they walked among the indoor bamboo trees on the terrace. It was still early evening, and the sun shot a quivering bolt of fire into the river. A crowded, rolling waterbus crawled along close to the banks, the tap-clack of its engine piercing the evening. There were tree trunks and flowers, rotten fruits and other greenery floating peacefully by.

Lieutenant Katsumata was sitting at the table as they arrived. He got up to greet them. Hedges noticed the flash of unmistakable affection race between the Japanese and Derek as their faces beamed. Katsumata dismissed the sergeant and the guards.

'Tonight we shall be alone. Just like we were that first day in Singapore, but not in a cell. We shall dine out here.' He was speaking in English, not Spanish.

There were six chairs around the table.

'Who are these for?' Hedges asked.

'We will shortly be graced with the company of ladies.'

Jimmy glanced at Derek's expression.

'You look like a boy caught smoking in the school library. There's nothing wrong with a bit of crumpet.'

'You ought to be ashamed of yourself.'

'I call a spade just that, not a bloody shovel. We have been summoned here to get a fuck, compliments of the Japanese Imperial army. I'll have yours too, Pritchard, if you prefer to abstain.'

Katsumata looked away and did not see Derek's blushing face.

And then the girls came. Three of them. Young and slender with flowers in their hair. Their feet did not seem to touch the ground as they glided towards the table. They clasped their hands prayer-fashion and bowed their heads. Their coal-black hair shone with the last rays of the sun from across the river and they smiled shy smiles. Jimmy Hedges was stung. He did not expect the feeling of chastity that governed their posture. There was purity and grace about them.

'I take it all back, Derek. Your friend Katsumata has style. This is paradise. Thank God for this mission. Can you imagine the alternative? We would still be rotting in that cell in Singapore right now while such heavenly creatures walked about this town waiting for someone to ravish them. They can shoot my arse off after tonight, my boy.' He remembered regretting using the bad word. There was subtlety around the table, and elegance. Lieutenant Katsumata did not hear him. He was talking to one of the girls while the other two watched him and Derek.

Katsumata spoke the language well.

'The local food is a mixture of Indian and Chinese cuisine, with a touch of Burmese and Malay. There is an abundance of seafood and three crops of rice a year. We shall share a bottle of whisky for the occasion. Tomorrow you can get up as late as you wish. Please disregard all the uniforms around this table, especially mine. The sword you see is no more than a ceremonial part of my attire. I have never used it. If I have to use arms in the near future, it will only be in your presence and for your protection.'

He spoke in Spanish now, and Derek, relieved to busy himself with something, translated it word for word with great conviction.

'Don't you believe any of it,' Hedges said. 'He is trying to get our mind off reality, but there's no need. I am quite relaxed as things are. You can tell him to save his pacifist shit for someone else.'

'Don't you have any trust at all?'

Jimmy was going to reply, but the arrival of the food stopped him. There were fried shrimps and chicken wrapped in banana leaves, small plates of coconut milk mixed with curry and herbs, deep-fried *placapong* fish on the bone and crabs and crispy lobsters in hot sauce, and tons and tons of steaming white rice. The evening was giving way to night and a cool breeze blew from the river, but no one noticed the darkening horizon as the lights came on. From the other side of the river, above the mist, pagodas speared over the palms and the sound of crickets was all about.

Jimmy Hedges was tired. He almost fell asleep right there. His meal tonight had not been at the Oriental Hotel, but Kung Chi was almost as good. The memory of that night all those years ago had made his mind up for him. He would go back to the Orient.

The memory of Thailand had its pleasant side. It was as inviting as his bed upstairs. He got up with a groan, went upstairs to his room and sat down on the bed. The mattress sank and the springs creaked under his weight. He turned the bedside lamp on, got up again to switch off the Tiffany lamp that hung down from the ceiling. It was a pretty lamp with dark green leaves hugging its beige rims. It looked softer when the bulb was off. Jimmy lay on his back and looked at the open curtains. He would have to get up and draw them if he was to sleep late, the way he had done on that last morning in Bangkok. But his eyes were heavy and he was pleased with his memories and his food and he did not undress. He could always sleep for a bit and then get up for the curtains. He could sleep with the sun filtering into the room. He was scared of the dark, and always slept with a glaring bedside lamp on. That was why he did not allow most of his ladyfriends to spend the night with him. It was a secret he did not want to share. Only Trudi – his current girlfriend, a forty-eight-year-old German widow – stayed all night at times, and she never commented. He loosened his tie, kicked his shoes off and turned sideways with his back to the light. He slept.

CHAPTER EIGHTEEN

He could not stand the way Trudi called him 'Jamie' instead of 'Jimmy' or 'James'. She had a thick German accent and had tried without much success to shake it off. She was a war bride who was brought back to England from the ruins of Munich and, like most Bavarians, she was jovial and laughed a lot without reason. Her husband was dead and her son had emigrated to Australia. The travel agency she managed enabled her to live well and travel freely. She had simple tastes and did not require too much entertainment. She liked to cook, although he did not like her food.

On and off, Jimmy Hedges had been sleeping with Trudi for some five years. It was a lazy affair. He did not need to chase, woo or court her, and she was happy with a bunch of flowers and a beer. To her, Jimmy was the epitome of the English gentleman whose female gender she longed to be. She was a buxom, well-shaped woman with healthy skin, and she always dressed elegantly. She would come to him at all hours and then leave, and would not insist on waking up with him by her side if he did not want her to. She was passionate and attentive and she knew how to make him feel masculine, strong and important.

That evening he had taken her out for a meal at a small restaurant in Knightsbridge. She was driving as it was his chauffeur's night off, and she was all set to drop him off at his flat above the surgery and go home by herself when he suggested she come up for a nightcap. Trudi smiled to herself because he always asked her for a nightcap before making love to her.

He slid out of the car. Trudi parked and locked the door and followed him. The echo of expectant pleasures inched up her spine and her nipples hardened. He used to be a little selfish in his lovemaking, but over the years she had learned to grab her own pleasure. The thought of it excited her as she stood behind his large frame and she fought back an urge to touch him. She could almost feel him entering her body and her throbbing flesh contracted.

He led the way up to his bedroom, sat on his bed and took his shoes off and then his socks. She helped him out of his jacket. He loosened his tie and released his suspenders. She sat by his side and her hands stroked his chest. He was sweating.

'Would you like me to open the window?'

'Better undress me.'

She wished he would be a little softer. She wished he could call her 'darling' and whisper something sweet and silly in her ear. She felt a tear coming down her cheek as she released his belt and peeled his trousers off.

'Don't bother to hang them up,' he said. 'They're going to the cleaner's tomorrow. Come down here.'

His hand touched her back and he pulled her towards

him. She got up and wriggled out of her dress. She took off her shoes, her stockings and her brassiere and threw them all on the floor.

'Go on,' he said with a smile. 'Fold them and put them on the chair. You won't be happy unless they all sit there neat and tidy and Deutsch.'

She did as he said and she chuckled to herself because he was right and because the swell below his belly pushed visibly against his boxer shorts. She came back to the bed and bent over him. Her full breasts rubbed against his enormous thighs and she watched his manhood rise. She touched him through the cotton. It was large and hardening and it was exciting. He could say whatever he wanted. He was big and fat and short-tempered and cruel and rude to her, but he was a man and tonight she wanted him. She squeezed him and came closer and pulled his shorts off and up it came and touched her face. She wanted him to hug her and rub his hands hard on her back, but she knew he would not because tonight he was tired and lazy. She kissed his flesh and sucked it and he sighed and murmured something about her being an expert. Almost as good as calling her 'darling', but now the heat was going through her and what he said did not matter. She climbed on top of him and guided him into her. Her hips rose to him and came down again; she stretched backwards then came back at him, her lips touching his, and she kissed him. He pushed her off and laid her at his side, and for a moment he was far away. The throbbing of him was gone. Then he turned her on her back and came above her, mounting her, and she felt his flab fall on her. He entered her and she cooed as he moved. There was anger in his face, but she did not ask him why he was angry because he was rubbing her insides and it was sweet. She rose and fell while he uttered obscenities she did not want to understand. A new energy was emerging out of his heavy body and he bit her shoulder. She knew it would hurt her later, but it felt oh so good the way he filled her, and he moved and she did and she dug her nails into the small of his back, caressed him and pulled at him. She wished it could go on for ever, but then her desire reached the point of no return and she rose closer and tighter and then it came and she blew up like a balloon.

She could feel the blood rushing to her face and her nipples dug into his chest. She said 'Jamie' quietly, but he did not hear her because he was still grinding and moving and cursing and then he groaned and fell on top of her and exploded inside of her as his head rested on the pillow.

'Shit,' he said, 'that was good.' He rolled off her and lay in the centre of the big bed, exhausted. 'Rub me down with a wet towel,' he said, and the softness of his voice sounded sweet and gentle and caring.

'Yes, Jamie,' she whispered, and got off the bed. Her head felt light. She would walk in the rain for him, but all he wanted was for her to wash him down and dry him and make him comfortable.

Ah well, she said to herself, all men are children. No. They are babies and can do nothing for themselves. She felt cool and strong and needed.

She came back with the cup of tea he would have asked for and she saw him sitting up under the sheet. He looked fresh as he took the mug from her hand and smiled.

'I wanted to talk to you about a trip to the Orient. A sort of pilgrimage, you might say. A visit to see if the gods of war are still as youthful as they were when I was there. I would like to go to Thailand, maybe Hong Kong and Singapore too. I've been there before, but I take it you could get me there for a month without sticking me on a troopship. I am going to splash out. First class all the way. The best hotels and chauffeur-driven limousines. I want to see the place again, but this time in comfort. I've done the economy bit already. This time it's caviar and champagne.'

She took a piece of paper and a pen and she made notes.

'Don't be such an ass. Surely you don't need to write down everything. It's so bloody simple. All I want is to spend some time in Bangkok, yes, and a few days on the coast at Pattaya . . .'

'That's where all the men go to pick up young girls and syphilis.'

'Last time I saw the place it was a small fishing village. A long, palm-lined beach and a few houses.'

'You were in Pattaya before?'

'We were taken there from Singapore by the Japanese. Myself, another Englishman and two Burmese civilians. I saw no girls there, I promise you. It's not so much Pattaya, but a tiny place called Bang Saray I'd like to see again, if only for an hour or so. That was where my captivity ended. A lucky place for me. Not too lucky for the other chap. Chap called Derek Pritchard. He died there.'

'I am sorry to hear that.' She put her hand on his arm. 'I never knew you were taken by the Japanese. That must have been terrible. They are the most cruel people in the world.'

'As a matter of fact, things were not too bad for us in Thailand. The Japs actually got both me and Derek laid in Bangkok. Why they let us spend the night with those gorgeous women I can't say, but boy it was fun. The woman – what am I saying? – the girl, young as she was, was a genius. She got me going again as soon as I was through. Unbelievable, five or six times. Of course, I had not been near a woman for almost a year. I was eager and young and sort of free for the first time. The other chap, Pritchard, was not too keen. I'm sure he did nothing. His wife thinks he did, though.'

'His wife?'

'I mean his widow. I keep in touch with her for old times' sake. Over the years she has convinced herself her husband was one hell of a swordsman. Anyway, that was quite a night even if Derek did keep to himself. I don't know. I was either screwing or asleep. Sorry, tonight was just as great, Trudi, I promise you . . . I would never have thought of Bangkok if it wasn't for you. Perhaps you are even better. The years tend to make one imagine things, you know. You only remember the good things, right?'

She nodded. It was nice of him to say what he did, even if it was a lie. He was a child. He was not using her. He was dreaming moments of lost youth and hours of greatness and maybe he wanted to impress her as any child would. Tonight he was reminiscing, yet still it was her night because he did it with her. She knew how to listen.

He lay on his back, his face lit by the table lamp, and he talked.

CHAPTER NINETEEN

The river had changed its pace as they sat for their breakfast. It now bustled with boats and the loading of people and goods and engines of all sizes. The glare of the water came to their table. Katsumata said they still needed the all-clear sign and could have a day sight-seeing. He knew the town well, and there were lots of things to do and see. The old capital, Ayuthaya, was only a few hours' boat-ride away. There were temples and the flower market and a river where crocodiles swam free. There were cinema houses and the gold market in Chinatown. The local Chinese were not too friendly with the Imperial army, Lieutenant Katsumata said. They were mostly first-generation and shared the hatred their old country felt for Japan. A lot of them, Katsumata said, were communists and potential guerrilla fighters, but mostly they were merchants and, being aliens, they had little influence in Thailand.

'You can't seriously be surprised,' Hedges said to Katsumata. 'Not after the way you murderers behaved in China. We have heard all about it in England. How you burnt their cities and raped their women after 1931.'

'Get off his back,' Derek whispered. 'He's not responsible for that.'

'Are you defending the enemy?'

'Let's go and see the Emerald Buddha.'

'It's not really made of emerald,' Katsumata said. 'It's just a dark green rock. We can go to a few temples on the way and see a film in the afternoon. I like the cinema.'

'He likes the cinema,' Derek said, parrot-fashion.

The two men then proceeded to waste thirty minutes on dissecting *Gone with the Wind*. Katsumata had seen it in Tokyo in 1938. He said his wife had cried and he cried a little too. Derek said he had seen it in London, but did not remember when. He had read the book.

'We Japanese used to fight each other too, just like the American Civil War. Wars between brothers are cruel.'

'All wars are cruel.'

'What a beautiful woman Scarlett O'Hara was. Did she really exist? Did the big man ever go back to her? I have forgotten his name.'

'Rhett Butler. I don't know if he did. Anyway, it is fiction. Only a story.'

'A beautiful story.'

'The woman who played Scarlett O'Hara is English, you know.'

'It was the longest film ever. There was an intermission in the middle of it.'

'Let's get going, for Christ's sake,' Hedges said.

For once things seemed to go his way, and the party set off. The city they were driving through was full of contrasts. It was poor and dusty, yet all the temples were covered with gold and their gardens well tended. The priests seemed to be starving while the Buddhas were fat and lazily reclining, watching their guardians with an almost smug eternal smile. There were huge stone male organs which had been covered with flowers by shabbily dressed young women.

'A sign of fertility,' Katsumata said. 'Childless women come here to pray.'

'Can I be of some help?' Hedges said, but no one laughed.

They took a narrowboat which slid along the river to

see the floating market. It was a hot day and Jimmy was sweating, but Derek and his Katsumata were talking in superlatives of admiration. There were fruits and fish and house utensils and electrical goods and millions of flowers and vegetables, all spread on boats mostly tended by women. He had never seen so many beautiful women in his life. Dark, gentle and forever smiling. What a place to spend the rest of the war in.

Lieutenant Katsumata left them in the care of the sergeant while he went off to meet someone. They strolled into a small roadside eating place with a corrugated iron roof and wooden tables and chairs.

'Let's dump him and run,' Hedges said.

'You're mad. Katsumata will be back shortly. Anyway, where are we going to go? We're too obvious.'

'It's our duty to escape.'

'You're being childish. We wouldn't last an hour, German uniforms or not.'

'Are you scared of the sergeant? He wouldn't dare shoot, you know.'

'You know nothing of war. You forget I was a real soldier. I assure you he means to let us go.'

'If you believe that, you're a simple-minded fool.'

'I may be a fool, but I am not simple-minded. I wish I was.'

The sergeant must have guessed something. He got up and he took his pistol out of its holster and checked the safety mechanism. He polished the butt on his bare arm and returned it and smiled.

'Look at his teeth,' Hedges said. 'Smell that foul breath. Must be all that raw fish they eat. Come on, let's see what he does.'

With these words Hedges got up. The sergeant

followed suit. He looked at both of them and sat down again. There was a hard expression on his face. Hedges pointed at his crotch.

'I need a pee,' he said, and gesticulated.

The sergeant nodded and pointed to the back of the room. Hedges went off. The place was swarming with people eating, drinking and belching. One got up, lifted his arm and said *'Heil Hitler'*, then sat down and fanned himself to chase the flies away. Hedges was taking his time and the sergeant got up. He shouted something. Jimmy looked about him in search of another door, but saw none. He turned and walked back to the table. The sergeant was pointing the pistol at Derek.

'This is it,' Hedges said. 'He's got instructions to stick with you. I'm going to give it a shot. Coming?'

Derek shook his head.

'See you in London.'

A bus came to a noisy, dusty halt by the kerb. Derek shouted, 'Don't!' Jimmy looked at him and then sprinted past the table, knocking it over. Must get to the other side of the street, he thought to himself.

'Stop!' Derek shouted, and then he heard the shot. A waiter holding a steaming pot full of rice fell in front of Hedges, the food spreading on the dusty ground. The bus started to move.

'He'll only kill some passer-by,' Derek shouted. 'He won't kill you. He can't.'

Hedges crossed the street. There was another shot. He turned and waved at Derek as the two soldiers came out of the shadows behind him, bayonets at the ready. They prodded him back. Across the road, a stern smile appeared on the sergeant's face.

'That's smart,' Hedges shouted. 'Bloody smart,' he

said, and lifted his arms. 'Okay, okay, I'll come quietly.'

People were running everywhere. They were shouting and gesticulating and some screamed. A dog was nibbling at the rice on the ground. The waiter got up and wiped his face. There was no blood. Hedges reached the table and sat down, the soldiers behind him.

'He can't even shoot. Some protection we've got here,' he said with a sneer, and one of the soldiers hit his back with the butt of his rifle. The sergeant slapped his face hard.

'I'll behave,' Hedges said.

The sergeant was just about to hit Hedges again when a sharp word of command stopped his hand in mid-air. Lieutenant Katsumata stood over them, his face taut with anger.

There followed a short exchange of words amongst the Japanese group. The soldiers were sent away and the sergeant walked to the bar. Katsumata sat down. His face was open. There was a hint of a smile around his mouth.

'You didn't really intend to run, did you, Dr Hedges?'

'Of course not. Where would I have gone?'

'Well, don't try it again. I am not a fool and neither are my men.'

'No,' Hedges said. 'You're cunning little yellow monkeys, aren't you?'

Lieutenant Katsumata ignored him, and Derek looked upset.

'Our time in Bangkok has come to its end,' Katsumata said. 'Captain Kato has given us the green light. We are leaving for Burma this very afternoon.'

Captain Kato had got them cars for the first part of the

trip. An English Austin, which used to belong to an English *gaijin* who lived in Bangkok before the war, and an American Ford. No harm had come to the Englishman, Katsumata assured them. He had left for London on his holidays and had not come back. Captain Kato had told him that the Englishman had left his Austin with Captain Kato for safe keeping. He had left his maid, too.

Captain Kato had lived in Bangkok for many years and before the war he had worked for Mitsui. The Englishman was a dealer in precious stones and knew Captain Kato because they were neighbours and had played golf together. The cars would take them as far as the border and then they would continue on foot.

'Another tall story,' Hedges said. 'The bloody captain was probably a spy and killed the fellow. If I didn't know better, I'd say your friend Katsumata is a mug. He seems to believe the story himself. You're a fine pair.'

'Thanks,' Derek said.

'We do have a small problem,' Katsumata said. 'We are taking a driver who will look after the cars while we are in the mountains and guard the petrol. One of you two will have to drive the Austin. It should be easy for you, it being an English Austin.'

'No problem,' Hedges said.

'It is a personal favour Captain Kato is doing for us. He does not use the car very often. He intends to give it back to its owner when he returns after the war. Anyway, we won't be able to enjoy the cinema here in Bangkok. I am sorry. *Maipen lai*. That means "never mind" in Thai.'

'*Maipen lai*,' Derek said. 'Good words to know. *Maipen lai*. The whole world has gone berserk. People are dying at sea and in the desert and in jungles far away from where they should be. Perhaps the world will stop to think for a moment and regain its senses, ask itself what is happening and put a stop to it. *Maipen lai.*'

'And when, Moses, do you think that will happen?'

'Look around you, Jimmy, see the smiling faces and the flowers. Smell the fried shrimps and the rice there. Look at the people eating. Not a care in the world. *Maipen lai.* What a beautiful expression. You and I and Lieutenant Katsumata are sure to go to the cinema together one day. We'll watch love and jealousy and we'll even watch death. But that will only be make-believe death with make-believe bullets and make-believe hate. Harmless. *Maipen lai.*'

The sergeant did not understand a word and no one bothered to translate for him. Derek was in ecstasy and there was no stopping him. He was talking about the peoples of the world sitting on the beaches of the world, holding hands. He was talking about the exchange of ideas and poems and music and art between people, and he talked of love. It was the first time Jimmy Hedges had noticed the strong baritone of his voice. Clear-cut, crisp shit about international understanding based on an ideal family.

'Poppycock,' Jimmy said. 'Members of the same family can hate each other worse than their enemies.'

'One day the people will speak,' Derek said to a hypnotized Katsumata, 'and then we'll all throw our cannon into the sea and plant trees.'

'You should have been a preacher,' Hedges said, and Katsumata nodded enthusiastically.

'Was he crazy?' Trudi asked.

'No. He wasn't.'

'He was on drugs maybe?'

'If he was, I didn't see him take any.

'So what was wrong with him?'

'I don't know. I suppose he was a hero.'

CHAPTER TWENTY

TOKYO, OCTOBER 1975

She wasn't getting any closer to him. She must make him like her. Want her. Want her? Her mother would die. But this was Anna's party, and she would make him think she was after him. He would then be on the make and, like all men, he would be blind. He would not be able to think once he felt she was available. He would promise and open up and talk and reveal.

'Sorry you couldn't reach me yesterday,' Anna said. 'I had to go out at short notice. There was a reception at the British Embassy and my husband had forgotten to tell me. My hair was in a mess when he called, just one hour before we were supposed to be there. You wouldn't embarrass your wife like that, would you, Mr Katsumata?'

'The custom in Japan is different, Mrs Bellingham. A wife does not go to official functions unless her husband is a VIP. My wife has only been to a business dinner two or three times. And a Japanese woman would never criticize her husband to another man.'

He was right, of course.

'A wife can help, though, can't she?'

'In Japan, a woman's place is in the home. To make it safe and pleasant and permanent. When a Japanese wife does go out, she makes sure she is ready well in advance, and will never embarrass her husband with her behaviour or dress. Our women are not spoilt, Mrs Bellingham. They are brought up to accept that the man's first duty is to his company.'

Male chauvinist pig.

'This conversation is a bit heavy for the phone.'

'What do you suggest, Mrs Bellingham?'

Why was he so sure of her? He was treating her like a tart. Well, that was what she wanted. No. Not a tart.

'What about tea this afternoon?' Was she being too forward?

'Where would you like us to meet?'

'How about the Imperial coffee shop?'

'That's fine. Would five o'clock suit you?'

'Five o'clock is perfect,' she said, and felt sick. He apologized for being in a hurry. There were other calls on his line.

What should she wear? It might get cooler later in the evening. Her green dress would be best. Not the grey wool. She had worn that on their first meeting and he would not be flattered unless she wore something different. The skirt of the green dress had a slit at the side and showed her leg a good way up. The green dress it was. What would her mother do in her place? You can't walk up to people in the street and shoot them. This was not the Wild West. Her mother was old and bitter and far away. Could Anna not think for herself? Had she been her mother's slave that long? She would do it her way. Meet Katsumata at the Imperial and see what happened. He must pay for his father's crime, her mother had said. Do not feel pity for him. His father had no pity for Derek.

Not the same man. Not the same time. Not the same place.

Excuses again. Well, something would turn up to

guide her.

How could they be sure Jimmy Hedges was right? Of course they were sure. Her mother had extracted the whole story from him down to the last detail. With her Latin quest for salvation through pain, she had to share Derek's fate by suffering. No one had ever told Anna any details. She was old enough to know them now. She would ask Jimmy.

If only she could have been a child again, sitting by the window and running to him like her mother had said she did. Feel his arms. No one had arms like that, warm and reassuring. But she must not daydream now. Jimmy Hedges was coming east as far as Bangkok. She could go there and meet him. He would make her feel safe and she could ask him exactly how her father had died.

Jimmy Hedges had come to see them the night before they left for Japan. His food and drink and tobacco were catching up with him. He had become quite enormous. He could not walk more than ten paces without a protest from his lungs. The freckles on his face grew larger and darker, his red hair had gone grey and greasy. His body was taking revenge on him for the lifelong abuse, but his brain was as lucid as ever.

'I hear Thailand is in vogue. Pattaya is dreamland.'

'For dirty old men like yourself.'

'Quite right. Now that I'll have you out east I can start planning.'

'Let us get there first.'

Jimmy arranged for his chauffeur to take them to the airport in the morning. Leaving Jimmy in the sitting-room, Jonathan followed Anna to the kitchen.

'Why are you so curt with him? He has never been

anything but kind to us. Don't you remember? He gave us our first holiday when I wasn't doing too well at the bank . . . and the car.'

'He doesn't take it like that. We have an understanding . . . oh, maybe you are right. I don't know what it is. I am sorry.'

'Don't apologize to me. Apologize to him.'

She did not get a chance to do that since Hedges was fast asleep on the couch when they came back.

She put on the green dress, consulted the sky and decided to take an umbrella. The maid smiled her embarrassed smile as she came out of the bedroom all made up.

'*Kirei desu ne.*'

Anna said '*arigato*' because she knew *kirei* meant beautiful.

Outside, the rain had started falling onto the narrow street. People hid under the canopies of their umbrellas. With the rain, the city had assumed the colour of grey, its ginkgo tree-lined roads curving like muddy rivers, and yet there was no gloom. It was early enough to find a taxi. Walking to the main street in the drizzle would give her time to think.

Later, at the coffee shop in the Imperial Hotel, she sat down on the street side. The waiter came and she ordered a coffee and then she saw Yoshiro Katsumata emerge from a taxicab. He was coming in any moment now, and she braced herself for the encounter and lit a cigarette.

He saw her sitting by the window as soon as he got out of the cab. It was early. He had left the office in time to browse around the shopping arcade. The *gaijin* woman was saying something to the waiter. It was his daughter's birthday and he was looking for an elephant for her. She was fascinated by the animal and someone told him he could find one at the Imperial arcade. Perhaps the *gaijin* hadn't seen him yet. Even if she had, she might not have recognized him. All Japanese look the same to *gaijin*. The Australian girl had told him that and an outspoken American had confirmed it was true. He himself needed time and practice to learn how to tell one *gaijin* from another.

They were big and hairy and tall and had big noses and looked older than their years. Some of them were darker than others and some had more hair. Some had different colours in their eyes. Above all, the difference lay in their character. Not all were friendly and open and eager to be liked. Some were moody and hated to come to Japan and could not wait to get away. Those were the impatient ones who would never succeed.

The *gaijin* woman did not see him enter the hotel. He did not mind making her wait because she was one of the impatient ones. Yoshiro knew that *gaijin* had the habit of exploding when they got angry, and when they exploded they were truthful. She might do the same and he would know what it was she wanted with him.

He descended the stairs into the arcade and made for the toy shop, but the only elephants he saw there were metal battery-operated ones on wheels.

'There is no demand for soft toys these days, sir. All they want are noisy toys you don't get attached to. How about a bicycle?'

'My daughter loves elephants. Big, cuddly ones, soft and warm. Like Papa-san,' he said, and the sales girl nodded.

'Try the furniture store on the other side. I saw an elephant-shaped stool in there. Strong, it was. Even you could sit on it. I think they make them one at a time, so do not be disappointed if it's gone.'

'Thank you,' he said, and left.

He saw the stool in the shop window. It was beautiful. It was grey and had big shiny glass eyes and the carpet on its back boasted endless coloured stripes. It had a golden crown on its friendly forehead and glass gems adorned its rear. The owner of the shop told him a master craftsman from Sendai had built it. He had never seen a real elephant, not even in the zoo. He had fashioned it after a film he had seen about an Indian boy called Kim. Rudyard Kipling, an English *gaijin*, wrote that film, she said. She liked the elephant so much she really wanted it for herself.

'I was thinking of giving it to my grandson,' she said, 'but he prefers racing cars and war planes. I am afraid of war because I remember the bombs. You are too young to remember, but I do. I saw my street burning.'

'My daughter would love to have this elephant, if you agree. It's her birthday tomorrow. Of course, she does not expect such a magnificent elephant.'

'I hope your daughter will be very happy with the elephant. She will probably give it a name. Shall I wrap it for you?'

'I would prefer to take it as it is. I'd like to look at it on my way.'

'I cannot blame you for that. But mind the rain.'

'Thank you.'

'I wish your daughter a very wonderful party.'

'I hope so.'

His daughter was special to him. It was her unruly independent nature that made him chuckle every time he saw her notes. She left him notes everywhere. Always in places he was sure to discover. Small, painstakingly coloured pieces of paper childishly scribbled and stuck on the bathroom mirror or the television screen. They contained requests or regards and sometimes a drawing to amuse him.

In the last few months, she had drawn nothing but elephants: small ones, big ones, grey and red and white ones. She would have never expected this present, he thought, and it made him happy.

As he walked into the coffee shop, people turned and pointed at the elephant under his arm, and when he stood over Anna's table she thought he looked almost human. He smiled sheepishly.

'May I sit down?'

'Of course,' she said, and the waiter came over.

'I'll have a coffee,' Yoshiro said, and lit a cigarette. The elephant stood under the table and Anna took her shoes off to rest her feet on it. Yoshiro leaned back and waited for her to talk. She had been insistent. She wanted to see him and was early. If she had seen him getting out of the taxi, she would have known he had been in the building for some time and would be angry. But this lady was hiding her anger behind the smoke. The Japanese, he thought, were better at hiding their frustrations, but then they had practised it for generations. A Japanese does not tell the world about his pain or rejection. He would use the energy to build himself up from within. 'What a lovely stool, Yoshiro. I can call you "Yoshiro", can't I?'

'The stool is for my daughter. It's her birthday.'

'I shouldn't keep you away from home, then.'

'It's not until tomorrow.'

'Is she going to have a party?'

'Yes. In the afternoon.'

'How wonderful.'

'Yes, but I won't be able to attend. I must be in my office.'

'That's unfair.'

He would never understand.

'You poor fellow. I am sure you'd rather be there.'

'In Japan, the company comes first. She will have her elephant. At that age, children only care about what they want.'

Cynical son-of-a-bitch.

'I suppose so. Perhaps it's really the same for us, only we don't admit it the way you do. Money is money everywhere.'

'We all have to play the game. The company comes first. That is the rule. The company pays my salary. I have to work hard and make sure it is strong enough to continue to do that.'

'The coffee is on me,' she said. 'Not the company.'

He did not like that, but did not say so. She was hiding what she really wanted of him behind a veil of cynicism and crude humour. He was going to flush it out of her. Do the *gaijin* thing.

'What was it you wanted to see me about?'

She did not show any sign of surprise. Only her eyes, the window to human souls, flashed vibrantly.

'I was given your name by my old boss in London. He said you were a forward-thinking Japanese business-man who could help me understand the country better. I am writing a book about the reasons behind Japan's success in world trade. I am trying to find out why you don't seem to have the same problems we have. Strikes, pay disputes, inflation, trade unions, you know what I mean.'

'How can I help you? You can go to the Ministry.'

'You people are very cagey about yourselves. Your way of life is a state secret. We have no idea what makes a Japanese company tick. How do you manage to keep the discipline you have in the midst of social upheaval? The younger generation of Europe is against everything that represents law and order. The establishment is under fire all over the world while in Japan it thrives. I would like to know why.'

It was an intelligent question. As she spoke, he watched her face and her eyes and saw her expressive arms gently sway her breasts. Perhaps she was not quite as beautiful as he first thought. She was close to the earth and practical. Along with her alert, analytical mind, she was all woman.

'Life has been too easy for your young people. They are children who have been understandably indulged by parents who grew up in wartime deprivation.'

'I know what causes our problems. What I want to know is how come you don't have any? You talk about children. Okay, what about children? Don't you pamper your children? Don't they play games and run about, wild, unruly and disturbing?'

'Not like yours. *Gaijin* children have an easy time at the beginning. The learning of language is easier for them because your writing is simpler. A Japanese child works harder at school because he must master a few thousand Chinese characters. At the same time, he must learn the Japanese alphabets and all that can cause conflict in his mind. On top of that, there is the Latin alphabet later on. Japanese children do not run wild because they have no time. They are encouraged to excel because there are so many of us and competition is fierce.'

'Discipline again . . . is that all there is to it? The

Germans are disciplined too, yet they have had problems on their streets.'

He thought for a bit and closed his eyes as he spoke.

'It could be that we are blessed with Shinto.'

'Religion, you mean . . .'

'Shinto is the way of the gods. A feeling of respect towards things, like respect for a mountain or a waterfall or a tree that has always been there. It is difficult to explain.'

'Are these your gods, then?'

'No. They are *kami*. You might think of *kami* as gods, but it really means things above or superior to us. Things we respect and revere. You see, a peasant might respect a large rock at the end of his field because it has been there, in the same place, in his father's day and his grandfather's day and it stood where it is and inspired them all to revere it.'

'The same, then, as your dedication to the Emperor, your willingness to die for him during the war.'

'You could be right,' he said thoughtfully.

'That's it, then. That reverence, that discipline you had for your *kami* you now have for the company.'

'You could be very right,' he said, and he smiled, but his eyes were serious. 'I've never thought of it like that. It could be that naïve reverence of a rock in someone's field has developed into . . .' He hesitated.

'Into a no–strike, no–nonsense way of making cars and watches and cameras.'

She must know a lot more about Japan than she is letting on. There is something else behind that frank smile. He'd have to wait until she told him.

'You were not spoilt, then, yourself? Not even a tiny bit?'

'No, I was not. When my father came back from the

war, he was a changed man. For years he kept to himself and hardly spoke to me. No, I was not spoilt. It is the younger generation you are talking about, not mine. I am thirty-nine years old.'

'You don't look it.'

'I can teach you something useful. To you, a Japanese always looks ten years younger than he really is. To us, a *gaijin* looks ten years older than he is, but when we reach sixty, we start going downhill faster than you.'

'My turn to say you could be right.'

'This is a proven theory. Whenever you look at a Japanese and think he is thirty, you can be sure he is really forty.'

'How old do you think I am?'

'There are exceptions. Thirty-four . . . thirty-six?'

'Do you mean I look ten years older?'

'I said there are exceptions. *Gaijin* are larger and fatter and their skin is different to ours. They lose their hair faster than we do. It's to do with food. The younger generation here is changing, too, as is their diet. They eat too much meat like you do. Do you know what a *nisei* is?'

'No.'

'A *nisei* is a Japanese who was born and raised outside Japan. In Brazil, for instance, there are five hundred thousand people of Japanese blood. They are taller, they are fatter, they lose their hair, and the texture of their skin is different. It's the food.'

What was she doing with this man? Why couldn't she just tell him the truth? Tell him what his father had done. He knew.

No, he did not.

Tell him she came to Japan after his blood? No, she wouldn't need to. Once she told him what his father had done, he would punish himself. No, he wouldn't. He was too modern. She would have to do that all by herself. She would not say anything until she knew what she was going to do. She must appear happy. Keep surprising him. Amuse him.

'What are you doing this evening, Yoshiro?'

'Nothing in particular.'

'Does that mean you are free?'

Her frankness was attractive, as was her face. It was an oval face, and it was open and alive, yet her sparkling eyes, fearlessly looking at his, hid something.

'I suppose it does.'

'So am I,' she said, and her face lit up. She was beautiful now that her voice became hoarse and far less sure of itself.

'Would you like me to buy you dinner? We can have fish. It won't hurt your complexion. Seriously, though, I do hope you can help me with my research. I'll need to meet all sorts of people – the young, the old. You can give me an insight into Japan, yes?'

He was not sure how much of what she said she really meant. She could have said it all before. But then she could be nervous. She talked too much. Just like his father's Taisho.

Mr Sakamoto had called him earlier in the day to say he was going away for a few weeks. He was going to Europe for the first time since his visit there in his youth. It was going to be a most interesting trip because he was going to visit Berlin and Paris and Amsterdam. He was going there by himself, just as he had when he was eighteen. He was going to visit his cousin's grave in Paris to coincide with his birthday.

'You remember him, Katsumata?' the Taisho had

said. 'The one who was a diplomat in Paris and was run over before the war.' Yoshiro did not remember, but did not say. The Taisho was going to fly all the way because shipping lines were not as frequent or as good as they used to be. Hardly anyone went by boat now. The Taisho said they still had a lot to talk about and he would tell him more when he returned.

'Go and visit the temple,' he had said. 'Say a prayer for me too.'

The woman was still talking. He saw her face, but also saw the Taisho's face and in his heart he was thinking of his father, thinking how much he would have liked to have been in his place now. This conversation would have given him the answers he had searched for in the cinema houses.

The woman was saying something to him. She was not just talking as she did before, because she talked in a different way. Slower, softer, and she expected him to react.

'Sorry,' he said, 'can you repeat that please?'

'Sure. I was asking you where you would like to go. You must know all the eating places in town. We mustn't be too late as you must get home.'

He looked lost again, yet there was energy behind his eyes, as if he had been charging his batteries all the while. Don't feel sorry for him. I don't, mother, I don't.

'We Japanese eat early,' he said. He called the waiter and paid the bill. Anna picked up the elephant and handed it to him. She walked ahead of him and he looked at her rounded hips as they swayed to an imaginary tune. Japanese women did not move like that. Not in public. He felt an urge to touch her, but the weight of the elephant reminded him who he was and who she was and where they were.

She turned, saw him looking at her and smiled. She had a generous smile and chiselled lips.

'What is it?' she asked, and he said it was nothing. She flung her head back and her hair flew across her face.

She enjoyed leading him. The indecision and the helplessness emanating from his eyes seduced her imagination. He was trotting behind her, content for her to lead.

All the men she knew were different. They were aggressive. They had to make the first move and have the last word.

Her father must have been like him. Her mother had been the initiator; she had become Derek's housekeeper and his manager and leader. How obscene. Yoshiro Katsumata like her father? She looked at him as his eyes searched for a taxi and she wanted to embrace him. Motherly? Yes. Motherly.

Yoshiro Katsumata was not a man at all.

Not like Jimmy Hedges.

He stood there with the elephant under his arm as people poured out of their offices into the cold streets.

All the taxis were taken.

'Sorry,' he said, looking like a child. There was no self-pity in his face. A good face. How could that be?

Yes, a good face.

The cold wind came from nowhere and her hardened nipples hurt. It came then, in a lightning flash. She had to take him to her bed and cuddle him. Wrong. All wrong. He could never be her lover. But he had to be, if she was to get close to him.

Why not? She would never enjoy the conquest. A conquest it had to be, because he would never make the first move. She would have to initiate it all. It had never happened like that. Exciting, but wrong. Why? She would hate him better if he could force himself on her the way Jonathan did sometimes.

He turned to her. She was sure he could see what was in her mind.

'Sorry,' he said. 'We will have to wait. Why not go back inside?'

There was something warm in the way he tried to please her. Rubbish. They all did. That is why they were so successful. He looked ridiculous with that large elephant under his arm.

Her wanting of his body was a mortal sin, but she was the hunter and that was tantalizing. It was all a big mistake. She was planning the seduction of a man only to bring death to him, but all she could think of was the chase. That masculine prerogative she was assuming on her father's behalf. Lethal. Disgusting. Beautiful.

'Shouldn't we give up and walk?' she shouted into the wind. 'We'll be here all night the way things are going.'

'Let us wait a little longer. Please,' he said, and then the rain came pouring down. He tried to stuff the elephant under his jacket, but it was too big. He was getting soaked. Anna opened her umbrella and fought to keep it overhead in the wind. Hibiya Street had become dark in a second, and he shook his head and gave up, his face reflecting failure.

It is not the end of the world, she wanted to say, but that would mean she cared. He assumed the defeated look of a housewife whose Sunday roast was overcooked. He came over to her.

The urgent sexuality had given way to an instinct she did not recognize. She wanted to be alone with him somewhere, and put him on a bed and undress him. She took his arm and turned him back towards the revolving doors.

'We will eat Western, Yoshiro,' she said.

'If you like.'

'I like, but let's hurry. There are no ceremonies with Western food. We just eat it.'

Perhaps it had been hunger all the time. She had eaten no lunch. Yes. What she thought and felt and was puzzled by was plain hunger. An empty stomach always did things to her. Strange reactions; sudden decisions to act, to explode. That insanity would disappear once she had eaten. Take him, yes. She may well have to. Enjoy him? No.

Could she have been aroused by this man's lack of aggression? Maybe, but food would soon make it all clear.

CHAPTER TWENTY-ONE

'There is no good in people nor bad,' Yoshiro said. 'People are motivated by fate, not will power.'

'What about character? Isn't being mean or decent part of us, like a nose or an arm?'

'You must separate our physical existence from the mental. Being cruel or kind is not a permanent part of us, like an arm or a nose. Characters change.'

'Nonsense. Don't you think murderers are born evil?'

'No. There is only the great wheel of circumstance. It rolls in on people and wills them to act. It creates situations that make them act. When fate decrees a man is to kill, he will kill because the circumstances for that will be there. You can't fight destiny or change it. You might think you are here because you have planned it this way, but it is fate that brought us here. Think a minute. Sometimes you choose a particular dress because it is there or because you like it, yet you end up wearing another because it is cold outside.'

Fate brought them here? Not her mother . . . not those years of anguished planning . . . not . . . what was he saying?

'You mean we could be sitting here minding our own business and suddenly that wheel of yours drops in and starts dictating our next move? Casually, just like that?'

'Oh yes. My father used to come to Tokyo to visit. Fortune was smiling on him when he bought the ticket. We'd make arrangements. He'd look forward to seeing me and then circumstances changed. I would be busy or away on a trip.'

'I think I understand. It takes time. I am sorry.'

'We have time enough.'

'Time is the only thing we are short of.'

'Time is eternal.'

Should she tell him about the room she had booked? The key was burning a hole in her handbag. They had been meeting for a few weeks now and today they were in the district of Takanawa, a good distance from the centre of town. She had asked him to meet her at the Takanawa Prince for coffee. It was a discreet place, and with the extensive Japanese gardens outside it was peaceful. The agonizing ups and downs of her mind were over for now.

'Do you really believe that?'

'I do. I should do. And yet I confess I may not. My father has moved into the so-called eternal realm and I should believe he has found his peace, but I cannot get used to it. I cannot believe I shall never see him, or hear him, or get angry at his indecision again. I should believe, but I belong to a confused generation. I find myself wanting to ask him things. Silly little things. I miss the guidance he never gave me because I rejected it.'

'You mean fate rejected it, surely.'

'Yes. He might have felt I did not respect him, but one can't be blessed with the same feelings all the time. Fate sees to that. He was a quiet sort of man. Gentle and soft. He would have been able to help you and would surely have been helped by you. You would have liked him.'

You must be mad.

'I am sure I would have done.'

'Why are we here, Anna?'

'I like it here. It's the most elegant coffee lounge in town. And it's private. I suppose my wheel of fate wants me to be naughty. I want us to be alone somewhere. Away from the telephone and the traffic. Nothing wrong in that, is there? I want to look at some greenery, not people and cars. Are you nervous?'

'No,' he lied. 'We are alone, aren't we? I can't see anyone I know.'

'I didn't mean it that way. I wanted us to be somewhere without people at all. By ourselves.'

'We'll have to go to the moon for that.'

Bastard. He knew exactly what she meant. All that shit about a wheel of fortune and being good and being bad.

'Are you trying to make me blush?' What else must

164

she do?

'Where can we go in the middle of the morning?'

She put her hand into her handbag and fished the key out. She dangled it and played with it.

'I have rented us a room,' she said, watching his face.

So that was what she was after all the time. Curiosity. He had heard *gaijin* women were puzzled by that. How different it might be. The Australian whore had said that she, too, was curious about Japanese men until she found out it was all the same. He must have been blind. He had opened up to her because he thought she was a friend. Did he suppress a desire for her?

'There is no hurry,' she said. 'I can always give the key back. Are you afraid of me, Yoshiro?'

He was not afraid of anyone or anything. He did not like surprises, that was all. His face was pale. God, she hadn't meant to shock him. What had got into her? His face fell and an embarrassed look masked his eyes.

'We can forget the whole thing.'

But he did not react. Across the hall, a figure from the real world came into Yoshiro's vision. Mr Sato, the chairman, was walking through the coffee lounge towards the gardens. With him were two other men. The chairman walked through the glass door and towards the waterfall beyond. He did not see him. The other two rushed forward to open the door for him. That meant they were lower down the social scale, and yet it was unnecessary because the doors were automatic. Yoshiro smiled. He would have done the same.

That's better, she thought, and suddenly he said, 'Let's go.'

The waiter came and she signed the bill.

'I hope you enjoy your stay with us,' the waiter said

in English. Out in the garden, the sun was shining and Mr Sato turned around. He stopped to admire one of the Yoshinori lamps, then started to walk back towards the hotel.

'It's room number 328,' she said. 'Why don't you meet me there.'

She was saving him from an impossible confrontation. He wondered whether she realized it.

She left the table first and got to the lift. The doors opened as soon as she pressed the button. Lucky day today, she said to herself, and repeated it to cover her nervousness. Well, they could go up there and just sit. It did not have to happen. That wheel of fate might yet think it out and do it all for her.

She thought of him and his attractive face and the way it had been between them lately. What was she thinking about? Fate. Not attraction. Remember that.

She was his master and the power she was wielding over him intoxicated her, and yet she must not linger on it because it all had a purpose. She would find it someday, or maybe she had known it and had forgotten. Well, she had never done this before. That was why she was so confused.

In the room, she took her shoes off, sat on the bed and lit a cigarette. She had left the door ajar. He was following her somewhere in this big hotel and he would soon be there. She did not feel edgy now because he was coming up at her instigation. All hers. No mother. No Jonathan. Yes, she did feel funny and her fingers itched.

What about Jonathan? This had nothing to do with him. Or anyone. Besides, maybe nothing would happen. Then there was a knock on the door. She could make him wait there for a week. Or crawl in on all fours.

'Come in, Yoshiro,' she said. 'It's open.'

He was wearing a pair of grey flannel slacks, a navy blue blazer and an English school-style tie. His shoes were impeccably polished. He looked small and manageable and his hands dangled about his body. The blind leading the blind, she thought.

'Go and sit down by the window, Yoshiro. Would you like a drink?'

'No, thank you. Do you mind if I smoke?'

'Of course not.'

'How is your book doing? Did you see the man at the Ministry about the figures? I made the appointment for you.'

'I spoke to him on the phone. It's no good. I don't think you understand the kind of book I'm trying to write. It's nothing to do with figures and statistics. I don't care how many people work for Yamaha. I want to understand the whats and whys and hows of Japan, and that I can learn by observing you and getting to know you.'

'I think the main difference between us and the *gaijin* is the time off business. Leisure. I think *gaijin* are far more interested in how to enjoy themselves after work. How to spend the money they earn rather than worry too much about earning it. We supply the West with instruments of leisure. Cameras, stereo systems, you know.'

She was not listening to him. She had to stop this charade. She had to get to know him. Yet how could she ever hope to know him? Her mother did not know her. Jonathan? Well, he knew her body and what she looked like in her sleep.

What he thought she loved or hated was what he wanted her to love or hate. Just like her mother. Like anyone who controls you. She couldn't really put the blame on anyone. She herself had chosen to be guided. She dressed to please Jonathan and raved about things he wanted her to rave about. Most of the time, anyway.

Fate had made Yoshiro into an extension of her will. She could put words in his mouth and action in his limbs. She was now his wheel of fate.

'Come and sit by my side, Yoshiro,' she said.

He got up and walked to her and sat. Why was he obeying her? He had never listened to his father nor taken his advice. Even as a little boy, when his father came back from the war and did not talk. He had heard his mother call his father names and tell him he was weak and stupid and useless and other words he did not understand. He had called his father some of those names after he had hit a tree while skiing at Yoichi.

'You don't know what you are saying, son,' his father had said, but did not hit him, and Yoshiro felt ashamed of himself. His mother had told him often enough he did not need a father because he was strong and knew where he was going and took his character from his grandfather. She said the war had damaged his father and he might never recover and Yoshiro might need to fend for himself. And yet she said he'd have to respect his father like any good Japanese.

It was the time his father did not speak at all that he remembered best, because he thought his father did not want to speak to him. He might not have been the best pupil in the class, but he never failed an exam and when he proudly showed his paper to his father the man said nothing. No. He did not listen. And yet something made him obey the *gaijin* woman.

'Do smoke another cigarette,' she said.

His father went to the cinema often to find out about

the *gaijin*. What would his father have told him about this woman? She had a cigarette in her mouth and he lit it for her and she held his hand. Her fingers were strong and naked. She looked at him, then put her hand round his neck and pulled him closer. She kissed his tight lips and she bit his chin and he stiffened. She took his tie off and threw it on the carpet.

'Take your shoes off, and your jacket, or do I have to do it for you?'

Still he said nothing and she puffed smoke in his face and he coughed. His father had told him to try and give the habit up, but that only made him smoke more. His father's old Taisho had told him, too. She started undoing his shoe-laces, then took his shoes and his socks off. She rubbed his feet. Was he sad, or was it the down-slant of his eyes that made him look so?

'Take your shirt off,' she said gently, but he did not, and she did it for him. It seemed he could do nothing for himself and she remembered how many times her mother had told her the same thing. What fun her mother must have had thinking her helpless. She switched the bedside table light on.

'Go and draw the curtains, Yoshiro,' she said. He looked petrified and she got up and shut the daylight out. She came back and gently pushed him down and lay beside him. He did not move a muscle.

'Will you put your arm around me?' she asked. She looked at him. 'What are you thinking about?' She knew she had heard the sentence before, but did not stop to think because all of a sudden she was in heat and it was urgent.

The thought of undressing the muscular body by her side was compelling. She longed to feel him close and inside and she itched for his touch, but still he did not move.

She kissed his forehead and his eyebrows and his neck. She bit his shoulder, her hands travelling down his chest and his belly. She undid his belt and her fingers wandered down and felt his soft manhood.

'Do you want me?' she whispered in his ear, but he did not reply. 'I know you want me,' she said, and squeezed him gently there and felt him harden. 'You can't fool me, Yoshiro. Just lie still and let me. You are used to being served and I will serve you like you have never been served before.'

He was thinking of his next visit to the temple. What would he tell his father when he knelt down by his remains? But his body was far from his brain and he felt a strange passion crawl up towards where her hand was.

He had been used to quiet, submissive women who smiled shyly. They capped their mouth with the palms of their hands to hide their smiles. Their voices were soft, as was the expression of their desire, and they talked little. Sometimes they did not talk at all. They did not sweat or scream in his bed. They groaned and sighed and closed their eyes in the dark and, rarely, they whispered. They did not tell him how great he was or how bad and never confessed their past lovers to him. He knew the *gaijin* woman would. Her neck released a gentle fragrance of perfumed sweat and her lips were hungry for his, but he lay still. What was he doing there at this time of day? He should be back at his office. He was next in line for promotion. They were waiting for Mr Sato's cousin to retire. He would have to prove his commitment and his worth even more now. But there was no stopping her. He knew she wanted him because of the uncontrolled movement of her hips, getting ever closer.

So she was after a close experience, but why him? And why in the middle of the morning? And why did she not go to that place behind Akasaka where *gaijin* women went for that? Did she feel it was expected? No. She did not because there was no pretence in the soft moisture he felt now that she had taken her skirt off. She breathed heavily as she climbed to lie on top of him.

And all the while he hardened until it was paining him and she touched it and smiled and said, 'I know you want me.' She rested her head on his shoulder and he looked at her small ears and her dark red hair while she pulled at his trousers and with her feet kicked them off. Her skin rubbed his. The room was hot and dark and her legs surrounded him and she whispered things, but he did not understand.

Something was running amok inside her and she was losing control. Something was willing her to press and squeeze and bite and suck and tear at him. No one was telling her what to do. No one was asking her if she was enjoying it. She never knew how to answer that because things were done to her. She imagined herself alone in the bath and the door was locked and she was touching herself, except she was doing it with someone else's body. She was coming close to that safe relief she could only get when she was by herself. Now she was on top of the body of a man and she felt him growing down there, and as her legs spread she guided him inside and all hell was breaking loose. She bent over him and grabbed the small of his back and screamed, 'Move, you bastard!' But he did not follow her orders and she rolled off him and tasted him, tasting herself and all the while her tension was rising and he lay as still as if she had not been there at all. She touched him everywhere and touched herself and then she mounted him again and her hips moved and she could feel his hardness grinding. She sat up and raised her arms as if in a dance and she moved and gyrated faster and faster. Her eyes were closed and her nails were at his shoulders and all the while her lower body rolled and pitched and shook and he was in there.

Suddenly, very suddenly, his hands rose and gently he touched her hips and her sweating back and guided her rhythm. His fingers hesitated over her breasts and she opened her eyes and thought she saw someone there with her. She must have been in the water and alone, as she often was, and her body was moving ever faster towards salvation and she felt his stomach harden and his hips were moving in tune with hers. She heard herself say, 'Faster, you bastard, faster and harder and more.' She was screaming at him to wait and he did and they both moved and then she exploded into a million tiny bubbles and her body felt limp and fell on top of him. She felt him move fast without control or words and he pushed more and again and once more and embraced her. It was wet and hot and her sweat was pouring all over him and all the while he moved while she was still and then his climax shuddered through him and he fell back. He could hear her palpitations and his own.

She was crying and he did not know why. She said, 'Don't go. Stay a little longer.' She felt him slowly going limp inside her and then she eased herself off him and rolled over to lie by his side. The bedside lamp was on, but where she was it was dark as the tiny spasms receded and when they died away she took a cigarette off the side table and lit one. She lit one for him.

'*Domo arigato gosaimasu*,' he said. 'Thank you.'

She was aware she was not alone, but she did not talk. How terrible. How wonderful. She should not feel like this, but she had never felt like this before. There was total release and no nervous talk and she saw things on the walls and colours and shapes. There were no fears in her bones and the cigarette tasted sweet and she was hungry. She wanted someone to kiss her and caress her and tuck her in. There was no one there but him, and she knew she could not turn to him for that. Doubts crept into her and she slipped off the bed to the floor.

'Where are you going?' he asked. She did not answer. She was hot and wet and she could smell herself all over the room. She needed to shower the sweat off her body.

'I'll soon be back,' she said. 'Very soon. Would you like to order a cup of tea for me?'

He did not understand why she had gone cold on him.

'Would you like something to eat with your tea?'

She said, 'Yes', and disappeared into the bathroom.

He felt tired. His eyes were heavy and he fought the web that tried to wrap them. Perhaps he could sleep for a little while. Five minutes or so.

He had received a postcard with a French stamp from Mr Sakamoto. Tight, orderly characters and no address. What was Mr Sato the chairman doing at Takanawa? Could he have noticed him? Mr Sato was not noted for his tact. The *gaijin* liked him because they mistook his talkative manner for frankness. He would surely have said something had he seen him. Too much to lose now.

His daughter had left him a note last night. A little poem and a drawing of snow and mountains and rain and rivers. His mind wandered back and he remembered an almost cruel smile of satisfaction on the *gaijin* woman's face. Was she using him? Was he her whore and about to be offered money in payment for services rendered? She had no inhibitions or humility or shame, yet he was the object of her desire and that made him proud.

Yoshiro dialled room service and ordered tea and a club sandwich. He spoke in English and the girl on the other end said, 'Yes, sir.' He wondered whether Mr Sato was still in the hotel. He must never be caught out. It was Mr Sato who had acted as go-between after introducing him to his wife.

He put the phone down and again his eyes felt heavy. He did not hear her in the bathroom or think about his daughter's note or the Taisho's postcard.

Nor, for the first time in an eternity, did Yoshiro think about his father.

CHAPTER TWENTY-TWO

It was an invitation he could not refuse.

But it came in the midst of a problem he had with the Nagoya branch of the company. He had dealt badly with it, allowing a man lower down the company ladder to be rude to him. The department had sold Nagoya two thousand cases of tinned crab meat from Taiwan. A report stating the merchandise was out of condition had been sent to him and Yoshiro had signed it without actually reading the contents. There was a danger of food-poisoning and two customers needed hospital treatment. The health authorities were threatening to release the story to the press unless the goods were recalled. As the man talked about the problem, Yoshiro kept asking him to repeat himself and the branch manager from Nagoya became livid. He was close to one of the Sato nephews and could easily draw his attention to the way Yoshiro had neglected a possible law suit against the company.

He could always find some money out of the department's expense allowance to pay small sums of compensation, but this was going to be big. The accounts department would have to authorize it and the chairman would find out. No one was safe until they reached the eighth floor. From there you could put the blame on someone further down the line. Failure was the exclusive domain of the peons in the general office. He was not playing the game. He was allowing the Nagoya branch manager to stab him in the chest. Face to face.

'The chairman wants to know if you can meet him for lunch.'

'Today?' His mind was on the tinned crab, but the chairman's invitation was a summons.

'Twelve o'clock at Maxim's,' the chairman's secretary said. 'This is a private lunch. It is the chairman's birthday.'

He had forgotten.

'Of course,' Yoshiro said, 'I shall be honoured to be there.'

His mother was about to visit Tokyo for the first time since his father's death. She'd find out about how rarely he had been spending nights at home. She'd see his drawn face and worry. Bonus time was close and he had not written any recommendations yet. An important American customer had been in Tokyo for over a week now and Yoshiro had not found time to see him yet.

Nor had he been to the temple.

The Englishwoman's descent on his soul was total. They had been lovers for a few weeks now. She had been open and talked freely of her sex life with her husband. She said she used to think sex was something one did to please men. Her frankness made him blush. He was sure the whole office was listening in on what she said.

Did she hide something from him? Was she lonely? Was there something painful driving her to use words no Japanese woman would ever dare utter?

And she was taking chances.

'Twelve o'clock at Maxim's,' the chairman's secretary repeated, and Yoshiro bowed over his desk and said again that he would be there.

Mr Sakamoto was waiting on the phone. He said he was surprised he had not heard from him for so long. He had tried to reach him at his home, too. He had taken the precaution of calling his friend Mr Sato. Were they keeping him too busy?

'Did you know it's the chairman's birthday today?'

'Yes, Mr Sakamoto. I have been invited to lunch with him.'

'It is a great honour to be asked on such an occasion, and a rare opportunity. I have been asked too, indirectly, to join the two of you, but I think I shall be best advised to decline. The invitation was only issued, I think, by way of good manners.'

Naturally, Yoshiro thought, what is ever direct in this ancient society?

'We could meet for coffee after your lunch,' Mr Sakamoto said, 'or for dinner.'

The *gaijin* woman was going to call him about dinner. She had made a date with him earlier, but had cancelled it again. He did not know what she was playing at, but he needed her. He felt her soft hair on his face and he could hear her talk. Not yet, Yoshiro. Wait. Not yet.

'Mr Katsumata,' the Taisho said, 'are you there?'

'Yes, yes. Of course I am. Someone just passed me a note. I am sorry.'

'I keep forgetting how busy you must be. There is much to talk about.'

'May I call you after my lunch?'

'You do that. Do enjoy your lunch, and give the chairman my best regards. That way I won't need to refuse his invitation. Social graces must be preserved, don't you think? Or else we'll get lost in a *gaijin* sea.'

We might all learn to swim together then, Yoshiro thought. The Taisho talked a lot. Perhaps all his friends had died in the war or of old age.

'Do not neglect your duties to the company by meeting me,' the Taisho said. 'In this country, unless you have family connections, you can only get to the top by sheer hard work. The well-born lead the work horses. They have no choice, because they have given their ancestors their word that they will continue to lead. The workers must follow because they have to eat. That way we make the country great, together.'

'I'd never thought of it like that,' Yoshiro said.

'I shall be expecting your call,' the Taisho said, and hung up.

He was not a man to pry into other people's private lives, the chairman said, but sometimes one is forced to interfere when an important member of the staff is about to make a mistake.

'Thank you, sir,' Yoshiro said.

'Who is the *gaijin* woman, Yoshiro? Why do you

keep meeting her at such odd hours and why in a hotel? If it's business, she can surely come to the office. I have not seen her myself, but I hear she is very attractive. This is a private lunch, and you can remain silent if you wish. I don't expect you to be a saint, but I do expect you to be discreet. A man must be allowed to play, but the game must never interfere with his life. You have not been sleeping at home lately. You have been absent from your desk. I do not expect a comment from you, Yoshiro, all I expect you to do is listen and think. You will be forty years of age next year. You are the head of the Katsumata family now and you will be a member of the board of Sato Kaisha. There is no telling how far a small indiscretion can lead you. Now let's enjoy my birthday. The manager tells me they buy all their fish and vegetables from us.'

The company's gossip network worked both ways. The story had filtered upwards. It occupied an important slice of the chairman's thoughts. He would not have mentioned it otherwise.

The last important man to get into trouble was the former finance director. His intimacy with a company typist ended in tragedy. The girl disappeared and the director left and joined a *gaijin* company. He lasted two years there before he was caught stealing. He sent letters apologizing to everybody and then committed suicide in a small hotel at Atami Spa. That was what the chairman had meant when he said there was no telling how far an indiscretion could lead. The two men were known to have been very close. Mr Sato, who had never missed a day's work, took a week off after the finance director's body was found.

'What is wrong with the way we Japanese treat the *gaijin*?' the chairman asked.

'It's simple,' Yoshiro said. 'We must learn to think of the rest of the world as an equal partner. We have been living on these islands for thousands of years. We've had wars. We have a class system that was established by battles won long ago. We had a difficult time learning to live with ourselves and we find it impossible to look outwards. For us, there is no one else. Trade is more than the exchange of goods against money. It's the exchange of culture, history and thoughts. We are protecting our own interests.'

'Isn't everybody?'

'Maybe, but then we are scared, that's all. We Japanese are only comfortable with each other. We never describe foreigners as Italians or Germans or Americans, do we? They are *gaijin*. Foreign men. Barbarians. A common title to describe someone who does not belong to us and is forever to be suspected, kept out. Like a leper.'

'I wouldn't say that.'

'Look at our nationality laws. A Japanese born in the United States or in England or anywhere will automatically get the passport of the country he was born in. The Russians, the Jews, the Chinese, the Indians, all those people whose parents came to live here before the war and were born here can never become Japanese citizens, can they? Call it what you will, but they are not considered worthy. Behind our famous inferiority complex there lies the greatest conceit in the world. We are not particularly loved. We don't even love each other. We tolerate each other because we are all Japanese and sons of the Emperor and better than others.'

'What about tradition? Don't we owe something to our ancestors? Our heritage?'

'We should be proud of our heritage, not just

worship it because we are told to. How can one be proud of one's heritage without learning about other people's? We are accused of stealing other people's innovations, designs and ideas. We take them away and make them here cheaper. This is how we are seen because we are a mystery. No one knows what we are like. Why are we required to look into other people's hearts without allowing them to glance at ours?

'I am not saying we must break with our past. The class system and discipline have solved the problems of labour for us. They give our companies the loyalties of their members. They pulled us out of the devastation. They keep our jails relatively empty and our streets safe.

'We have more to offer than cars and watches and cameras. How many *gaijin* know about our gardens and our pottery? Some obscure professor talks about our culture on American television while everybody watches baseball on the other channel. Exporters, that is what we are seen as, and one day the Chinese and the Koreans will do it cheaper.

'There are few foreign cars in our streets and even fewer foreign students in our schools. Unless we change our ways radically, the world will one day be forced to declare a trade war against us. There will be barriers, such as the ones we have put on them. All you need is one big recession in the West and people out of work and that will happen. Our only salvation is to become a part of the world, not only in words, but in fact and action. Have factories outside of Japan with the backing of Japanese capital.'

'What about those millions of mouths we have to feed here?'

'Family planning, Mr Sato, and emigration. Both

North and South America have been built by immigrants. There are half a million Japanese in Brazil.'

'No one wants our people.'

'If we were to establish plants overseas, if we gave jobs to people there, no one would stop us from coming.'

'Do you want to drain this country of its population? Lose that heritage you claim you are so proud of?'

'Forgive me, Mr Sato. American–Italians have not lost their heritage and on St Patrick's Day you can see thousands of Americans remembering their grandparents who came from Ireland. The positive side of our heritage is indestructible.'

'You are a radical.'

'I am not. I want to survive. I want the company to survive and others like it. They have a common market in Europe. Old enemies like Germany and England all working together for a common prosperity.'

'We tried that before the war.'

'That was not the same. The idea was great, but it fell flat on its face because there was no equality. We saw ourselves as leaders. You cannot have a partnership based on a master race. You need equality. That is what was missing then and, alas, is missing today.'

The chairman's face was aghast. The man did not understand what he was talking about. He was treading on dangerous ground. Mr Sato yawned into his handkerchief and he smiled. Yoshiro raised his glass.

'May I wish you a happy birthday? I have served the company and you for many years now and hope to do the same in the future. *Kampai!*'

'Thank you. By the way, Mr Sakamoto tells me he is meeting you today. He thinks very highly of you, Yoshiro. I suppose he does not know how you feel about

Japan's future. If I were you, I would not discuss that with him. He is an old-fashioned man.'

'I don't talk like that to everyone, sir. I know you are open-minded. You will be able to correct me if I am wrong because I respect your ideas and your talents. Happy birthday, sir.'

They drank their wine and Yoshiro felt sick.

'I have gone through a difficult time lately and sometimes a man must be allowed to say what is on his mind, right or wrong. In the absence of a father, I took advantage of your kindness.'

He had shamelessly used his father's death to seek favour with this simple-minded man. He was much too early. This was still an old man's domain.

'I am aware of what you are going through, but watch yourself with that *gaijin* woman. This large city is just a village.'

'Thank you,' Yoshiro said as the chairman, as host, got up to leave first. He bowed.

'Give my regards to Mr Sakamoto.'

'Thank you, sir.'

They parted company and Yoshiro went to call his father's old Taisho.

CHAPTER TWENTY-THREE

—————◼—————

'You look disturbed,' Mr Sakamoto said. 'Was lunch a failure? We should not carry our hearts on our sleeves. Some of our feelings are best kept in check. It is not always easy. Not when you are young, but I should not worry if I were you. The future is yours.'

The hell it is. Old men rule. Tired ideas.

'How did you like Europe? It must have changed since you were there last.'

'It has. The whole world has changed. It's become less different now. People wear the same clothes, drive the same cars and eat the same fast food. The same films are shown in all the capitals and identical brand names are displayed everywhere. In the old days, you knew you were leaving one country and entering another. Nothing is foreign any more. The excitement of travel is gone. Only the languages are still different and the currency. The people all look the same. The buildings seem to have been designed by the same architects. Everybody is following the same trend. Everything is predictable. I am sorry I went there. It would have been nice to have remembered Europe the way it was in my mind. I shall try and forget what I saw.'

'I am sorry to hear that.'

'Yes.'

'Do you have children, Mr Sakamoto?'

The old man's face fell. It was the wrong question.

'I did have a daughter, Yoshiro. She would have been your age now. Like others of my generation, I did not see much of her while she was a child. It seems I have been a soldier for ever. I was in Manchukuo when she was born. When I saw her first, she was two years old. You didn't get around much in those days. Then came Burma and Singapore. Perhaps I saw her for a total of three months during her life. We had a small house in Yokohama near the bay. Difficult to believe it now, but you could actually swim there then, before the factories and the tankers came. We used to spend long summers there when I was a boy.

That is where I learned to fish. Yes, there were living fish in Yokohama Bay once. It's too depressing. The family still owns that property, but we now let it to a Chinese family. They have a large restaurant in Chinatown.

'Both my wife and my daughter were drowned one afternoon in Yokohama Bay. The little rowing boat they were in was found on the sand a few days later. Their bodies were never washed ashore. It happened one month before the end of the war. In 1952, I married my wife's younger sister, but we have no children.'

'I am sorry to hear that, Mr Sakamoto.'

'Thank you. That was a long time ago. When the telegram arrived we were in Singapore, in the process of surrender. I was angry. We did not know about the devastation of Hiroshima and Nagasaki and the bomb that prompted the Emperor to capitulate. We felt betrayed and humiliated. For me, there was nothing to go back to. The soldiers in Singapore did not suffer battle fatigue. They were ready to fight and so was I.

'The natural reaction of any man would have been to come straight back, but I was a prisoner of war. I could not get drunk or lose myself in the arms of a whore. I had to face the death of my wife and daughter by myself. Could not talk about it to anyone. And in my cell, I learnt perspective. Mine was just a small tragedy in the midst of a monumental disaster.

'I suppose I was not a good father. I have forgotten what the little girl looked like. The pictures I had with me were destroyed. The pain I suffered blended in with that pain of losing a war. I have never been given another chance and I cannot say what sort of father I would have become. Probably the same. I am sorry to say that, but you asked me.'

'I am deeply sorry, Mr Sakamoto.'

The Taisho did not comment. He took a last sip of his cold green tea. His face hardened.

'We shall talk of other things. I gave my word to your father. I shall tell you about his time in Thailand. I think we got to the party I gave your father at the house of that Chinese merchant the night before he left.

'He used to get import allocations from us in return for small favours. Local gossip, we used to call it. Boats that came into small uncharted creeks, goods that were smuggled onto the island, new faces in the streets, that sort of thing. He was making money while we were able to keep an unofficial tab on the situation. It was important to have supporters locally, because mostly they hated us. The Chinese merchant became a very rich man towards the end of the war. He was found dead in his office two weeks before we surrendered. His throat was cut, but not a penny was taken out of his open safe. He had made enemies, as all of us do. Yes, that was as far as we got last time we met. I remember now.

'Your father did not come to Tokyo that often, did he? I suppose he was trying to do something with his time. It is hard for a man without an occupation to pass the time in this city. There are millions of people and buildings and shops and cars. Your father and I knew this city before they took the narrow streets and the trees away to make toll roads and skyscrapers. When you work, you spend two hours going to your office and two coming back and there are never enough hours in the day to do what you have to do. There are museums and bars and foreign foods to sample, but there is not time. But when you are retired and you do have time, you do not want to go into the stores. You look for human contact. Maybe your father searched for that in the cinema houses he loved. No one has the time for a retired man and your father could not bear pity.

'People never change. They just get older and they die. A stubborn young man becomes a stubborn old man. Your father ended up an outsider in this city. He preferred to study foreign faces on the screen and listen to their conversation rather than make new friends. I remember when he came back to meet me in Bangkok he had had a blow. Something had upset him and he needed to share his low spirits with someone, but he kept silent. He did, of course, tell me what he was obliged to tell me. He did not miss, as you will see, one bit of it. Yet he never mentioned what had depressed him after his return. Where was I?'

Yoshiro did not reply. Let the old man find the place himself. It was afternoon and he was hoping to meet Anna Bellingham at the Takanawa Prince Hotel. She still kept her thoughts and her feelings and her plans to herself, hiding behind a sensual wall of sex. These past few weeks had confused him. With his father's story unfolding and his own emotions in disarray, he did not put the old effort into the department. They seemed to manage well without him. His priorities had moved from his desk to the *gaijin* woman's arms and her bed.

'Let me tell you more,' the Taisho said.

CHAPTER TWENTY-FOUR

'That afternoon your father, the two British officers and the sergeant set out for the border in the Austin. The Burmese and the two soldiers went up in the other car. The English medical officer was driving the Austin.

'I shall now reveal something very few people knew at the time. The real reason behind the mission. The high-ranking officer we wanted brought back was a traitor. He was looking for ways to end the war. He had given himself up to the enemy to show them how to weaken the influence of the army on Japanese politics. The army was then at the peak of its success. Ever since Mukden, Japanese foreign policy was dictated by the generals. As long as things went well, the ministers and the public were happy. At the time of your father's mission, we were watching the reverses our German allies were suffering in North Africa. The Allies were concentrating all their efforts on Europe and that gave us some time to consolidate our position in Asia. We would then continue from a position of strength.

'That high-ranking officer was a member of a group of officers who were suspected of plotting to parley with the British and the Americans. No one knew what he had in mind. Perhaps, since he had spent some time in Moscow before the war, he was acting for the Russians in some way. Peace with Japan would allow more Allied troops to be deployed in Europe and take the heat off the Red Army.

'He had given himself up in a very sophisticated way, visiting a part of Burma he had no business in and where there was a large presence of British commandos and Burmese guerrillas. He did not tell his captors who he was. He was waiting for instructions from his colleagues in Tokyo. We were waiting too, since we needed their identity in order to deal with them. The man who was captured with him was loyal to us, but he died soon after they were taken.

'The plan he had was elaborate. It included the dismissal of Tojo and three other ministers as well as the arrest of every commander-in-chief in all the occupied territories. We suspected the replacements were already on the staff of those generals, waiting for an order to move. It was imperative for us to find out who they were. In a command post such as Singapore, it could have been anyone.

'The high-ranking officer was the key to everything because he had chosen to offer his services to the enemy. He was the only one who knew each and every one of the plotters. We knew he had memorized the list rather than commit it to paper and this was why he had to be brought back and interrogated. He would be executed once everyone else had been dealt with. Neither his existence nor the plot was ever to be disclosed. Everyone on the mission had to be eliminated, including your father. It was Captain Kato's responsibility to see to that. I had tried to change my superior's mind in the case of your father, but I had failed. I could not overdo my pleading without becoming a suspect myself. In those days, only a handful of people were considered safe.

'Captain Kato was different, because he had been working for military intelligence for a long time. He had been on the payroll of Mitsui before the war to give him cover and was a member of all the social clubs in Bangkok.

He reported on political opinions and powers in the area. Remember, we were planning to form a co-prosperity area in South-East Asia and our success in defeating the invincible *gaijin* by force of arms did a lot to boost our leadership role. Captain Kato was an important man. He was finally killed by communists a few months before the end of the war.

'Do not judge me by today's standards. You may say I had used your father, but I was used myself. No matter how high a position one attained, in times of war we were all expendable. I did not want this war, nor will wars cease when I have passed on.'

And so they left Bangkok.

The car had a walnut dashboard and leather seats, and it went like a rocket.

'You sit in front with the red-haired *gaijin*,' Lieutenant Katsumata told the sergeant. He knew the medical man was planning to get away. He did not understand why Hedges wanted to risk an escape when his freedom was nearly guaranteed. He settled in the back with Lieutenant Pritchard. They were both looking at the road, and watched the mountains in the distance. They drove past coconut trees, banana plantations and sugar cane. In the valleys, they saw rice fields swaying in the wind like a pastel green lake.

'They grow good rice here in Thailand,' Lieutenant Katsumata said. 'Tastes better than our own. The earth is rich and fertile and everything multiplies in abundance. In Japan, we have to dig the rocks to find the earth and then nurse it and feed it to get anything to grow. Our fields are small and orderly and symmetrical . . .'

'Farmers are the same the world over,' Pritchard said.

'They have a hard life and they are simple. As soon as a country boy moves into a city, he is smitten by the sin of envy and his fertile mind becomes a target for outside influence. Usually bad.'

'This car was built for better roads,' Jimmy grunted.

'Did you know the class system was born in the country?' Pritchard said.

'The country is for the birds,' Jimmy replied.

'The class system is the curse of England and Japan and the world. Until the masses are educated, democracy stands no chance. We have tried to change all that, but the odds were too heavy against us.'

'Do you mean you have given up?' Katsumata asked.

'I will now strive to make myself a better provider to my wife and daughter. The world will have to be a better place after the war because it will have lost, and losers try harder.'

Everywhere the countryside was at peace with its greenery. The pastoral scenes enchanted both the officers in the back. Tanks and cannon had made them both forget about fields and trees and smiling peasant women laying flowers at the feet of Buddhas along the rivers.

'I have not seen the war yet,' Lieutenant Katsumata said.

'I have. It destroys and burns and cracks the earth to starve the people. Fruit trees die and meadows go barren. Dead horses and charred cars lie where once old trees gave shade and cleansed the air. Wells and rivers are clogged with the waste of battle, and farm animals are slaughtered by shrapnel. It's ugly, Lieutenant Katsumata, and you are a fortunate man not to have seen it.'

'Rubbish,' Hedges said. 'He must have seen the taking of Singapore and Malaya.'

'I did not,' Katsumata said. 'I only arrived there a day before I met you.'

'And I suppose you were living on the moon before they shipped you to Singapore. I suppose you did not see what your gallant armies had done to China and the Philippines and Indonesia.'

'You suppose right, Lieutenant Hedges. This pistol has never been fired.'

Nothing much had happened, Mr Sakamoto said, until the party got to the border crossing. They joined up with the other soldiers and the Burmese, and were lodged in the empty house of an absent Japanese businessman. They were given back their British uniforms and their German uniforms were packed away. They ate fruit and curried fish and cold rice. They were told they would cross into Burma very early in the morning, before the sun rose.

It was a quiet little town and it had no street lights or buses and only one or two cars. The air was clean and it was cool. The house was furnished Japanese-style and Lieutenant Katsumata showed the *gaijin* how to set their *futon* on the *tatami* for the night. He was hoping he wouldn't have to kill the *gaijin* now that he had begun to understand their minds. They all retired early. Derek Pritchard stood by the window and sighed in admiration.

'Look at the pink sky above those mauve mountains, Jimmy.'

'Fuck the mountains. I'm hungry.'

'You wait. Soon the stars will appear. They will spray the darkening canopy with a golden glitter. That's what the sky in Spain looked like one night in 'thirty-seven, when I married.'

They had not noticed Katsumata coming in. He

191

listened to what Pritchard said.

'There was no such romance when I met my wife. We were children together and there were no surprises for us. I was hoping to emigrate to Brazil and start a new life there with her. To be free of the enslaving tradition I was born into. Rich or poor, in Japan you follow your family. Rich or poor, your hands are tied because your life and position are governed by your origins.'

'It's that cursed class system,' Pritchard said, 'but the old monster is on the run, hanging on to dear life in a new world. It can hang on because it is rich and experienced and refuses to die.'

'It seems our social structures are very similar,' Katsumata said, 'in spite of the distance.'

'The feudal system is still here, but when this war is over people, having paid in blood for their country, will demand a share in its destiny.'

'I hope so,' Katsumata said.

He left the room and bowed from the door.

'Idealistic crap,' Hedges said.

CHAPTER TWENTY-FIVE

———◼———

'They woke us at the ungodly hour of three o'clock in the morning,' Jimmy Hedges said to Trudi.

'We had nothing to eat or drink and the bastards expected us to walk in the dark streets of that fucking city on empty stomachs. We were prisoners and thought we were walking through our final humiliating hours, being led by a bunch of cruel Nipponese. They were going to offer us in exchange for some bigwig who was being held somewhere in the mountains. I don't think that Lieutenant Katsumata knew where he was.

'Those little Thai border towns have no suburbs. Where the streets end, the jungle begins. The air was cool, but I was sweating like a pig. Every time I tried to open my mouth, I was pushed by one of those tiny soldiers. Derek Pritchard was playing the hero. He did not complain and walked immediately behind Katsumata like a schoolboy following his teacher. For a man who never played any sports, he was as fit as a bull. He walked on stones and in wet tall grass and across trees and prickly bushes. I kept thinking of snakes and tigers and other dangers, but Derek strolled behind his beloved Katsumata as if they were on an afternoon walk in a park somewhere. I had to admire his stamina. We walked for four solid hours before we stopped.'

'Good God,' exclaimed a tired Trudi. 'That must have been terrible for you.'

'I was not the ruin you see today. I was all muscle in those days, even though I had been a prisoner for three months. Could take on anyone at anything. Derek was as tall as I, but he was tired and brittle and all will-power. He had a rocket up his arse.

'We stopped in a little clearing on top of a hill, midway up the mountains. Below us, the morning sun revealed a few huts in the valley – not far, a mile away at most. It was seven o'clock in the morning and we were exhausted, but Derek stood and admired the view. He was talking about shades of green and perfumed air and how the lifting mist reminded him of some ballet he had seen in London on his wedding anniversary. They had the same sort of mist on the stage. What are you laughing at, Trudi?'

'The word "mist" in German means "shit".'

He laughed. 'Dead right. Lifting morning shit in the mountains. Shit and flowers and royal palms. The heat was coming at us with the sun and I was hot. Shit is right.

'The two Burmese were huddled together on one side. The Japanese were not too nice to them before, but now they were offered cigarettes. We were in their country, I suppose. They were not young, and I do not know how they managed the trek. I think they were civilians, government officials of some sort, I believe. Anyway, Lieutenant Katsumata was talking to the sergeant, pointing at the huts. Whoever lived there was still very sensibly asleep. Pritchard talked like a tourist. "I wish I had a camera," he said. Shit is right. I myself wished he would stop admiring the countryside, and stop being so friendly with the lieutenant.

'Katsumata ordered the sergeant to go down to one of the huts. He took a soldier with him, bayonet at the ready, while the rest of us stayed behind. The sergeant got to the first hut and knocked on the door with his pistol. The soldier stayed at a safe distance behind. The sergeant knocked a few times before it opened and the small figure of a woman appeared. We could not hear what was going on. Katsumata told Derek that his people had gone down there to buy some food. The place where they kept the bigwig was not too far from here, Katsumata told Derek and he told me. Didn't I think those little huts were charming? No, I did not. He wondered what the people up there lived on. There were no fields anywhere. Perhaps they grew tea or tobacco. "Why don't you ask your boyfriend Katsumata?" I replied, and having no sense of humour he did just that.

'Katsumata knew nothing. We all waited for the

sergeant to come back. He was taking his time talking to the little woman, who did not move from the door or invite him in.

'We waited more than half an hour before the woman went back inside. The sergeant and the soldier squatted down right where they had stood. I did not understand why Katsumata bothered to be that polite. I would simply have ordered my men to go in there and get whatever there was. Derek said the Japanese were trying to create a benevolent impression on the Burmese. Especially those who were with us. Besides, Derek said, Katsumata was not that sort of a man. He was no thief. He was only a murdering son-of-a-bitch, I said.

'The woman came back. She held three large packages in her hand and the Japanese jumped to their feet to collect them. The soldier looked up at us and lifted his gun three times into the air by way of a signal. Katsumata got up and said, "*Vamanos*", which even I knew was "let's go" in Spanish. We all walked down, the Burmese and the soldier, with Derek following Katsumata. The Burmese walked faster and they overtook us.

'"Look at their faces," Derek said, "they are so happy. You can tell they feel their own earth under their feet. I do hope things work out for them. Can you imagine, Jimmy," he said, "if the huts down there were the port of Dover?" I said I did not believe in magic, not while a Japanese bayonet was pointing at my backside. He said "good luck" to the Burmese, but they didn't acknowledge him.

'The valley was much smaller than I thought it would have been. There were five or six dirt roads running across its centre, each pointing in a different direction. There were, perhaps, ten buildings in all, wooden buildings with thatched coconut-leaf roofs. There was a sort of mud puddle in the centre of the valley and the smell of dung suggested it was used to water the animals. Some of the huts were bigger than the others and looked like miniature warehouses. Here and there, there were remains of fires. There were heaps of cut wood by each burnt-out space and I thought perhaps the place was a kind of signal station for something.

'There was a real meal waiting for us by the hut. The sergeant actually paid the lady for the stuff with Burmese notes he kept in his leather rucksack. There was steamed rice and curried chicken and vegetables and fruit and cold boiled crab. There was a cold brew which looked like beer and, boy, with the thirst killing my dry throat it tasted like Moet and Chandon. Katsumata and Derek walked about like geese while the others ate. I don't think there was much left for Derek once we were through. Lieutenant Katsumata had had a selection of food put aside for him by his people and he offered to share it with Derek, who accepted. I would have done, too. The bastard had the best pieces put aside for himself. Those Japanese officers lived like kings. They sat there, Katsumata's sword sticking up in front of him like a stiff cock. He was a large man for a Jap, with an enormous moon-shaped face and short-cropped hair. He did not sweat. He ate his food and took a few swigs from the brew. Had his own jug of the stuff, as befits an officer. Derek did not eat much. He just picked and nibbled, but then he always did that. I don't know how he managed. He behaved like a spoilt child, but then if you ever sampled his wife's cooking, you'd understand. Superb. I go down there for the occasional Sunday lunch. She's Spanish, you know. He brought her over after the Civil War.

'Anyway, we stayed there for the rest of the day. It was becoming very hot, a sort of dry, clear heat. All kinds of people kept coming up the valley, some on horseback, others on foot. Most of them were laden with jute parcels and all went into the woman's hut and stayed there for a bit before they went on their way. Derek said we had been sitting on a delivery depot. Smugglers, that's what the people in this valley were. Rubies, cigarettes, booze and marijuana. Perhaps even opium. It turned out that the village was a meeting place for smugglers. They stopped there on their way in and out of Burma and Thailand and other places. Sometimes they made their delivery right there, sometimes they went on, but payment was made at the village. Lieutenant Katsumata told Derek that, and it amused him no end. Sometimes, Katsumata said, there was more money there than in the Bank of Tokyo.

'We were waiting for some Burmese gentleman to arrive. A sort of smuggling king with whom we were going to do business. The two Burmese were quite interested in what was going on. I suppose they were able to understand it better, with it being their own language. Derek said you could find out the price of gold and coffee and God knows what else. He said they knew more about the way the war was going than the combatants.

'"This is a strange kind of war," Derek said. "We are far from the shells and cannot smell the dead, but this is war all the same and we are in it. In Spain, the war was near. Results were immediate and you could see them right away. Either you were dead, or the enemy was, and the one alive was the winner for the day. The commanders were right there with us and you really did hate the enemy, I am ashamed to say."

'I did not understand what he was talking about or

why, but Katsumata drank every word of it as if it had been nectar. Derek told me later Katsumata was not cut out to be a soldier. He was well brought up and gentle. Well, as things turned out, Katsumata was no softie at all.

'For the time being, we were sitting right in the centre of that smugglers' beehive. All around us, there were arguments over prices and goods and, as the day progressed, the two Burmese became more relaxed. One of them came over to where we were sitting. He spoke English as well as I do. Been to Oxford, read law at Caius College there. Was even called to the bar in the UK in the mid-thirties before going back to Rangoon where he entered some posh English law firm. He had a flair for business, and in 1938 he started on his own. His company advised Burmese businessmen on investments and took cuts by way of payment. He was a real opportunist and managed to make himself a tidy sum before war broke out. At the same time, our Burmese got himself involved in politics. You could do no wrong in Rangoon with an Oxford education, especially if you wanted the British out of your country.

'I suppose the little bastard felt free to talk to us that way because we were in Burma and in the hands of the Japanese. What a cheek! Comes to England, gets a degree with our compliments and then goes back with an English accent to make his fortune and kick us out. Anyone could sense he was wildly anti-British. Hated our guts. "I admire your honesty," Derek told him. "Everybody wants his country to be free. We English taught you all about liberty. You must have read John Stuart Mill? You know our own history. No dictatorship will ever get a foothold in Britain. You have learned your lesson well."

'The Burmese lowered his eyes as Derek spoke. He

wanted to answer, but Derek was in one of his lecturing moods and for a long while he did not let him say a thing. "I may not agree with you," Derek said, "but I will defend, until my last drop of blood, your right to be wrong. That is what we English are all about, or should be. Of course, you will have your independence, but leaving school does not give you the right to kick the teacher, does it?"

'Derek could be quite forceful when the spirit took him. I saw him come out with dynamite a few times before, but he tired easily and with that last barrage he smiled and asked the Burmese to tell us how he got to Singapore.

'It turned out that our smart Burmese lawyer was not too clever in choosing his clients and friends. He was big in the anti-colonial movement in Rangoon, but that was a clandestine affair. One of his clients, having struck it rich in construction, was not keen on changing the state of affairs in Burma. He preferred the stability the British presence was giving the country. For a man who had never been out of Burma, he was a staunch supporter of the Crown. That building tycoon was sharp. And as soon as the Japanese arrived in Burma, he shopped our lawyer as a British spy, citing his English education and his English clients. To add to his troubles, our Burmese lawyer had an English wife who was in London when the Japanese invaded. His correspondence with her and the other factors tipped the scales. He was arrested as a spy and sent to Singapore.

'This was, the Burmese lawyer told Derek, a real comedy of errors. Here he was, a great nationalist and an actual supporter of the Japanese plan for the area, sharing cells with officers of the British armed forces. He had nearly been shot on several occasions until someone in Rangoon intervened on his behalf. The Japanese were told he was not a British spy at all. In fact, he was earmarked to play a big part in the independent Burma they were trying to bring about once the British were beaten. His colleagues in Rangoon wanted him back to help with the pro-Japanese local administration. That was how he was saved from execution and brought back with us on the mission. He was important, and if the man Katsumata was after was being held by Burmese, they were sure to let him go in exchange for his freedom.

'In the new Burma, the man told us, he was going to be a minister. He was educated and dedicated and could even make prime minister. The Japanese were right, he said, the English and the Dutch and the French had no business in the Orient. Asia for the Asians. He did add that both Derek and I were nice chaps, but we had no reason to try and liberate his country from the Japanese. We would all be kicked out of an independent Burma after the war. We should concentrate on protecting our little cold island from the Germans instead.

'I suppose he was trying to impress Katsumata with all that pro-Japan stuff, but the Japanese officer did not understand half of what he said. He was not listening too carefully, either, because he kept dozing off. Derek said he had had a little too much of the local brew and was not accustomed to alcohol. The sergeant and the soldiers constructed a tiny tent over his upper body to protect him from the sun.

'"What makes you think," I asked the Burmese, "that you people are ready for independence?"

'"You are ignorant," he said. "We are an old, proud nation which had its independence before your people could read or write. I shall use what I have learned from you, because you have used us. You sucked our wealth away."

'"Do you think the Japanese are going to be any different?" I asked, and he said they were.

'"You would," he said, "be surprised to hear how many Burmese agree with what Japan is trying to do."

'"This," I said, "is what British soldiers are dying for in these jungles."

'The Burmese did not bother to answer. He got up and joined a circle of Burmese smugglers a few yards from where we were. Lieutenant Katsumata woke up and smiled that smile of his at Derek.

'"Get some rest," he said. "The smuggler we are waiting for will soon arrive and then we have to leave. It's not too far, but it won't be easy. We may even come under fire."

'Lieutenant Katsumata smiled again and then he yawned and went back off to sleep as if we were all on some beach somewhere.'

Trudi stared at him, her eyes alert and sparkling. She was sharing the bed of a real warrior.

'Get me a stiff drink. And get one for yourself, too. Then you can rub me to sleep. Watch it. Anything can happen at this hour.'

Trudi smiled to herself. Yes, he was curt and rude and sometimes unpleasant, but that was his way. All men are really children. Anything could happen.

CHAPTER TWENTY-SIX

◆

'The most striking thing about your father was his courage,' the Taisho said to Yoshiro. 'I am not referring to his physical courage. No officer in the Imperial army was a coward. No, I mean his mental courage. His willingness to admit his unconventional opinions to me at a time when such revelations could have easily meant execution. His life was in my hands and still he spoke his mind in a way that made me envy him.

'He was a man of contrasts. I tried to understand him then, as I am trying to now. He disliked the army, of that I am sure, yet he never tried to get out of a task. He was big and strong and could have been mistaken for a *gaijin* if you looked at him from the back, yet he had a quiet voice and was a just and fair officer. During the mission he had killed, yet he was a pacifist. He could have stayed away when we capitulated, as other people did to get themselves a clean start with the Americans after the war. They pretended to oppose the regime, but not your father. He never accepted the so-called New Japan of the late thirties, but never tried to desert either.

'They were in the mountains, your father and his *gaijin* and the rest of them. They were waiting for an important Burmese smuggler to come and meet them. In exchange for freedom of movement, the smuggler fed our intelligence with vital information. He was one of Captain Kato's best sources. He could get his hands on anything we needed. Spare parts for vehicles, different calibres of ammunition and Scotch whisky. And he knew where the high-ranking officer was being held. Captain Kato could not move without him, and this was why he was allowed to run his business across those borders. We did not pay him any money. He was not a supporter of our ideology, nor an enemy of it. He was a useful man to have on your side because he never failed to deliver. He was supposed to meet your father's party there in the village and lead them to where the officer was.'

When the Burmese smuggler finally arrived, it was four o'clock in the afternoon. The two Englishmen were asleep in the sun and the Burmese, having had a fair amount of alcohol, were unable to move. The smuggler noted the state of Katsumata's party and suggested they leave at midnight. The place they were heading for was no more than four or five hours' walk away, and they would arrive while it was still dark. The guerrillas were alert and would shoot at anything that moved, and there was an English soldier with them, which could complicate negotiations.

Lieutenant Katsumata arranged for an empty hut for his people to spend the rest of the time in, then he crouched with the Burmese smuggler, a bottle of *gaijin* whisky between them, and they talked. The smuggler spoke in English and Keichi asked him to speak slowly so that he could understand every word. He wanted to know about the people he was going to meet and what they were like.

'Things must be as clear as possible,' he said. The smuggler laughed.

'In my line of business, you have to play it all by ear.'

'You are a successful man, by all accounts. Your goods arrive at their destination in time and you get paid. That can only be achieved by proper planning and a high degree of delegation and discipline. Just like the army.'

'Correct,' the smuggler said. 'I do not employ a lot of

people. Important matters I deal with myself. Have a drop of this.'

'I cannot take much hard alcohol. We can both get drunk together this time tomorrow when we finish this mission.'

'You're the boss. Whisky to me is a medicine. At the moment, I am suffering from a bad back. Nothing like whisky for any pain. In my business, you don't get to see a doctor often.'

'We have a doctor with us. An English doctor. Would you like him to look at you?'

'No thank you. He'll only tell me to stay in bed for a month, and that can't be. I have been walking around these parts for twenty years, sometimes carrying heavy weights on my back. It's only getting back at me for all the punishment I dealt it.'

The whisky was loosening the man's tongue. He said he was born in a small village outside Rangoon, and started life as a shepherd. At the age of sixteen, he ran away from home and joined the British army, where he was a pathfinder for twenty years. That was how he came to know the country so well and learned to speak English, too. With his discharge money, he bought a few crates of whisky and cigarettes which he sold across the border in Siam, having carried the whole lot to the border by himself, little by little.

Over the years, he said, he began to realize that smuggling had become a drug. He had started to live for the tension and the excitement and could not stop. He had a large apartment house in Rangoon and a chicken farm in his home village. He had a huge stock of goods and gold sovereigns and cash and he did not need to work any more.

He did try to stop and took trips to Hong Kong and Yokohama and stayed in hotels, but the mountain paths soon beckoned him to return. Everything in the outside world was predictable. You ate your dinner and the waiter was sure to come for the money. In his world, there was tension. Would the goods arrive? Would the policeman look the other way?

'I deal in human greed and weakness. These are commodities that come in different shapes and sizes, but they are always there. Every man has his price, and if he is not for sale, he's got his breaking point. Then there is fashion. Seasonal stuff. Profitable, but risky. Whisky and cigarettes always move.

'We had a boom in crocodile skins a few years ago. Everybody was bringing them in from Siam. Bales and bales of crocodile skins. They were selected right here by an Italian expert. These skins found their way through India and the Suez Canal to Europe, not paying one cent of customs duty anywhere. The Italian expert came up here every few months. You could set your watch and your calendar by his visits.

'That was beautiful and safe and easy money, but the fashion changed overnight and the crocodile skin business died off. Sometimes you sell people and sometimes you sell gold or information, but above all you sell yourself.'

'Fascinating,' Katsumata said.

'This is a big industry, with people from every nationality. You begin to wonder what all these policemen are being paid for. Only two months ago we had a Russian up here. Don't ask me how he got as far as this, considering there is a hell of a war on, or how he knew where to find me. He was selling Russian emeralds and diamonds and amber, and came to buy English sovereigns.

You would think he'd go to England for that.

'He was a funny man and we were all sorry to see him leave. He knew I had a horde of sovereigns in India, and while we waited for those to arrive, we sat and drank a whole crate of Scotch together. He even told me to come and visit him some day. But when he left, he was sober and sharp and businesslike and he got everything he came for. Only his local Buddha knows what he wanted sovereigns for.

'How can I retire to some terrace or coffee house and listen to old people talk about their pains and their children and the weather when I can be here with you today? All we do is take a little money away from governments. They still have enough to spend on state palaces and wars. We are not thieves or criminals. If I die before paying a bill or making a delivery, my son will do it for me. Can you say the same about governments? As soon as they change, the new man in the palace says he did not make any promises. We provide a service. We do not harm anybody. Only governments, and I don't mind that at all. I hate them.'

'But you are working with a government now. The Japanese government, aren't you?'

'No, young man. I am working with Captain Kato who is a man of his word. Secondly, it is Captain Kato's government who is working for me. They save me the cash I would need to corrupt the border police. With your government behind me, I can do things, but this won't last forever. One day Captain Kato and his army will go away and I will have to find someone else. Until then I shall stick to the arrangement.'

'What about the man we've come for? Have you actually seen him yourself?'

'You Japanese officers are all the same. All work and no play. You really should take a drink some time. You should have seen the British officers at night in their mess. By ten o'clock they were drunk. They relied on those who were on duty and sober, and they were friendly, I can tell you.'

'Perhaps they were too relaxed. They are losing the war.'

'They haven't lost it yet. In their own words they are suffering a few setbacks. I am speaking of another time. There was no war when I was in the British army.'

'Do you think they will win this war?'

'I am not a fortune-teller.'

'Don't evade the question. I won't report you. This is a private conversation.'

'I am not a politician, young man, but it does not take a genius to guess you can't fight the British, the Americans and everybody else all on your own.'

'But look where we are. The British Empire is nearly gone. The flag of the Rising Sun is flying everywhere.'

'Not in Africa, Lieutenant Katsumata, not in Europe, not in America.'

'Japan is only concerned with Asia.'

'I am not in the mood for a political argument. Let's just say you have done very well so far. The British and the Americans are going to get the Germans first. The Italians are on the run and the Russians will eventually come into the war against you. Please, Lieutenant Katsumata, let us stop this. Anything can happen. There are many in my country who wish you well.'

'What about you?'

'You asked me about the prisoner. I saw him the day before yesterday. I don't know what you want him back for. He is a quiet man who sulks a lot. I have been paying his captors to feed him well for weeks to keep his strength up, but that doesn't do much for his spirits. He keeps asking for a British officer to talk to and all they have there is a sergeant-major, a regular army man, in for twenty-five years. Good at organizing food and ammunition dumps, but not a negotiator. I thought of dressing him up as a colonel, but your man would find him out in two minutes flat.

'The man keeps insisting on having a British colonel at least. I promise you, in all my years with the British, I never even saw the colonel more than once a month. Anyway, they told him they will find him a colonel pretty soon and he has quietened down for now. Let's wait until you get there.'

'Do you think his captors will agree to deal?'

'Hard to say.'

'What sort of people are they?'

'They claim they are anti-Japanese guerrillas, but their leader is no freedom fighter.'

'What do you mean?'

'That one is a bad egg. Used to rob banks before the war. Small banks in small cities. He was not too good at it until he found himself some partners. Two women, believe it or not. They used to plan the operation for him from A to Z and pull it off great. They did a few large branches and made a lot of money. I think he was sleeping with both of them. Anyway, a week after you lot arrived, the two women were ambushed by your army and shot dead right in front of the cashier. The cashier was shot dead, too. That was the end of the fellow's career and he was very upset about it. He said the English never got him because they were good sports. The Japanese were too serious and efficient, that is why he joined the guerrillas. As a freedom fighter he will be pardoned for his past if the British win. Yes, you may be able to deal with him.'

Lieutenant Katsumata was amused.

'Money?'

'Of course.'

'He must be a very colourful character. Just like yourself. I do not mean to offend you. I have never met anyone like you before.'

'That man is not colourful at all. Devious, yes. Nasty, yes. Two-faced son-of-a-bitch, yes, but not colourful. He is a criminal. He is dishonest.'

'I am sorry. I meant you are both unusual.'

'What is unusual about a bank robber? Don't you have them in Japan?'

'What sort of a deal could we offer him?'

'I cannot answer that, Lieutenant Katsumata. All I am supposed to do is to get you there safely and introduce you to them. I am going to make sure you will be treated as a friend under a truce for five hours. After that, if you don't strike a deal you will have to fight it out or run for it.'

The Burmese smuggler did not want to talk any more. He was tired. He asked Lieutenant Katsumata to have him woken fifteen minutes before midnight, in time to get himself ready for the trek. It was not going to be an easy trail to follow. It was way up in the mountains and impossible to approach without being seen, heard or smelled.

He got up and, heavy on his feet, he walked away.

'Your father actually enjoyed that evening,' the Taisho said to Yoshiro. 'He could not stop laughing as he was telling me about the smuggler. Captain Kato confirmed to

209

me that the man was genuine. He was fond of him, but Captain Kato was killed and never saw the end of the war. I found out what happened to the smuggler, though. I even told your father about it during one of our meetings here in this coffee shop. He laughed his head off when he heard.'

'What did happen to the smuggler?'

'You do look like your father. He was just as curious as you. He had a broader face, and he was taller than you, but you do have something of him.

'That occasion I have just described to you was the last light-hearted time your father was to enjoy on that mission. The memories of it produced some relief for his profound misery about Lieutenant Pritchard and the circumstances of his death. Not enough, I fear, because Pritchard was to haunt your father for the rest of his life. He told me that himself. He would have liked to have met with him again after the war and got to know him and his family. You might dismiss that as sentimentality. I did. I told him the army is not a bank or an insurance company where you plan meetings and cultivate relationships to suit yourself. A war is a sad occasion for losers.

'Your father was a reluctant survivor. He slipped away from death both during and after the mission, yet I felt he did not really want to get away. He questioned the divine right he had been offered to see you and his grandchildren grow while that Pritchard did not. He held himself responsible for the Englishman's death, but that was wrong. I gave him explicit orders that if the prisoners were not exchanged they should not survive. Your father only survived because Captain Kato succeeded in changing Tokyo's mind.'

'Did my father kill Lieutenant Pritchard, Mr

Sakamoto?'

'I don't know the details. That happened after the mission. After we met in Bangkok. We did not take the boat to Singapore together as was planned. He took a few days off, and he went to a small place south-west of Pattaya. A place called Bang Saray. He was no longer under my command and did not have to report to me. I only saw him briefly after he came back from Bang Saray, and he said Pritchard had been killed. He did not give me any details.

'A few months ago, while we were sitting here, your father asked a favour of me. He said I was a banker and had connections overseas and offices everywhere. He asked me to find out all I could about Lieutenant Pritchard's family. He had the Englishman's address in England and was going to write to his widow. She is still alive and so is his daughter. But your father did not know that.'

'Did my father kill Lieutenant Pritchard?'

'Killing in wartime is no crime. The last time we met, he asked me to make contact with Pritchard's family through our branch in London. This I have now done, and I have all the information, but it is of no use to your father now.

'I don't know what he had in mind. Perhaps he wanted to make amends to the family or ask forgiveness or something of that nature. I thought of leaving a note with my findings in the temple for him. It's not much. Just facts.'

A feeling of impending doom closed over Yoshiro's mind. He was alert and had listened to every word. The sentences were crisp and his brain was lucid as it had not been for days. He sat and he listened and waited for the old man to speak, but it was as though he knew what was coming.

'I did not get a chance to tell your father about that,' Mr Sakamoto said. 'Imagine, had he lived he could have met with Lieutenant Pritchard's daughter right here in Tokyo. I have all the details. I don't know what he wanted to do. Was he going to come up to her and say, "I am the man who caused your father to die years ago"? I do not believe in bringing ghosts back. Would he have wanted her to kill him? The custom of *kataki uchi* is not applicable in wartime. Any *gaijin* I meet in the street could be the son of someone I have killed.'

It could not be. It must not be. He did not want to hear any more. Perhaps the old man was going to forget. Keep the name to himself. His mind was racing and hoping and he said:

'It is a story without an end.'

'I suppose you would like to know what happened to the Burmese smuggler and how the mission ended. That will take one more meeting, I am afraid. I am too tired to continue now. It's an old man's privilege. But I will tell you about the smuggler. He died an envious death. He was shot by a jealous husband five years ago in Rangoon. He was eighty-three. You will understand why your father laughed so much when he heard this. Funny, don't you think?'

Yoshiro did not think at all as he composed his last question.

'Are you sure Pritchard's daughter is in Tokyo?'

The Taisho looked at him and yawned and smiled.

'I am a banker, Mr Katsumata. We deal in facts.'

'Never mind.' Perhaps it was better not to know.

'I have had two of our London people check this information very carefully. They had Lieutenant

212

Pritchard's address and serial number and employed a local agency to verify their findings. You must remember I was doing a service for a friend. Of course I am sure she is in Tokyo. Her name is Mrs Bellingham, the wife of Jonathan Bellingham. Her name is Anna, her maiden name was Pritchard. They change their names upon marriage, the same as we do.'

CHAPTER TWENTY-SEVEN

By the time he got to the door, he was almost running. He had uttered a quick goodbye to Mr Sakamoto and on his way he bumped into one of the waiters, knocking his tray to the floor. He did not stop. He had to get into the air.

He was going to see her this very afternoon. They had not met for a week because she had gone to Hong Kong with her husband. There was a little bar on the other side of the street. They served drinks there.

A little whisky was all he needed. He could then call the *gaijin* woman and cancel the meeting or something. But would he have the strength to, once he heard her voice?

He stopped and looked across the road. All eight floors of the Sato building stared at him, each one of the windows frowning in anger. The company flag shook disapprovingly from the roof, motioning to him to get back to his desk. You are wasting your life, the big red letters said to him.

He could not think. Pictures came into his mind, and were gone and came back again. Words. The bitter-sweet scent of Anna's sweat mingled with the sound of his father's voice. Or was it the Taisho's? All he needed was that small drink. She was waiting for him at the Takanawa Prince Hotel.

He ran down the steps into the bar and ordered his drink as he sat down. The barman watched. The dashing young executive who usually took pride in his appearance was dishevelled. He had seen people hit by something before and often they would drink and talk to him, but this man did not speak. He would take long to recover. Silent ones always did.

The Ginza was bright and clear and the air blew cool. The tall glass buildings reflected the sinking sun and the sky and the cars below. There were new goods in the windows. A black line of close-cropped schoolboys passed by, following their teacher.

He went up to his office to sign his post. He went into the men's room to change his shirt and shave. He stayed at the office long enough to make sure he was seen. He then scanned the room and left down the stairs to go to the woman.

The evening was descending on the district of Takanawa. It was only five o'clock, but darkness comes early in winter. From her window, Anna saw the lights coming on. She had been waiting since lunchtime. The remains of her American club sandwich were still on the plate, bitten corners of cold roast on a sea of soggy lettuce.

They did not come to collect it because she had left the 'do not disturb' sign on the door which she had left ajar. Yoshiro was coming any minute now. He had called to say he would be here at five. He was always on time.

She had had all that afternoon to herself, reflecting on

what had gone on between them and what was to come. The more she had thought of Yoshiro's wheel of fate, the more she understood. The circumstances that had brought her to Japan occurred over thirty years before, between two men who were now dead. Yet their meeting had scarred her life. She was committed to one single act of revenge. And she was as far from it today as she had ever been.

Jonathan's assignment was coming to an end. He had told her that while they were in Hong Kong. They would soon be back in London and there was a promotion on the cards. 'You don't really like it here,' he often said. 'It must be a bore.'

She had used the hunt for Yoshiro for her own pleasure. That was a sin. He had become the solution to a problem her excitement had created. He should have been a target, and every time they met she was going to hit out at him. But then he would come into the room and stand in the corner or sit far from her in the chair. First she would identify with him and then she would crawl up to him like a cat and rub against his skin and touch him, and still he would be passive and make her dizzy and she would forget what he was there for.

Away from him, she could hate him and plan his destruction because, far from him, she could not feel him or need him. Her time was running short now, and with the knowledge he had given her of his customs and code, she knew it would be easy to turn him on himself. He could not bend. He was a machine and machines could be destroyed.

He had been almost human the time he bought the elephant, but even dogs have passion for their young.

He had talked so little of himself, so unlike the men

she had known. Today she would get him to do something that would ignite her anger right there with him, not at a distance.

He knocked on the door and rang the bell. He always did that, even though he knew the door was open. He knew she was there and that she was waiting for him, but that was their ritual. He never came in immediately. He heard her voice invite him in.

Today he did not come straight in after her words because today was different. Today he had been informed by his wheel of fortune that the Katsumatas owed a debt of honour to the woman inside the room. Today his dead father had told him he had killed the woman's father long ago, when she was a little girl. He did not say it in so many words, nor why or how, but he did say it had been his responsibility.

'The door is open. Come in,' the woman said. Today there could have been the love he so missed, but the wheel of circumstance had interfered.

On his way to the lift, Yoshiro saw Mr Sato, the chairman. He was in the main lobby with the financial director. Yoshiro thought he had seen his chairman in the hotel before, but he was not sure. He was not sure of anything.

Mr Sato called out to him.

'What are you doing here? I suppose you are meeting with an overseas visitor? This is a beautiful place to meet and the gardens are enchanting. They have Japanese and Chinese food here, and their French place is the best in town.'

The financial director nodded in servile agreement.

He had pretended to listen to what Mr Sato was saying, but did not react. He continued his walk towards the lift without a word of parting. He knew he was doing something wrong, but then he was there at his father's command and the dead have priority.

'Mr Katsumata,' the chairman called.

'Mr Katsumata, the chairman is talking to you,' the financial director shouted after him, but Yoshiro did not stop.

'The door is open,' she said again. 'Come in.' He walked into the room and silently shut the door behind him. He stood there, motionless.

'Come in and sit down,' she said as she had done many times before. 'What would you like to drink?'

He sat down on the big chair and he opened his jacket and asked if he could smoke. He looked paler than before. He looked thinner and the springy zest in his movements was missing. His skin seemed dry and his eyes were small. He looked grey and tired. His hands rested on his thighs as he slumped down on the chair.

'You look like death,' she said, forgetting what she had promised herself. Instead of hate, she felt compassion. He looked at her and she saw the ocean of misery in his eyes. 'What is the matter?'

He could not talk. What could he say to her? Here she was, trying to comfort him, and all the while his father's spirit was commanding him to stroke her hair and cry with her and tell her he was guilty.

Did that wheel of destiny force the son of Lieutenant Katsumata and the daughter of Lieutenant Pritchard into a bed? To pray for their fathers by getting into each other's bodies, closer than any two men could?

Her compassion turned into pity and then the frustration came and a hint of hatred.

'What the hell is the matter with you?' she shouted.

He did not appear to notice her at all.

'I have been here alone all afternoon waiting for you. Who do you think you are?' Not a word came from him. He raised his head and looked out of the window.

'You arrogant son-of-a-bitch,' she screamed, and then she looked at his face and saw his agony and she was sorry. She got up and went to him and took him by the arm and led him to the bed. She turned the lights off. Only the television was on. A sumo contest. Two baby-shaped giants, their skins gleaming with sweat, their long hair in shiny oiled topknots, were throwing each other about, trying to remain inside a circle of sand. It was grotesque. It was funny, but in their faces there was fear and hate. She looked away from the screen.

Yoshiro lay on his back and she turned to him and pulled his shoes and his trousers and his underwear off. She touched his flesh and it remained limp and small. She was in heat again. She had aroused herself all day without even knowing. All week, ever since she had last seen him, she craved to extract that peace of hers out of his body. There was nothing in him now.

'Say something to me.'

He looked. Her face hung over his. A drop of sweat rolled off her brow onto his chin. Her lips moved and her hand touched his, but he could not hear her. He should have listened more carefully to the Taisho's story, but there was nothing to tell. The Taisho did not know what happened.

'Talk to me, you bastard.'

The chairman was going to think his behaviour very strange. To be ignored by an employee in front of another director is a loss of face. The chairman had only been making small-talk. He did not really want to know what he had been doing at the hotel. Yes he did. And Yoshiro had been rude and offensive. But this was not really him. It was only his body being manipulated by his father's spirit.

'Talk to me,' the woman said.

Then the animal came into her and she went down on him and kissed his chest and his legs and his hands and held on to him and touched him, but he did not harden. She climbed on top of him and rubbed it against herself and she grunted and gyrated and screamed obscenities.

'Come on,' she said, and held him in place while she moved like the wind, her body rubbing against his. What was she doing to his body? Was she using him to please herself? This was not the time.

'Make me come,' she growled. 'Please make me come.'

Yoshiro was not there. He thought of the Taisho's story and his father's instructions. Mr Sato was in the lobby. That was his end.

Perhaps it did not really happen. Perhaps his over-taxed mind was making him see things. Her nails were in his flesh and the pain was real, but maybe it was someone else's pain. Another place.

He would have to meditate hard and find out what was real. The woman's father was dead and the Taisho said his father had caused it. That meant his father had killed him. The Japanese language can be vague. Words mean many things. Maybe his father never told him about the war because he did not want to load him with his obligation.

'Get a hold on yourself,' the woman said. Her body was drumming into his soft self. She was in a hurry now. She wanted him to swell as she forced him inside and moved like a piston, but there was no satisfaction. There was no peace within her body.

Bastard. Killer. On the screen, there were two other sumo wrestlers and the crowd came alive as one flew out of the ring. The announcer's voice sounded like a high-pitched ship's horn. The magic was gone from it. She got up and she was angry. On the screen, Chinese letters appeared, covering the picture like white, evenly spread snow.

Yoshiro lay where she had left him. Her anger knew no bounds as she looked down at his crumpled flesh. It looked like a bored snake grovelling in the black grass of his hair. He looked stupid lying naked on the bed. His socks were on his feet and there were holes in them. He had no pride. He was small and helpless and ridiculous, and yet he must be laughing at her. He didn't even want her any more.

'Come on,' she said in a strong, resolute voice. 'Get up and out of here. I don't want to see your arrogant face again. Get up, get up!'

Yoshiro obeyed. He rolled off the bed and collected his clothes and got dressed. He had to tell her now.

'Anna,' he said.

'Don't bother. Just go.'

He did not know what brought her anger out. He had to tell her, but how? When he got to the door, she called him back again. He had to tell her now or never. She took a faded photograph out of her bag and showed it to him.

'My father,' she said.

'Lieutenant Derek Pritchard,' he said. 'I know.'

He thought his voice had sounded like his father's. Perhaps his father was there with him. There was quiet acceptance in his voice. He must tell her now.

'My father killed your father,' he said. 'My family owe you an obligation.'

Her anger knew no bounds. It came down on her from everywhere and in all directions. So he had known all the time. And still he let her court him and chase him and kiss him and make love to him and he knew.

'You shit!' she screamed, and she came at him and hit his face. 'You fucking son-of-a-bitch! You murdering bastard!'

'You are right,' he said in silent resolution.

'Go kill yourself,' she said. 'You have never been any good at anything. Go and screw your little slave of a wife, then shoot yourself. Now go. Get out. Out of this room!'

He wanted to look at the *gaijin*'s face again, but her temper was on fire. She could do herself harm, he thought as he left the room. He heard her rant and rave behind him, and then she came to the door and opened it and screamed at him down the corridor. She threw his shoes and a plate after him.

An elderly couple waited by the lift and watched them. The woman looked the other way. The man looked embarrassingly at Yoshiro. They would have to share the lift and share his shame and ponder what the *gaijin* woman was saying to this man and why. The trip downwards lasted forever and when they got there Yoshiro remained inside. The man nudged him to show him they were on the ground floor. He came out, his shoes in his hands, and bowed his thanks to the old man.

He walked out through the lobby and did not notice Mr Sato standing there. He walked straight past him to the street. He could walk the streets tonight and then at dawn go to the temple to bid his father farewell.

The debt had now passed on to him. That was the

whole point of the Taisho's story. He was to meet Lieutenant Pritchard's daughter and confess and receive her pardon, and now that she did not give it to him his path towards death was clear.

He would live those moments with her once more. The hours. The days. The things she did to him and said. The shame. Feel the shame and let it enter his soul and humiliate and hurt. Tonight he would go to the Dai Ichi Hotel, or the Ginza.

Or should he go home? It was early yet, but a dishonoured man has no home. Just like his father before him. He could never go to the office again and embarrass the chairman by showing his face. He could think about it all later, alone in his bed at the Dai Ichi Hotel, once he had had a few drinks to clarify his mind. Not now.

Not even the Taisho could help him now. This was a family affair. A question of honour. He could not – and should not – load anyone with that. It was between him and his father and Lieutenant Pritchard's daughter.

It was all part of being punished.

CHAPTER TWENTY-EIGHT

There is nothing like the Ginza at night. There are lights and millions of people. There are thousands of drinking places for a man to get lost in.

You can sit and listen to loud music and gobble the snacks and hear how human suffering becomes common gossip.

There are small girls in kimonos, hostesses in make-believe geisha houses, tall girls in miniskirts with long legs and *gaijin* eyes. You can talk about your troubles and pretend the girl is listening while she makes sure your glass is always kept full.

There are happy people in the Ginza bars and there are sad people, people from the country and from the offices. They are all there, and on their way they see the lights dancing up and down the tall buildings.

There is French can-can music and rock, and there are Italian *cancione* and Japanese love songs and pop music. You can listen to records or a band and you can have a microphone and sing for yourself.

It was Mr Akashi who had introduced Yoshiro to the Ginza. He knew every bar and every brand of every drink. He knew every mama-san and had slept with many of them when his rows on the top floor had become acute. He used to go there early in the afternoon while the office was still like a beehive. Yoshiro covered for him and finished his work and made excuses for him over the telephone.

Mr Akashi used to call him from the bars and say, 'Stop slaving for Mr Sato and come and join me here.' Yoshiro went, because Akashi had been like a father to him and had taught him all he knew. He would go to the Ginza to meet him and take him home in a taxi because he was too drunk to go by train. He used to listen to Mr Akashi's whisky-sodden complaints about Mr Sato and the system. There had always been a chairman called Mr Sato on the eighth floor of the building. There always would be. It was the custom. Some things never change.

Now Mr Akashi was no longer in charge of the department. Yoshiro Katsumata was. He was confused and beaten, just like Mr Akashi had been. But Mr Akashi had been beaten by the system. Yoshiro Katsumata had not. He had simply been caught by his father's wheel of circumstance, and since his father was no longer on earth, it fell to him to do his duty for him. Simple, if one really believed. He did, and yet he did not understand it all. He was taking orders from a living man. His father's Taisho. Why? Was the Taisho *kami*?

Unimportant.

He had accepted his father's punishment himself. It was the custom. A matter of honour. Some things never change. He flagged down a taxi.

'*Ginza dori*,' Yoshiro told the driver. He remembered his shoes were still in his hands and he put them on and settled back for the drive.

BOOK 4

THE ROAD TO
BANG SARAY

CHAPTER TWENTY-NINE

BANGKOK, DECEMBER 1975

She was hot and she felt sticky. The trip from the airport to the hotel took over two hours. The reception chief at the Siam Intercontinental apologized. The roads were bad in Bangkok and the traffic chaotic. They were building motorways which were going to shorten the trip, but he hoped that her stay in the hotel would compensate her. Everybody comes back to us, he said. There is a swimming-pool and sixteen acres of tropical gardens and a little zoo, all in the grounds. The best seafood in town is right here at our Talley Thong Restaurant and we want you to consider this hotel as your home away from home.

The reception chief had a haunting smile. It matched the airy, pagoda-shaped lobby. He had an American accent. His voice was deep and reassuring.

'Dr Hedges left a message for you, Mrs Bellingham,' he said. 'Have a nice day.'

She would have gone straight to London had it not been for Jimmy Hedges. He had written to say that his trip to the Orient was imminent. He would like to meet her and Jonathan there on their way back. Spend a few days together in Thailand. Go to the coast, perhaps. Anna wrote back saying Jonathan was expected in London immediately, but she would be pleased to come.

How she was looking forward to seeing him again. A wholesome slice of home without the pressure.

'Have gone out on the town to chase a few memories,' Jimmy Hedges wrote in his note. 'Would have waited for you, but you will probably want to have a swim and a rest. Anyway, where I'm off to is out of bounds for good little girls. Have reserved a table for two at the Talley Thong for nine o'clock. One of the seats is for you. Love, Jimmy.'

A bellboy, golden-turbaned and white-jacketed, rolled her suitcase along the tiled path that led to her poolside room. The plants imprinted their shapely shade along the way. A refreshing breeze shook the palms and their thick trunks rubbed lazily against the hibiscus below. She would go and have a look at the gardens as soon as she'd had a little rest. Later on, in the evening, she would call her mother. For the third time this week. She would tell her again it was nearly done.

Anna followed the luggage cart. Yoshiro was on his last lap. She knew he was because she had spoken to him more than once since that day. He had, for the first time ever, pleaded with her to meet him.

'I have not been at my home in weeks. I hardly go to the office now. Do you know they won't let me take any papers out of there?'

'I couldn't care less,' she had said.

'I shall take the consequences of my father's actions upon myself.'

He sounded pathetic and his voice was foreign and tinny and insignificant.

'Can you imagine, Anna, what would have happened if we were not who we are? Not the daughter and the son of two lieutenants? We could have been anybody. We could have been other people. It would not have lasted, but it was magic while it did. I don't blame anyone for what happened. It was that wheel of fate.'

'Who cares?' she said, and hung up on him.

The little bellboy reached the door.

'May I open it for you?' he asked. They all had such beautiful smiles. 'Your first time Bangkok? Beautiful, no? Good food and happy people.'

'Thank you,' Anna said, as he laid her case on the chair. She gave him twenty baht and he clasped his hands and lowered his head.

'Flowers and tropical fruits for you on table. Compliments of hotel. *Sawadee kap*, madam. Enjoy the stay. You pretty lady, madam,' the boy said, and was gone.

The room was cool and the curtains were drawn. She tore her dress off and kicked her sandals onto the floor and lay on the bed. There was a cream-coloured, flat ceramic image of two elephants on the wall. There was another with a crowned goddess. She turned the piped music off and looked at the elephants. One looked like the stool Yoshiro had bought his daughter a hundred years ago.

She hated what Yoshiro's begging was doing to her. She would have preferred him to have kept his dignity and pride. If he was going to do himself in, he should go away somewhere and die quietly. No goodbyes. On that first call, he had been doing all the talking, and the sound of his voice was humiliating. Where was the thrill his downfall should have given her? He did not ask for mercy. All he wanted was her company.

'I have become an alcoholic,' he had said.

'Really?'

'I have been watching other alcoholics. They sit and drink and they do not talk. Not even to themselves, like I do.'

'You bore me.'

Someone hung up. She did not remember who.

Her mother had told her not to feel sorry for him. He called her back again afterwards and she did not want to think of what he had said. Now she was going to build a life of her own. Right after she had visited Bang Saray and had heard about what happened there. Her father's soul would rest in peace, just like her mother said.

Yoshiro said something like that, too, the last time they spoke. This very morning, just before she left for the airport.

There were no introductions or pleasantries.

'In the other world we will be allowed to put the past to bed,' Yoshiro had said as soon as she lifted the receiver. 'Your father and Bang Saray plagued my father for over thirty years. I shall bring peace to us all with my own hands. I shall be watching you and shall pray for your happiness and imagine how things could have been, had we been allowed to be two other people.'

She had been angry because she was losing her composure. The taxi was waiting outside.

'Do you think that? Do you think we ever could be two other people? I knew from the start whose son you were, Yoshiro. That is why . . .'

He interrupted her.

'I know why you are saying that . . . it's because you feel guilty about it all. You have committed no crime. You have cheated on your husband and I cheated on my wife, but they will never know about it. Look for the lights in our afternoons. Don't be sharp and clever and insulting. Remember how good some of it was and how it could have been. Blame it on me, or fate, or on the book you never wrote. Not yourself.'

Why was he so condescending? She did not need his help. She did not feel guilty.

'Are you quite finished? I have a plane to catch.'

That time he must have put the phone down and that

was the last she had heard.

Her phone rang and she picked it up expecting Yoshiro to come on the line. It was the hoarse voice of Jimmy Hedges.

'*Sawadee*,' he said. 'That means welcome in Thai. Did you have a good flight? Did you get my note?'

'Yes and yes,' she said, and he laughed his lecherous laugh.

'Are you saving on words these days? Don't tell me you've got someone in your room already. You haven't been here long enough. They tell me you arrived half an hour ago.'

'I was just having a rest. The heat is tiring.'

'I am sorry. I'll see you in the lobby at nine.'

'I look forward to that.'

She stared at the ceiling and there was a void inside her. Could she have been disappointed it was not Yoshiro?

Along the corridor in his room, Jimmy put the phone down. A few hours of shut-eye would do him good. It was his fifth day in Bangkok and he had spent each one of the five afternoons in the same Turkish bath. The flight had been long but comfortable since there were only three other passengers in the first-class compartment. Two got off in Bahrain and the third in Bombay. Jimmy had slept most of the way. Trudi had booked him a bunk on the upper part of the Singapore Airlines 747. He got out of bed for meals and consumed enough brandy to make him sleep again as soon as the feasts ended. He landed in Bangkok early in the morning and an air-conditioned limousine whisked him to the hotel without fuss.

With first-class service all the way from Heathrow, Jimmy Hedges arrived back in Bangkok thirty-three years after he left it. The trek from the border to the hideout in the Burma mountains was hard and long, but the passage of time had attached a romantic aura to that experience. His current visit was comfortable, but that other one, with Derek and Lieutenant Katsumata, that was fun.

He had never gone into details with anyone about the rest of the mission. He did not tell Trudi about what happened after they all left the huts with the Burmese smuggler. He did not tell her any more than he did when, after his release, army intelligence debriefed him. It was humiliating, he confessed to Trudi, to be interrogated like a spy by your own people. Three days and three nights of questions and maps and demands for accuracy and more questions.

He had only told them simple, uncomplicated facts. Not all. And it was coming back to him now. No power on earth could stop it.

It was fifteen minutes before midnight when they all stood in front of the hut. Lieutenant Katsumata knocked on the door. A dog barked at them from within, and then the door opened and the Burmese smuggler stood in its frame, fully dressed. His face was clean-shaven and his oily hair was combed backwards, thirties style, with a parting in the middle.

'You are punctual,' the Burmese smuggler said to Katsumata in English. 'Let's get moving.'

Katsumata asked him to lead the way and motioned to Jimmy to follow. Behind him marched the two Japanese soldiers with the Burmese, Derek and the sergeant following. They crossed the clearing and entered the jungle single-file.

The path they started their trek on was reasonably

detectable. It must have been in daily use because no grass or shrubs grew on it. In the moonlight, it assumed a chalky, white colour and it cut through the trees like a fluorescent light. They had all been issued with rubber-soled boots and the sergeant could not hide his satisfaction at the way the boots fitted every member of the party.

The silence that greeted their feet as they hit the ground was eerie. They looked like nine ghosts walking a path of mystery, Derek said later.

Two hours into the march, the Burmese smuggler led them off the path and into the thickly leaved growth of the jungle. The ground kept changing rapidly. At times, it was rocky and then soft, and often they were walking ankle-deep in water. Jimmy's neck and face were covered in mosquito bites. The jungle was everywhere and branches hit their arms and cut their faces as the smuggler intensified the pace and they began going uphill.

He is leading us into a trap with me the first to go, Jimmy thought. He could hear the men behind him breathing heavily as they climbed. He felt his own sweat running down his back, his legs and his eyes. After three hours of marching, the Burmese smuggler stopped. Jimmy Hedges, who had been watching the ground, crashed into his back. Lieutenant Katsumata came running up.

'What's the matter?'

'Two hours to go,' the smuggler said. 'There is a little stream just here. We could use some fresh water.'

The water was cool and sweet. It entered their bodies and caressed their faces and shocked their skulls into awareness. They were all lying belly-down by its side, friend and foe alike.

As soon as everyone had a drink and the water bottles

were filled, the smuggler jumped to his feet with the elasticity of a youth.

'We better get moving,' he said.

The single file snaked its way behind him into the mosquito-infested jungle.

In his plush bedroom in Bangkok, there were no mosquitoes and his feet were dry. There was enough liquor in his bar and room service was only a telephone call away. Yet, as he lay on his bed watching the window and the trees outside, Jimmy Hedges wished he was back there, following the Burmese smuggler with thirty-three years less on his limbs and abdomen.

God, I was fit, he said to himself with a sigh. A woman like Trudi would have known how to appreciate that. In those days, it seemed he could go on and on and never have a rest. His telephone rang. It was the driver he had hired for the duration of his stay.

'Sir? You want another massage?'

'What do you take me for, Superman?'

'What time you come, sir?'

'No more massage parlour today. You go now and come back tonight at ten.'

'Okeedokee. Me come back ten tonight. You sleep now.'

'Thank you.'

'You sure no quick massage?'

'Very sure. Maybe tonight. See you at ten.'

Maybe Anna would like to see Patpong, the naughty part of town, after dinner.

It was cool in the room. It was six o'clock. He called the receptionist and asked her to wake him at a quarter to nine. He was not as young as he had been, and the afternoon at the massage parlour had been tiring. Maybe he should take a day off. He tried to doze a little but his mind was in turmoil and wrenched him back to Burma.

In the mountains they had reached where they were going. The smuggler announced that as they stopped for the second time. It was five o'clock in the morning. They could rest until eight. They were expected at that time and an earlier show would be a surprise. The guerrillas might open fire.

The two Burmese came closer to their countryman, but he did not appear to be interested. He curled up under a tree and, having asked Katsumata to wake him at a quarter to eight, he went silent. A few minutes later, they could all hear his snoring cut through the humid air.

Katsumata and Derek Pritchard sat down by Jimmy's side. They were speaking in Spanish again and Derek was translating. Jimmy tried to listen, but he must have fallen asleep and only woke up when the sun came directly over his face. The others were all making themselves ready. The Burmese smuggler watched the countryside through his binoculars. The mist was lifting.

'What about food?' Jimmy asked.

'If that is all you think about when you wake, you will grow to be a fat man.'

'If I live that long.'

'You will. You look like a survivor. Let us go now. They are expecting us.'

Presently they were on their way again. This time Katsumata walked with their guide, while one of the soldiers followed Derek and himself. The Burmese walked a short distance behind, watched over by the sergeant and the other soldier. The weapons the Japanese were carrying were slung over their shoulders.

'They can see every move we make,' the smuggler said.

'Great. We'll be shot by our own allies. That'll be a laugh.'

'No, Dr Hedges, we've made an agreement. No one will shoot.'

'I wish I had your faith.'

The rock they were approaching grew taller as they got closer. A squat, fierce-looking man sat at the top with the menacing mouth of a machine-gun pointing straight at the party below. He held a white flag in his hand and waved it with enthusiasm. Katsumata waved his handkerchief back.

They arrived in a clearing some distance away from the rock and stopped. The smuggler exchanged a few shouted words and smiles and gesticulations with the squat man above.

'Looks like a friendly chap,' Derek said.

'They all smile in this part of the world,' Jimmy answered.

'Business before breakfast, I am afraid,' the smuggler declared. 'The local commander wants to make sure you are going to keep to the bargain.'

'We have not made a bargain yet,' Katsumata said.

'He means any bargain. He does not want you to come back here with a whole lot of soldiers. He wants you to prove you are sincere. He wants to be able to trust you. Before they negotiate.'

'How do I do that?' Lieutenant Katsumata asked.

'He wants you to have one of your soldiers shot as a sign of good will. I suggest you accept that. He means it.'

The sun was up and it hit the back of their necks.

Behind them, the canopy formed by the jungle they had left was steaming. There was deadly silence as Lieutenant Katsumata weighed his options.

'Why is he hesitating?' Jimmy said. Derek's eyes were murderous.

'He must be going through hell. Do him the honour of keeping your mouth shut.' Katsumata approached the smuggler.

'Are you sure he is expecting me to do that?'

'Ask him yourself if you like. He speaks English.'

Lieutenant Katsumata moved two paces forward. The machine-gun barrel was lowered, but Katsumata did not flinch. The smuggler shouted something at the rock and the squat man nodded and smiled.

'What do you want, lieutenant?' he shouted down.

'Two questions. One, we would like to see the man we have come to see. Two, why do you want me to kill one of my men?'

The squat man got up, his smile frozen across his face. The sun was in his eyes and he shielded them as he spoke.

'Your man is here. We don't want him to see you before we talk. He says he does not want to be taken back. He wants to see an English colonel first. If he sees you, he might kill himself the way the other prisoner did.'

'Surely you have taken his sword away from him? How can he commit *seppuku* without it?'

'He can hit his head with a rock. He can find a snake to bite him. He can keep his head under water at night. You people are experts at killing yourselves. I saw a Japanese soldier dive head first from this very rock two months ago. It is more difficult to stay alive in this place, lieutenant, than to die. Now, shoot your man so that we can get down to business. The chief wants to make sure you can be trusted.'

There was silence again. Lieutenant Katsumata turned around.

He said a few curt words to the soldier who guarded the Englishmen. The soldier came forward.

He looked tense, but not frightened. The order he was given seemed strange to him, but he marched up to Lieutenant Katsumata and handed his gun to him. Lieutenant Katsumata said something to him and the little soldier bowed. He walked to the bottom of the rock and stopped. He turned around and smiled as if posing for a picture.

'The poor devil is doing it for us,' Derek said.

The Japanese soldier shielded his eyes and stood still, his face strained. He shivered a little as Katsumata lifted his gun, aimed and shot the little soldier in the head.

'There you are,' Katsumata said to the smuggler. 'You can tell him I am a trustworthy killer.' There was bitterness in his voice. The smuggler shrugged his shoulders.

Katsumata marched forward, his step fast and decisive. He stopped in front of the fallen body and bowed. He saluted and then turned and walked back with defiance to join the others.

'There,' Derek said, 'he has now killed a man for the first time in his life.'

'Would you rather he shot one of us?'

'I would rather he did not shoot anyone. I would rather there were no guns or bombs or submarines.'

One down, three to go, Hedges said to himself.

'Now,' Lieutenant Katsumata shouted to the man on top of the rock, 'get your chief to come and talk to us. He has wasted enough of my time.'

'I am the chief,' the squat man said. 'I welcome you to my base. Before we start talking, we shall eat.'

'A man after my own heart,' Jimmy said.

The guerrilla chief got up and motioned to the party to come closer. He told the smuggler to guide them around the rock. As they passed the dead soldier, Jimmy noticed his face. His eyes looked at eternity with a clear expression of surprise.

'He didn't know what was happening,' Derek said. 'He died with trust in his heart. I'd go like that myself.'

'I'd rather stay alive, thank you,' Hedges snapped.

Lieutenant Katsumata did not comment.

It was a large rock, more like a small mountain. It took them twenty minutes to travel round its girth. They walked close to the granite. It was hot and masculine and strong and old, its sheer drops racing down into the jungle. No green branches sprouted out of its smooth, muscle-like cavities. On one side, a rope ladder was lowered and the party started to climb up, one by one, following the smuggler.

As he waited his turn, Jimmy Hedges imagined the rock was a ship. The sight of the men climbing up reminded him of a film he had seen once about wrecked survivors being picked up by pirates.

As he reached the top of the ladder, the Japanese sergeant offered him a hand. Jimmy refused. Up on the ramp behind the edge, the guerrillas had prepared a little feast for them. He wondered how all those roast chickens and cans of vegetables and bully beef had found their way up there. With the food, there were jugs of steaming tea and a few jute-wrapped jars of a liquid he recognized as the local brew. Six guerrillas stiffened at mock attention behind the makeshift table. With them stood an English sergeant-major in fatigues. He saluted Jimmy and Derek before they all sat down.

'How's the war going?' Jimmy asked.

'No idea. There's been no action since I arrived. There's food and booze and other stuff,' the sergeant whispered. 'Don't trust these buggers. They are on nobody's side. All they're interested in is money.'

'What are you doing here, then?'

'I'm using them, that's all. It's a safe place and they like having me. They like people from both sides, at least until they're sure who'll win this bloody war. You can do anything with them if they smell cash.'

The sergeant looked around. No one had heard him.

'This is as far as I go,' the smuggler said to Katsumata. 'From here on, I am an outsider. You do the talking. I was paid to bring you here, and this I have now done.'

'You could have stopped them from forcing me to shoot my man.'

'I was paid to bring you here and to introduce you to these people. Ask Captain Kato about it, if you like. Anyway, you did the right thing.'

'I had no choice.'

'That is why it was the right thing to do. They trust you now.'

The smuggler took a flask of whisky out of his pocket and toasted himself. The others sat down to eat.

It was then, Hedges would later tell Toni, that he first felt there was a chance for them. There was something reassuring in the northern accent with which the sergeant-major had greeted them.

The telephone brought Jimmy Hedges back into his room.

'It's a quarter to nine, Dr Hedges,' the receptionist said. 'I hope you had a good rest.'

'Thank you, I did. Would you call Mrs Bellingham and remind her to meet me in the lobby in fifteen minutes?'

'With pleasure,' the receptionist said. 'Have a nice evening.'

Outside, the stars appeared, hanging down from a black sky. The reflection of the moon appeared on the face of the pool, rubbing shoulders with the palms. It was hot out there and the air stood still. Coloured lights surrounded the garden.

A good sleep always made Jimmy hungry. Lobster, he said to himself as he showered. Lobster thermidor with plenty of sauce, and perhaps a few fried shrimps to start.

CHAPTER THIRTY

The whisky was evaporating out of his system. Into his brain came the images of the day. Slowly, one by one they came, replacing the void. Yoshiro coughed and spat on the pavement. He might walk to the temple now, he thought, and then someone kicked him and apologized and he woke. He realized he had not been walking at all but lying on his side, gripping his empty briefcase. He was not sure how long he had been lying there or which bar it was they had thrown him out of. There were people about, walking and talking and laughing. There were cars. Neon lights flickered up and down, their images saying, 'Buy, buy, buy'. All around him, the Ginza was bracing itself for one last assault on the night people. Soon the cars would come and stop by the kerbs and take them all home. Soon the street cleaners would emerge from the underground train stations to sweep away the papers and the cigarette ends and the empty beer cans and the broken glass.

Shangri-la, the Smoking Dog and the Chanson D'Amour would dispense the last drinks. The mama-san would apologize and the girls would call for taxis or be collected by their boyfriends or pimps for the journey into daylight. He was no longer drunk and the words he had heard from the Taisho at dinner were fresh in his mind again, as was his resolve.

He got up from the ground and brushed down his trousers and jacket. He picked up his briefcase and joined the thinning lines of people on the pavement that had been his bed. Everybody was going somewhere. Soon the city's yellow trucks would come to spray the dust off the streets and brush them into a sheen. He felt his face. It was smooth. He had made himself presentable for his father's old Taisho. It was their last dinner and he had wanted to look his best. A matter of family honour.

He could go up the road to the station. There was an all-night coffee shop there where they served strong Colombian blends and buttered rolls. Iced water, too. The whisky had made him thirsty, but it had served its purpose to the full. It had obliterated the dark memories from his brain. There was plenty of time yet for the temple. The sun was not due up for another two hours. He could go through the Taisho's last story. He could write his notes. He could say a prayer for the soul of his father, Lieutenant Keichi Katsumata.

He did not need more sleep. He must have been out for a good few hours right there on the street. He felt refreshed and alert and he took in the details around him. He saw hostesses walking their clients to their cars. Others waved goodbye. Doors were being chained and locked up for the day and plastic bags placed by the roadside.

Clearer than daylight, his father's Burmese mission came alive again, and he remembered everything the Taisho had told him. His brisk cat-walk of old took him to the station. He felt agile and alive and he smiled at the waitress and asked for a coffee and two rolls.

She watched his attractive face from the corner of her eye as she lingered by his table, pretending to make notes of his order. Her customers on the last shift of the night were usually workers on their way to the factories out of town or drunken, abusive white-collar people back from a night out on the Ginza.

'Do you like cream in your coffee, sir?' He shook his head and she saw his warm, kindly smile.

'Black,' he said. 'You are very kind.' His eyes were distant. She would have asked him what was the matter had she known him, but she did not and another customer was impatiently clapping his hands for her attention.

'I'll be with you in a moment,' she said.

During their last meeting, the Taisho had been extra gentle with him. He had asked after his mother's health and that of his wife and children. He enquired about the company and Mr Sato, and he told Yoshiro he looked a little pale.

'There is just a little more to recount,' the Taisho said, 'and then my promise to your father will be fulfilled. You will know all about the mission.' This time Mr Sakamoto did not need to be reminded of where he had got to in his story.

The party was on that large rock, having breakfast with

the guerrillas. Keichi thought they were all enjoying their meal. There was a marked difference in the posture of the two *gaijin* officers. The medical lieutenant, Hedges, had become more comfortable in the new surroundings. He ate and chatted with the sergeant-major and he joked with the squat guerrilla commander. He seemed to be more confident of Keichi, too, and on a few occasions during the meal he had complimented him on the way he was handling the mission.

The other officer, Pritchard, became quite melancholic. He sat with the others and, as was his way, he nibbled at his food. Keichi wanted to reassure him, console him, find out what was troubling him, but he had other things to do first.

Judging by the guerrilla leader's first demand, nothing was going to be straightforward. The commander refused to talk about the exchange as long as they were eating and the meal seemed to go on for ever. The smuggler offered no help at all. He ate a lot and he drank more. His face was flushed and his speech slurred and soft, and he laughed too much and twice he fell on his side. He told Keichi he was not involved any more; he would guide them back to the village where he had met them once they were finished here. Until then, he intended to sleep. He suggested that Keichi take his time. The guerrillas did not see much action in their area and this visit was an entertainment they would surely want to prolong. Making them happy would help his cause, the smuggler told Katsumata, but he was not going to give him any more advice. He had overstepped his authority as it was.

The meal came to an end when the sun was halfway to the middle of the sky. There was not much shade up on the rock and the air was dry.

'People up here in the mountains live to a ripe old age,' the squat leader said. 'Unless they get shot beforehand.'

'Shall we start getting down to business?' Keichi asked, earning a disapproving glance from the smuggler.

'You must be very tired,' the leader said. 'It might be better for all of us to take a little nap and let our bodies digest the food. Some of the men seem to be asleep on their feet.'

'They are not going to take part in the discussion.'

'We do everything collectively up here. We fight together and we talk together.'

'I think this is up to the two of us alone. You and me.'

'No. My men have a say in this and they would find it disturbing if your people are kept out of it. You could, of course, call a vote and ask your party to give you a power of attorney to speak for them. But yours is not a democratic society like ours. A vote will look stupid to your sergeant and your remaining soldier.'

It was then that the leader told Keichi he much appreciated his shooting the soldier. It showed he was a sincere man and his stature grew in the eyes of the guerrillas.

Keichi would lament that to his Taisho later, and the Taisho would remind him that none of the soldiers was to survive. They were all due to go to the Pacific front, but that did not satisfy nor console him.

'Your father cashed all the pay slips due to him after the mission and had them sent to the soldier's family,' Mr Sakamoto had told Yoshiro. 'He was going, he told me, to support the little soldier's family after the war. But they were from Hiroshima and all perished there in 1945. Your father was a generous man and had a noble soul.'

Of course he did, Yoshiro thought, he was guided by honour and he expects me to do the right thing.

'Let's get back to the rock,' Mr Sakamoto said.

'The negotiations only started much later. It must have been a very quiet sector because Keichi did not notice any vigilance on the rock after the meal. Everybody went to sleep except for the Burmese prisoner who was a lawyer and pro-Japanese. He had found a piece of paper and a pencil somewhere and was busy writing something down. No one asked him what it was. No one paid attention to anything. Thinking of it now, I am sure that the guerrillas were not political. Perhaps they were not guerrillas at all.'

The afternoon came and slowly it crawled through the oppressive heat. Some slept and others played cards. Then, as the evening brought a gentle breeze of cool relief, the leader appeared. He ordered all his men and all Lieutenant Katsumata's people to come and sit in a circle where they had eaten their meal. Tea was served in serenity.

'We will talk now,' the leader said to Keichi. 'I'll bring your Japanese officer over when we're finished.'

'Fine,' Keichi said.

'What is it you want of us exactly?'

'We have come to ask you to let us take the Japanese officer back with us.'

'What is it you want him for?'

'Tell him a lie,' the smuggler said in a sudden splutter of Japanese. 'Sorry,' he said in English. 'Tell him the truth about the officer. Tell him why your people want him back to stand trial.'

The leader's face lit up.

'Trial? What did he do? Rob a bank?'

'He is accused of stealing money from the army,' Keichi said with a perfectly straight face. 'He was in charge of compensation payments for the Singapore and Malaya area. Large sums of money were to be paid for the damaged property of our allies. The Paymaster General has issued a writ. This is an embarrassing situation for the Imperial army and I want your word as a gentleman that these details will remain secret. I was specially brought from Japan for this mission. No one in Thailand or Singapore knows why we are bringing the man back. We want to find out what he has done with the money. This has nothing to do with the war.'

'Would you believe it?' the leader said with a burst of laughter. 'What are you willing to give for the man?'

'I could release the two Burmese gentlemen here and the British officers. If you wish to keep the Japanese officer, you may do so provided you let me interrogate him. He is really useless to us once we know where the money is and what his methods of diverting the funds were.'

There was naked admiration on the smuggler's face. Derek Pritchard said, '*Caramba, qué cabeza.* It's an old Spanish song,' he explained.

The leader scratched his head.

'How much will you pay for the officer?'

Katsumata's surprise was complete. His face went pale.

'Money? You are asking for money?'

'Yes. Why shouldn't I? You only want him because he stole money, don't you? How much cash will you pay for your officer?'

Katsumata pointed at the smuggler.

'You will have to ask him,' he said.

'He has nothing to do with it,' the leader said.

'Oh yes he has. This is new to us. We did not know money was involved. Of course, we can arrange payment for you, but only in Japanese money. You wouldn't accept that, would you?'

'Of course not. We need real money.'

'That is where our friend comes in. We will settle with him later. How much?'

'One thousand pounds English sterling,' the smuggler said.

'Rule Britannia,' Hedges mumbled.

'We would prefer gold. Get us the money in gold,' the leader said. His people were in obvious agreement. Some applauded.

'Gold is a little complicated,' the smuggler said, 'but nothing is impossible. Of course, the amount will have to be reduced . . .'

'By how much?' the squat leader asked.

'At least half.'

The game was out of Keichi's hands. There followed a heated argument between the smuggler and the squat leader while all the others listened in.

They finally settled on six hundred pounds in English gold sovereigns.

'There is a delivery of sovereigns waiting for me in Thailand,' the smuggler said. 'It is in a small fishing village called Bang Saray, some fifteen miles west of the port of Pattaya. All right. You let us have the officer and I will go and get the gold for you.'

'When will you be back?'

'As soon as I can. It depends on road conditions.'

'You must think we're all peasants up here. If you lot leave now, we'll never see you again.'

'You can send one of your thugs with us if you like. I

thought we all trusted each other.'

'We are talking about gold. I'll send two.'

'What will happen to the British while we're gone?' the smuggler asked.

'We keep them here until the gold arrives.'

'Who will guarantee their safety?'

'They are our allies.'

'In that case, you shouldn't ask for money. You should take them to the Indian border now. They are not safe here. The Japanese still control the country.'

'Are they safer with you?'

Katsumata jumped up.

'Yes, they are. They are safer with us,' Keichi said. The leader looked about him.

'Take them back with you, if you like. I don't mind. They are your prisoners. Let them be your responsibility. It's better that way. Less mouths for me to feed. Less bodies to protect.'

'That is fine. I would prefer to take them with me.'

'Yes,' Derek said enthusiastically.

'You're all fucking mad,' Jimmy grunted.

'And don't get any ideas, Lieutenant Katsumata,' the leader said. 'I shall send two of my best men with you. We have friends in Thailand too, you know. In any case, Lieutenant, you will guarantee safe passage for them while they are in Thailand. Once the gold is in their hands, they will bring the British officers back here and we will get them to India. If the gold is not forthcoming, my men will kill them.'

'The gold will only be given to you when they cross the border.'

'That is fine.'

The leader's face relaxed. He smiled.

'That's it, then. Let us have a drink. We're all friends and allies together now. Money is money everywhere.'

Lieutenant Katsumata's face oozed disgust. He opened his mouth to say something, but the smuggler touched his shoulder.

'The man is right,' he said, 'let's all have a drink.'

'Your father did not trust the leader,' the Taisho said to Yoshiro. 'He did not want to leave the British there. Perhaps he could not bring himself to part from Pritchard, about whom he always spoke with much tenderness. Anyway, that was no more than a detail because he had accomplished his mission. The fate of the *gaijin* was of no importance to the mission. Only, it seems, to your father. He could have argued with the leader, but he chose to take them with him. We can only guess at the truth. He might have engineered it all that way, but then I'm not sure. You know, Yoshiro, your father could have been in serious trouble. He was going to use Japanese funds for the release of British officers. Had this been at any other time, he would have been court-martialled and surely executed. But what mattered was he had our man and he acted in honour. In any case, that was how your father came to return to Thailand with his *gaijin*. That was the first time the name of Bang Saray cropped up. What happened there was to play a big part in your father's life later.'

The two Burmese prisoners were freed and officially handed over to the leader as a sign of trust. There were handshakes all round and toasts and then the high-ranking officer was produced.

He was a pale little man. He was clean-shaven and had a precise military manner. He looked bewildered when he saw the Japanese uniforms on Lieutenant Katsumata and his men. With an expression of great concern, he came closer to examine Keichi's insignia. He had an intelligent face that did not smile.

'We have come to take you home,' Katsumata said. 'It is late in the day and I apologize for having to keep you here one more night. At dawn we shall walk through the jungle to the border where cars will be waiting for us. My orders are to take you to Bangkok. I am happy to see how well you are, sir.'

The high-ranking officer had a deep, powerful voice that roared out of his tiny face like cannon fire.

'Who told you I am well? By whose authority are you here?'

'I am afraid I cannot discuss that. We have gone through a lot to get here and I am sure you will be delighted to return with us.'

'I am not a well man. I do not think I can travel on foot all the way to the border. Do you have a written order for me to see? What is your name, Lieutenant?'

'Katsumata Keichi,' the lieutenant answered. He ignored the other questions. The high-ranking officer sat down. There was now only a tiny hint of light in the sky. The golden horizon sailed into a sea of pink, then turned mauve.

'Your man does not seem too pleased to see you, Lieutenant Katsumata,' the squat leader commented. 'I suppose he still wants to see that British colonel he insisted on. Why don't you promote one of the prisoners?'

Six paraffin lamps were brought down and lit as he spoke. Keichi turned to the high-ranking officer.

'We do have a British officer for you, Colonel Derek Pritchard.'

He repeated the same sentence in English and Derek rose, saluted, and introduced himself to the prisoner.

'How can I help you?'

'Things are not what they seem here,' the high-ranking officer said. 'I need to talk to you alone. These people . . .'

'That is not possible. I am a prisoner of war myself and I cannot talk to you alone unless Lieutenant Katsumata is in agreement.'

'My orders are to take you back to Bangkok,' Keichi said. 'Until you are safely delivered to the Japanese Embassy there, the *gaijin* officers will remain prisoners of war. No doubt you will be able to talk to Colonel Pritchard on the way.'

The high-ranking officer seemed to accept his fate. His shoulders sagged and he sat there looking into space. He refused a swig of *gaijin* whisky and did not speak for the rest of the evening. Lieutenant Katsumata did not leave his side again.

That was the story the Taisho had told Yoshiro during their last dinner a few hours before. The weight on his father's young shoulders must have been immense. Yoshiro consumed the coffee and the hot rolls. He paid the waitress and thanked her for her kindness. He walked out onto the street. There was a thin drizzle in the air.

It would be best to make it look like an accident. His wife and his children would not need to live in the shade of his shame and his debt for the rest of their lives. His father would understand. He would tell him the truth once he reached the temple. It was just down the road.

At five o'clock in the morning, Yoshiro stood at the window of his hotel room. He opened it. Outside it was still dark, but it was not going to be dark for very long. Dawn was about to descend. He had been to the temple and had said his prayers. In his mind's eye, he saw his father. He looked like he did when Yoshiro was a small boy.

He had been extra cheerful with the night porter as he collected his key. The man said later Mr Katsumata was extremely happy. Perhaps he had had too much to drink, but he looked happy.

No one saw him mount the aluminium frame. The street, fourteen floors below, was still asleep. Up where he stood, the raindrops seemed thicker as they hit his face. He opened the window. The air was still clean. Soon the cars would come and bring the fumes. He stood on the sill and looked. He smoked a cigarette, but he did not cough. Look, he said to his father, no cough. Watch one more dawn. He took another puff and the smoke scratched his insides and he crouched down and took off into the air.

Never mind another dawn, Yoshiro thought as he flew through the air like a feather. It was going to be a grey day. He flew and he thought his father was there with him. They were watched by all the others, the little soldier and the *gaijin* Lieutenant Pritchard. He felt safe and he was not afraid and did not scream. He did not think of his youth or his past ambitions and what he had wanted to achieve. His mind was lucid and was still covered by a film of mist shielding him from pain and hope and memories.

Yet somewhere he did know what he was doing. There was no stopping now. No regrets. For a moment, he wanted to think of the *gaijin* woman, but he had no time to remember. There were no faces and no sounds and no time. Only the split-second image of a crowd: people from his father's past.

The pavement and the street were racing upwards to him and the void met him before his body hit the ground.

Too much pressure, some people said later. The police report indicated that Yoshiro Katsumata had had a flask of Scotch in his back pocket. What a waste of a man, people said. And others looked to the chance his empty desk was providing.

He could never take alcohol, people who knew him said. He could have been the first outsider on the board. The window sill was too low. He was too tall. Perhaps he wanted fresh air. Or wanted to see the morning.

The only time you get fresh air in this city is at dawn, just before the sun rises and the pollution descends.

'Bad luck,' Mr Sato said to his friend Mr Sakamoto. 'He was bright and had been doing well until the last few weeks. We were going to promote him. It's hard to find talented young men these days. He used to work late in the office,' Mr Sato said with pride. 'We demand loyalty at Sato Kaisha and we get it. That is why he stayed in town so often. Bad luck this,' he added, and handed Mr Sakamoto the menu.

The old banker was not hungry, but he ordered something anyway. They had been to the same school, and since Mr Sato had invited him for lunch he would be hurt if he did not eat.

CHAPTER THIRTY-ONE

It was a new, Western-style building. It could have been a warehouse or a supermarket because it was big and colourful and it had no windows. The driver opened the car door for him and Jimmy Hedges walked out into the heat, up the stairs, and pushed the glass door open. The cool air caressed his face as he got into the lift and pressed the button for the third floor.

There were bright electric lights everywhere. Coloured bulbs and indoor plants and paintings of heavy lipsticked Buddhas. The driver had told him this was the best massage parlour in Bangkok. He had been right. Jimmy had visited it every day since he arrived. This was his sixth day there. Anna wanted to take a tour of the temples. He told her he was too tired for that, but they could have dinner again tonight.

The lift stopped. More lights and more plants and waiters dressed in red welcomed him to the third floor. Across the way from the lift, an enormous glass wall divided the hall. Behind the glass, under the glare of floodlights and in rows, sat a myriad of sparsely dressed girls. They had numbers on their shoulders.

Some had green numbers indicating they went all the way. The others only massaged and washed and touched. The girls looked at the glass but could not see beyond it, and they were chatting and chuckling with each other. An aquarium of beauty, he thought, and sat down. The waiter brought him a brandy.

'Same girl as yesterday? Number twenty-seven?'

'Maybe yes, maybe no.'

Perhaps he should take number twenty-seven again. She was a green-numbered girl and she knew him now and pleased him. He had been with her five times already. She sat where she had sat the day before and the day before that. She was small, her round face surrounded by coal-black hair. She had a white dress on, a golden plastic belt and a golden highlight on her forehead. Number twenty-seven looked at her watch and smiled at the glass as if she knew he was there.

'You good man,' she had said to him. 'You give good tip, yes?'

He would have preferred it if she had not mentioned money, but this was a business house. She had golden Roman sandals and black panties with red flowers embroidered on them. She looked fresh and flushed.

'Ask number twenty-seven to come,' he told the waiter. 'Get me a good room like before.'

The waiter picked up the microphone and said something in Thai and the girl collected her golden handbag. She straightened her hair and got up. She walked past the statue of a golden goddess and disappeared.

Soon she was by his side and smiling.

'You come early for me. *Sawadee kap.* I happy girl today.'

The waiter took them to a room. The girl walked in first. Jimmy paid the waiter one thousand baht. This included another brandy, a Coca-Cola for the girl and a tip.

'Number twenty-seven best in the house,' the waiter said. 'You call for more drinks later?' He turned and shut the door behind him, leaving Jimmy stretched on the bed in anticipation.

In the corner, there was a bath big enough for two. It

was a pleasant room with pictures of American pin-up girls on the walls. The girl undressed him. She then pulled him gently up and led him to the bath. When he was immersed in the warm water, she splashed foam all over his body, and then she undressed herself. She had a fine shapely body and hardly any pubic hair. She stood over him with a sponge and rubbed his back and his big belly and below and then she rubbed his shoulders.

'You clean now,' she said. She sprayed the foam off with lukewarm water and he got out. She dried him with a series of small towels, lingering over his genitals, and he was aroused because he knew what was to follow. He wanted her to drag him into bed and mount him and make love to him, but that was going to interrupt her routine. She looked at his hardening flesh.

'Massage first,' she said, and laughed, and he did too because he was impatient.

'You bad boy,' she said.

She had magic hands and her fingers travelled over his skin, touching muscles and nerves he had forgotten existed. His desire subsided and rose and she turned him over face down. Her hands were on his back, on his head and everywhere, and Jimmy floated in a sea of calm pleasures. He was hovering between sleep and awareness and his mind wandered back into the past. He was young again and saw himself marching with Derek and Katsumata and the high-ranking officer back to Thailand.

Everybody was there. The sergeant and the remaining soldier and the two Burmese guerrillas and the smuggler. Jimmy and Derek were under the guard of the guerrillas, but they were, to all intents and purposes, free men now and the atmosphere was easy. They were walking more slowly than they had done on the way and often they stopped for a rest. Katsumata, the sergeant and the soldier kept a careful watch on the high-ranking officer. Subdued and slow, he dragged his feet through the changing terrain.

'I am sorry you have to come back with us, but it's safer this way,' Lieutenant Katsumata said.

'I don't trust those guerrillas either,' Derek said.

'I will go with you to Bang Saray,' Lieutenant Katsumata said, 'as soon as I deliver the man. I shall do it on my own time as a private citizen. I will see you to safety. It is a matter of honour.'

Perhaps he had been hard on Katsumata, Jimmy thought. He never admitted to Derek that the man was honourable. He had been hard on the Japanese, especially when talking of him to Derek's widow. But who would have believed their jailer was a gentleman who did not represent the horror of his uniform?

It was all such a long time ago, when the Japanese were all bad and people read about it and saw other prisoners coming back. His version of what happened in Bang Saray was so much easier to understand.

It was hard enough to have survived the war and faced Derek's widow and daughter. To tell them what really happened would have been too much. He had told her exactly what he had told the intelligence officer when he got to India. He had to stick to the same story. The truth would not bring her husband back anyway.

These were dangerous waters. There were rocks and rapids around. He had to change the subject of his thoughts. History, Derek had once said, is a description of events as seen by an individual. No one can contest what the Apostles tell us about Jesus. It might have been a lie, it might have been the truth. It was the way the story-teller had decided to tell it. You accept the official story of the past as written by contemporaries and that's all. Spanish children read about the Civil War as seen by Franco.

No one writes a history of defeats. That was what Derek himself had said. Jimmy was not going to tell about Bang Saray. The truth of it would always be Jimmy's truth, and with the passage of time he began to believe it himself.

Jimmy Hedges woke up. He had not really been sleeping. His mind had wandered away from the magic of where he was now. His body was awash with sweat. The girl pointed the electric fan at him and dried him off.

'You want sleep?' she asked, and he whispered no way and pointed at her hands and her lips and he pulled her head gently downwards.

'You big fat man,' she said. 'Like Buddha. I like fat man.'

'I don't,' he said. She had a flower in her hair and he took it out. She was touching him with her fingers and her lips were wet as she ran them over his chest and his abdomen and down and down. The room was cool, but he was still sweating and he covered his chest with the sheet and watched her head of hair down there. She was sucking at him and the room went a shade darker.

Perhaps he should have taken a rest this afternoon, he thought as his heart began to palpitate. He was sweating everywhere and he wiped his brow with his hand and all the while the girl was trying to please him. Number twenty-seven is the best in the house she had told him five times before as he handed her a tip. Number twenty-seven get reservation by telephone, she said with pride. She had a name, but he had forgotten it. He was a little scared now and he felt lonely.

The fear of death crept over him. It had happened before, but only very rarely, when there was no one about and not a drop of brandy to chase those dark thoughts away.

She was hard at it, but down below nothing was happening. Palpitations are not dangerous, but an attack could come at any time and he was overtaxing himself. He tapped her shoulder.

'You like?' the girl asked.

'Get me a brandy.'

'Coca-Cola for me, too?'

'Yes, yes. You can have your fucking Coca-Cola too. Get me a brandy now.'

Derek never used bad words, but Derek was a saint and you had to be dead to be a saint. Saints all die young because God wants them by his side. Rubbish. Saints die young because they do not have the chance to grow older and wiser and know better.

'Get the brandy now, please,' he said, and thought he had shouted, but all he heard was a whisper. What if he got a heart attack right there and died alone?

He did not notice the passing of the minutes. The girl picked up the phone and ordered his drink and then he dozed off. Good thing, sleep. He had all the time in the world. He had paid for two hours. The royal treatment. All included. He woke.

'You want sex now?'

He shook his head. He was in the throes of a self-imposed panic. He calmed himself and again he must have slept and immediately the images of the old road to

Pattaya came alive.

They were driving in that old Austin and he was at the wheel. The smuggler and the two guerrillas and Derek Pritchard were there too. So was Lieutenant Katsumata, out of uniform.

'I want to be sure of your safety,' Katsumata said, looking like a golfer. How they all squeezed into that car Jimmy did not know. They built those Austins to last before the war. He wondered whether the car was still in Bangkok. Chances were, it was. The girl touched his brow and wiped the sweat off. In her other hand, she had his second glass of brandy. She looked worried.

'You drink,' she said. 'Make sex later.'

He took the contents slowly. There was no burn. The pain in his chest had eased and the palpitations had gone. What could it have been? He was a little tired, that's all. Perhaps a little dehydrated. He asked the girl for two glasses of cold water and gulped them down.

What a stupid show, he thought to himself. He was overweight, but he had lost a few pounds in the heat and his clothes seemed roomier. The girl was touching him again and her hands worked miracles. Perhaps he should forget about it today. Come back tomorrow or something.

This was a city of total pleasure. The food, the women, the climate, the fruits, the agreeable smiles on people's faces. What had possessed him to work himself into such a frenzy? Wasn't he having one whale of a time? First class all the way. Thank you, Trudi.

Was it the recurrent image of Bang Saray? But that was long ago and he had long subscribed to his own chain of events. What difference did it make who slept with whom one hundred years ago? Did David write his story about Goliath to impress the Israelites?

He would have to concentrate hard on Bang Saray to piece the story together again, the way it was. He was not sure of it. He knew Derek had died there. Well, everybody knew Katsumata had agonized over it. Jimmy couldn't very well tell intelligence about that. Who would have believed a Japanese officer would spend days mourning for an Englishman as if they were blood brothers? He had to tell the tale the way he did, the way people would understand.

What nonsense. What a thing to think about when a girl a third his age was trying to make love to him. It could have been indigestion.

'I stay one more hour,' he said. 'I want to sleep now.'

'You go sleep hotel.'

'I stay here. You can go.'

The brandy had sunk into his brain and it made him stubborn. He could spend the rest of the afternoon here. A hundred baht more, a thousand. Who cared? First class all the way. Well, he'd have to get back before dinner tonight. Anna was expecting him.

And then Bang Saray sneaked into his mind again. He thought he was awake. He'd have to think that one out now. Think it all through. It would only take a jiffy. Now, while he was alone, he'd think of it and then it would go for ever. He lay back and covered his chest with the soft sheets and remembered.

The Austin took the dirt road from Pattaya with dignity. At times, the road was not more than a stretch of trodden grass and dung through a sea of coconuts. There were no signs to indicate where they were going. Katsumata did not interfere. He was on a week's leave, having delivered the high-ranking officer to his Taisho in Bangkok.

Katsumata's manner was now that of a relative on a family excursion to the seaside. They were going to witness the transfer of the gold sovereigns to the guerrillas, then they were returning to Burma and the *gaijin* would be taken to the Indian border. No one talked about the war.

'This road is fit for elephants,' Katsumata said.

'We should have had a truck,' Jimmy said.

'You are all spoilt city boys,' the Burmese smuggler said. 'There are many ways to reach a palace.'

Bang Saray was not a palace, but it was where his gold coins were stored. Payment for rubies and American fishermen's nets he had delivered.

'How do you get hold of American fishing nets these days?' Hedges asked.

'It is a trade secret,' the smuggler said, and drank some more.

'How come you keep that much gold here?'

'The Thais do not believe in paper money. They wear gold necklaces around their necks and they stuff gold in the ground to keep it for hard times.'

'What peace,' Derek said. 'Pastel green rice fields dotted by black-clad women bending over the earth.'

'In Hokkaido we have pine trees and ski slopes and cherry trees and rice fields too. Sometimes in the mountains you forget it is an island. They say Hokkaido is like Scotland. I would like to go to Scotland after the war.'

'We can all go together,' Derek said. 'I have never been there.'

All the while, Jimmy was driving the Austin, with one of the guerrillas and the Burmese smuggler by his side.

'We'll soon be there,' the smuggler said. 'As soon as

you smell the dried fish they hang out in these parts. Thousands of them drying in the sun for the market.'

'Dried fish is a delicacy in Japan today. In olden times, it was a necessity. My family have a fish-drying plant in Hokkaido.'

They passed a large isolated temple, a golden pagoda built on huge white columns amidst a palm forest. A group of priests wrapped in yellow gathered wood on the roadside, their shaven heads close to the grass.

'Everyone in Thailand has to be a priest at some stage of his life. He shaves his head like a schoolboy and walks about the country living on handouts. They claim it teaches humility. Even the rich and the royals go through that.'

'Not a bad idea for some of our politicians back at home,' Jimmy said, and then the smuggler pointed at a little bridge and said that they had arrived. Jimmy eased the car over the creaking wood. Through a thinning wall of trees, they saw the sea. It spread along an enormous bay with a chain of mountains in the distance. An orange bowl-shaped sun hovered over the calm waters. A sweet smell hung in the air.

'That's it,' the smuggler said. 'Dried fish.'

Lines and lines of them suspended on horizontal ropes hung between the trees. There were some twenty houses along the beach. Long, high-bowed boats rested on the golden sand.

'This is Bang Saray.'

Children came running from all directions. Barefoot, smiling, dark-skinned children.

'They seldom see a car here,' the smuggler said.

He guided Jimmy towards a large house in the centre of the village. The children, anticipating their destination, ran ahead then stopped, panting, by the only fence in the village.

'Stop here,' the smuggler said.

The house was built on stilts. Below the main structure lay a large country store. Brooms and cans and boxes, fruits and sacks of rice and pots and pans and fishing nets all lay about in disarray.

'I don't know how he finds anything around here,' the smuggler sighed, 'but he does know where everything is. He does not believe in paper money and keeps all his profits in junk like this. It's the only store for miles.'

There were barrels of dried fruits and nuts. There were painted jars of oil. There were spades and bicycles and there were straw hats and sandals. There were shelves of cloth, and there was rattan furniture and baskets.

'A proper department store,' Katsumata said.

'He is my partner,' the smuggler said with pride.

'How can you trust him from where you are?' Jimmy asked.

'He cheats,' the smuggler answered, 'but not that much, and he knows I know and so I trust him. I cannot see his truck, which means we may have to stay the night. No one else knows where the sovereigns are.'

The smuggler started towards the house. He turned to Jimmy, who stood by the car.

'He has a young wife. I am sure of it. He keeps marrying younger girls all the time. He buys them off their poor parents up-country. Every time I come here, he's got a different one, but his first wife is still there with him. She does the cooking. Better than any hotel anywhere. She is a good friend of mine. She will surely know when he will be back because he trusts her and tells her the truth about everything. Not, I am afraid, where the gold is.

'I had an uncle once who liked young wives. That was back in the days when I was still in the British army. My uncle produced a whole series of young aunts for me and my sister, and just like my Thai partner here, he kept his first wife because she was his bookkeeper. She ran the money side of my uncle's business and so he kept her. Also, she was the mother of his children. Anyway, my uncle went to Rangoon to collect his latest wife and when he returned to his village all the money was gone and so was my old aunt. She took his gold pocket watch and all his gold coins and notes and left. Of course, with no money in the house the young girl from Rangoon ran off with a fellow who worked for my uncle. She was my aunt for one week only. I have told the story to my partner here and maybe that is why he doesn't tell his first wife where the gold coins are. He is allowed more than one wife because he is a Moslem.'

Katsumata and Derek burst out laughing. The smuggler went into the house. Over the other side of the bay, in the distance, the mountains were changing colour with the descending sun. Six or seven boats were leaving for the horizon, all towed by a larger one whose old, spitting engine kept stalling.

'They are off for the night,' Derek said. 'Look at their silhouettes on the water.'

The sun was right behind them now, its rays wrapping their boats and their bodies with gold haloes.

The two Burmese guerrillas followed the smuggler towards the house. They paused at the store on their way and helped themselves to a few boxes from a shelf.

'Some allies we've got here,' Jimmy said. The road to India seemed further than ever.

The smuggler came back.

'My partner will be back the day after tomorrow. He has gone to Bangkok. The messenger I sent arrived too late to catch him, but we are welcome to stay at the house. You can go and have a swim now if you wish. His old wife will kill six chickens for us and we will have some lobster, too. She put a lot of beer in the icebox. I must go and look over the books.'

With this declaration, the smuggler returned to the house. The guerrillas stayed in the store and the two Englishmen went back to the car.

'They are not watching, you know,' Katsumata said.

'I was thinking the same,' Jimmy said. 'We could take the car and leave now.'

The Japanese officer did not answer. He looked at the bay.

'Here's our chance, Derek. Let's go now.'

'Lieutenant Katsumata has given his word,' Derek retorted, almost with anger.

'I suppose he'll shoot us in the back.'

'And I began to think you were almost human.'

'Why don't we all go for a swim?' Katsumata said. 'But we mustn't go out too far. There are sharks in these waters.'

'The smuggler is amazing, isn't he?' Derek said. 'He's like a character from a Joseph Conrad novel.'

'Who is Joseph Conrad?' Katsumata asked.

'He was a Polish sailor who settled in England and wrote sea-faring adventure stories of exotic places.'

'Romantic. Like my mother's brother who emigrated to Brazil.'

They peeled their clothes off and sprinted to the water. Jimmy Hedges stayed behind. A cold drink was all he wanted. At the end of the bay, behind the mountains, the sun was sinking and Jimmy saw Derek pointing at it as he talked to Katsumata in the water. The mountains were immersed in gold.

'It's like a stage,' Derek said. He looked thin and white and his flesh shone like a fish. A cold drink.

The silence woke him.

Someone must have turned the air-conditioning off. The heat made him thirsty. He looked at his watch. Seven o'clock. He was alone in the room. He got up, pulled the covers off his body and started to dress. His date with Anna was an hour and a half away. He could have a drink in the hotel. A cold beer or something. His thirst seemed to be old, but he did not remember where it had started. He'd enjoy a beer in his room at the hotel. He walked out of the room. The car was waiting for him outside. The sleep had done him good.

He dozed off a little more in the traffic. He could tell Anna about the Burmese smuggler over dinner. No. He could not do that. It was an amusing story, and after the way he had described Bang Saray to them, it was impossible. Bang Saray was a painful, evil experience. She would be full of her own day's experiences. He tucked Bang Saray safely away into his memory. It would take him half an hour to get to the hotel. He slept.

CHAPTER THIRTY-TWO

He must have been out of his mind to agree to this, but he had his back to the wall. She had sat across the table. The candle had quivered and the flame sparkled in her eyes. They were dear eyes, intelligent and beautiful and sincere. She had come down hard on him and her gaze had been strong.

'It is my right,' she had said. 'I want to go to Bang Saray. I must go to Bang Saray.'

'You don't really want to go there,' he had said, knowing it was useless. She was a strong-willed woman now, so unlike the inhibited girl she used to be. Derek would not have liked her.

'I am going to Bang Saray. With you or without you.'

'Yes,' he had finally said.

Now they were driving on the new Pattaya road in his hired limousine. She was not going to ask him again how her father had died. All she wanted was to see the place. Where the house was, and the country store, and the beach where her father had swum the day he died. And where the crate was where they had forced him to sleep. Where he had suffered his final humiliation at the hands of Lieutenant Katsumata.

She remembered it all well enough. No need to hear it again. No need to hear her mother's reaction again. Those constant *Dios mio* every time Jimmy described something particularly gruesome. And yet her mother would sit there and press him on, and ask and demand to hear it all again. How Derek was beaten. How he suffered.

And Jimmy had always obliged, and he told her of Bang Saray and how and how and how.

Antonia always cried when Jimmy talked about Derek's last *adiós* at Bang Saray. *Adiós*, he had said in Spanish. He must have been thinking of me, she said again and again.

Anna had heard it all and was surely immune to it. No. Not all. She would not ask him to go through that again.

The countryside had not changed much. Only the city of Bangkok stretched further now than it had when he drove that Austin to Pattaya thirty-three years before. The road was asphalted, it was broader and in places it had become a dual carriageway. The bridges were made of steel and concrete now, and there was more traffic on the road. They cruised past the same endless rice fields and temples and coconut plantations. The same water-crab sellers offered their wares from wriggling heaps of legs and eyes and feelers. On the rivers, the longboats now had Japanese diesel engines. Laden with fruit and goods and people, they sped along the water. The oars were gone, having been replaced by long, flexible shafts astern, with propellers at the end.

Years ago, on the same stretch of road, the smuggler had joked with Katsumata who joked with Derek. No one talked to Jimmy. He could remember the isolation as the limousine sped by the advertising posters. Toyota, BMW, Johnnie Walker. Sony. But this time he was not ignored. Anna was asking questions and she drank in every word he uttered.

Perhaps he could pretend to sleep. He could dig out the buried faces of Bang Saray and run them through his mind, then he would push them all back into the mineshaft where they belonged. They must stay there long enough so he could go back to where it all happened without any harmful apparitions appearing.

Where should he start? How? Should he close his eyes and imagine himself the way he was then, sitting alone with a beer while the others played like children in the sea?

Why not come clean? He had often thought of telling Toni, but it had always been a momentary impulse that passed with the first drops of brandy she poured for him after a lunch. Now that Anna was going to see the place for herself, they might never wish to speak of it again. He was making a mountain out of a molehill. Derek had died and his family lived on. Many died in the war.

But not like that.

They had passed Chon Buri and were now halfway to Pattaya and lunch. He was not going to take her to Bang Saray until tomorrow. They were booked into the Royal Cliff Hotel at Pattaya and he was going to take her out on the strip tonight. He had been told it was fashionable and bustling and littered with women and music and eating places and lights. He would work things out in the night. Right now he was too tired even to pretend. He should never have had that beer. The car moved at a constant, boring, sleep-inducing speed. His eyes felt heavy and he yawned.

Anna looked at his puffed face and watched his hands. They were big and beefy. There were freckles on his arms. His hair still had that hint of red, but mostly it was grey. He looked old and tired, but his strength was visible. He seemed to be at peace and did not snore. His hands fell on his knees and, in between them, his large stomach heaved with his breathing. His short-sleeved safari suit made him look almost like a soldier, but for the carnation on his lapel.

They were approaching the hills. It was such a beautiful country. The colours of its people and houses and flowers sparkled in the sun. Shades of green and blue and red and pink, a carpet of fluorescent paints. She could have bought every crocodile-skin bag she had seen, and the jewellery was half London or Tokyo prices. Jimmy had been right about the food. She'd have to watch it or else nothing would fit her again. Yoshiro once said he liked her fat.

To think of Yoshiro on the way to Bang Saray was wrong. No. Yes. It was obscene, but she was thinking of Yoshiro. The helpless sleeping figure of the man next to her reminded her of him. How easy it is to lead men.

All men.

Yoshiro had said how he'd wished they could have been two different people. He had asked her to remember happy hours. There had been a finality to his voice when he said that. It was a waste of a life and yet she was the injured party and Yoshiro accepted it. Tradition.

What was life going to be like from here on? Would she settle down, perhaps even try to start a family? Be her own woman, anyway. Across the rice fields and the palms she saw the blue line of the sea. It stretched for miles into the horizon and it beckoned to her. Take your clothes off. Run through the surf into the water.

More temples, large white columns and golden pagodas on top. Two policemen were questioning a frightened motorbike rider. One saluted her as they passed. She tidied her hair. Vanity. The driver offered her a bottle of Coke. The Rotary Club welcomes you to Pattaya. Twenty kilometres.

The thick hedge of coconuts hid the water. Only now and then did she get a glimpse of it. It all looked like that brochure Jonathan had brought home one night. Barbados. They did not go because they bought new furniture. Jonathan had nothing to do with this place. It was all her own. Was. She was never coming back. She should be thinking of building her life again, with her husband and herself at the centre of it, not her mother's obsession. The Spanish Civil War would soon be really over for her mother. There would then be no need to live with hate.

What on earth was she going to Bang Saray for? She always thought she wanted to see the place, but did she really? Her mother had wanted her to see it. She had been used for too long.

Yoshiro Katsumata had been an eye-opener. She had arrived in his life on someone else's strings, but now she was free. She had gone to the end of the earth for her mother. The man who died in Bang Saray was her mother's man. She had her own and she would learn to be his. Better still, she had herself and she would learn to like herself.

Yoshiro had been right. She would try to remember the good moments. There were many of those. She would try to be someone else's daughter, travelling to the seaside in Exotica. Did she love her father? Her mother said she did, but Anna could not remember.

How dare she think like that! Of course she loved her father. Did she not listen to his songs, his forgotten voice? Melodrama. Bullshit. She did not really remember all that, but it was all too old, too well entrenched. She had been programmed. Could she cut the cord again, as she did while she had things going with Yoshiro? That was her own and she would never share it.

They were entering the town. Pattaya, the driver said

with pride. Jimmy Hedges woke up and looked out of the window. He wanted to show her where they had landed after their voyage from Singapore.

'Difficult to find,' he said. 'There used to be a wooden pontoon somewhere along the beach. Hard to guess where. Probably where the port is now. There were hardly any buildings then. Nothing above two floors.'

He pointed at the hotels along the beach. They were all new. Over thirty years had passed and he would never have believed this was the same place. He looked at her. His eyes were serious, perhaps a little sad.

'I wish I was someone else. A man without a past coming here for the first time. No connection. No nothing. No thoughts of how things were. No memories, not even good ones. Nix. You wouldn't understand.'

Wouldn't she just. Could he have read her mind? She had never heard him talk like that before. His voice was soft and melancholy ruled his eyes. She should put her hand on his shoulder and console him, but then he said: 'We'll have a ball tonight. They say this town swings.' The moment of magic had gone. Wheel of fate.

Music and syphilis. She'd heard all about the sex tours. He must have had a bad moment, but he was back in his old saddle now. The self-indulgent dirty old man she knew was easier to handle.

He had to go on with the show. She would not notice. He must lock himself up somewhere. Underneath it all, his self-control was cracking. He looked at Anna and he smiled. She did not notice. She was looking at the beach. There were surf sailers and water skiers and parasailers and bathers, all exposing their European skins to the sun. There were chicken-fryers and coconut-milk sellers, heaps of fruit and T-shirts. Everything was for sale.

Corn on the cob and water-melon and mussels and dry fish and straw hats and hammocks and kites. Colours, colours and more colours. She longed to be out there.

'Let me get off here,' she said. 'You go to the hotel. I'll get a cab or something.'

Jimmy could hardly breathe. Control yourself.

'I'll send the car for you,' he managed to say. There is a God and that God loved him. He had brought him this far.

'The driver will come back and wait for you right here. I'll go and check in and have a rest. See you in the lobby at eight.'

She jumped out and waved and then she was lost with the breeze.

Jimmy sank back into his seat. He was sweating again and his heart was palpitating wildly. A bed. A solitary bed in a cool room. He knew what he had to do now. But he had to do that on his own. Better late than never. There is a God.

How he got through the registration process he did not remember. In the room, the boy put his cases down and pulled the curtains to reveal the sea and then he waited. Jimmy gave him a twenty-baht note and the boy smiled and said 'thank you' and wished him a nice day.

He knew the answer at last. He would write it all down. The truth. Yes, sir.

He sat at the desk and counted the sheets of paper. There were twelve of them, thin airmail paper. He would write it all down. She might never see it. It might all blow over. He wasn't much of a letter-writer. Usually he said what he had on his mind, but this was different. Thirty years of dirty washing was being pulled from under the bed.

Let the steam out or his head would blow up. Put it down on paper. Mistake? No, no mistake. No one will ever read it. What did he come here for? But it was late, too late now. There were two things he had to do.

The first note was addressed to his solicitors. In it he said he was sound of mind and body and wished this to be his last will and testament. His receptionist was to receive twenty thousand pounds, and the mortgage on her flat was to be paid off. Trudi, his travel agent, was to receive thirty thousand pounds and a new car. The rest of his estate he bequeathed to Anna Bellingham, daughter of Derek Pritchard and his wife Antonia. Her husband, Jonathan Bellingham, was to act as executor.

This will was final and irrevocable and was witnessed by the hotel manager and his assistant.

When the two men had gone, Jimmy sealed the envelope and called the desk for a bellboy. He handed the envelope to the boy at the door with a hundred-baht note. Registered, he said. This letter is to go to London this afternoon. I don't know what it costs, but you may keep the change. Leave the receipt in my key-box downstairs. I do not wish to be disturbed again this afternoon. He handed the boy another hundred-baht note. Make sure it goes, my boy. Do it yourself. The bellboy said he was going to the post office downtown right away. Dr Hedges could relax. The letter would be on its way within the hour. The bellboy said have a nice day and was gone. It was two o'clock in the afternoon. Jimmy called the operator. He wanted to have a rest. Would she make sure he was woken up at seven-thirty this evening? Sure she would. Have a nice day. Jimmy sat at the desk and stared at the page.

He put the date at the top of the sheet. 'Dear Anna,'

he wrote. 'This may surprise you. It will. It is a conversation we should have had years ago. So sit back and light a cigarette and read. Forgive this old hand-writing. It's accustomed to short notes. Prescriptions and postcards and descriptions of diseases. For referral to other practitioners of my illustrious profession. I am writing to you as a friend. I am also writing to you as one who has lied to you and your mother. Why I have, I don't know. Perhaps I was afraid. Perhaps I was ashamed. Perhaps I wanted to forget what had happened.'

The words flew out of his ballpen and spread. The words formed lines and the lines were moving down to the bottom of the page. He did not stop to think. He did not stop to correct his spelling. Some of the tenses were wrong, but as the pages filled his palpitations eased and his sweat dried up and he was feeling cooler.

At four-thirty that afternoon, Jimmy Hedges signed his name at the bottom of the tenth page. Right underneath the last line. The pen had become a part of his hand. A sixth finger. He got up. He looked at the sea. An old sailing junk battled the wind. It was going across to Coral Island. He felt easy, light-headed. They could take a trip to Coral Island in the morning, snorkel and swim and lie in the sun and talk tripe. The pressure was gone. He could take her to Bang Saray. He could sample the local delicacies, sneak in the odd steam bath and massage. She was not going to read this letter for a long while yet. He sealed the envelope and marked it for her attention. He underlined 'to be opened in the case of my death'. There was nothing to fear. He could sleep now. He had three hours to recuperate. Perhaps, after all, it had been a good idea to come back. He did not need a brandy now. He was going to sleep like an infant. He was going to send Trudi a postcard. She deserved that. Perhaps he would buy her a little present. They had good jewellery in this country. Someone had told him that. Anna? Perhaps it was Lieutenant Katsumata. He did not remember.

He had not felt better in years.

He drew the curtains and lay in the dark.

'Come on,' he said out loud. 'Come on in all of you. You can all talk to me now. I have survived you all and have thrived and have bounced back here once more. I have come clean. We are all off the hook. It's old Hedges again. The Cambridge loner. Let's have it, boys.'

His eyes were heavy and he saw his father. He looked like Jonathan Bellingham, only much older. He even spoke like Jonathan, but Jimmy did not hear him. He could say anything he liked. They could all sit in the corner of the room and chatter and gossip. He was king of the afternoon. They were talking about him. He was important. He had survived them all, and surprised them all, and he was not through yet. He slept. They could talk as loudly as they wished. Nothing was going to disturb him now. He had paid it all off.

He could not see them in the dark and because he was asleep he could not really hear them, but he knew they were there. Derek, Katsumata and the smuggler, his receptionist and Trudi and Kung Chi. A combination of past and present. He felt at peace with them all. The anger and anxiety and the fear that he had experienced were no more. A great sensation of relief descended upon him. His brow and his soul and his nervous system were clear and smooth and he was innocent like a child. Then the voices became distant as if someone had taken them all away.

Dark

CHAPTER THIRTY-THREE

He was an experienced driver. He had been working with *farang* for many years. He knew when to talk to them and when to keep quiet. He knew by their expressions what they required and how to offer it. The *farang* woman in the back of the car was in a state of shock. The *farang* take death heavily. They do not accept it like Thai do.

He could have told her the fat doctor was going to die. There was nothing sudden about it. He had bad colour and small eyes and his breathing was heavy. What was such a pretty *farang* lady doing with the fat old man anyway? But the driver did not make any comment because no one had asked him to and he watched the road carefully. Only sometimes, while she read her papers and did not notice, could he steal a glance and admire her beauty. She was pale and tall and had a generous mouth and long hair. She had covered her hair with a large scarf, but he could still see its reddish colour. He knew there was something wrong with the fat man as soon as he collected him from the airport a week ago. There was death under his skin and yet the man spent every day at the massage parlour. His friend the manager told him he had taken a fancy to number twenty-seven. She must have taken away whatever life he had in him. He must have been a greedy man because now he had this beautiful *farang* woman with him. She must have been his mistress and he must have had some good in him because the woman did look disturbed.

Still, the fat man had been kind to him and had always tipped him well. He had made it possible for him to go home early and earn extra money on the commissions.

The massage parlours and the tailors the fat man had visited were generous.

The driver was pleased they had sent the fat man's body back to Bangkok in an ambulance. As an experienced man who believed in the spirits, he knew it was a bad omen to have a dead body in the car. He could not have refused to take the fat *farang*'s body back to Bangkok in his own car had he been asked to do so.

Well, he wasn't going to lose anything because he had been paid in advance for his services and he could now work the limousine on his own until the company found out that their client had passed on. He would now be able to buy that refrigerator his wife had been pestering him for, or a small Japanese moped for his son. Still, he was happy he did not have to carry the body in his car.

The *farang* woman was quiet. She had changed from the way she was when they had driven here. She had been enthusiastic then, and talked a lot, and at the sight of the beach she had raced out of the car. Her hair was still wet when he had come back to fetch her, but he understood. She was much younger than the dead *farang*. He must have footed all her bills and the driver knew well how hard life can be for a woman on her own. She was a pretty girl, the driver thought. What a waste it was for the dead *farang* to spend so much time and money in the massage parlours. Even though it was number twenty-seven who had entertained him, he should have stayed with his own.

But he kept his thoughts to himself. He was known for his discretion and had worked hard to earn his reputation.

They were coming out of Pattaya, past the large temple onto the main Bangkok road. Anna lit another cigarette, refused a second Coke and settled down to read

Jimmy's letter. She still could not believe what had happened last night. Jimmy dead? It seemed impossible.

When he had failed to appear in the lobby for their dinner date, she tried calling his room. The receptionist told her he was not there because he had asked for a wake-up call at seven-thirty and had not answered it. He was probably out on the town. People did that sometimes, without calling to say they were up, and often they took their keys with them, although they were asked not to.

Anna had dined by herself in the coffee shop and had lingered there until ten o'clock. There was still no sign of him and finally she called the duty manager. It was the duty manager who entered the room to find Dr Hedges in a coma. He died a few minutes before the ambulance came. The receptionist should have alerted someone when he had not answered the phone at seven-thirty, she had yelled. It might have saved him. The duty manager assured her that the girl would be sacked, but that would not bring Jimmy back.

This morning, as she was checking out, the manager handed her Jimmy's passport and the letter addressed to her which had been found in his room, and now, on the main road to Bangkok, she picked it up and began to read.

Have you ever been lonely? (Jimmy wrote.) *To the outsider, I am bombastic, self-confident and brash. I seem to be full of my own importance yet I am a loner. I was not born a loner, Anna. I would have given my right arm to be noticed, to be recognized by that all-important group of Cambridge snobs in the thirties. I have come to find compensation in food. I looked for it in wine and in women and in raising my voice. I was funny and I tried to be generous, but people took what I offered and then left.*

I had learned to act the jovial Jimmy Hedges. The funny

man adored by his patients. As I grew older, I may have become him. I have perfected him and often I believe him to be my real self until something comes about to remind me of who I am: a social outcast. A leper. Someone people meet for a drink and then leave without exchanging telephone numbers.

I was welcomed to your mother's house. I ate there and drank there and wormed my way into your lives. I sat in Derek's chair and at his table and ate off his plates. I shared more hours with his family than he ever did and all the while your mother thought me his friend. The man your father was oh so lucky to have shared his last weeks with.

I was not a friend of your father's, Anna, I hated him. I despised him. I loathed everything about him. To me, he was the cause of all my tribulations. And he did not know. He was too conceited to notice the anger his mere presence evoked in me.

When we first met, I had been in Cambridge longer than he, and yet he took the limelight I had so long laboured to attain in one single evening. Until your father came up, I was able to hold my own at the Union debates. My views may not have been popular, but I was listened to because I made people laugh.

I don't think he even remembered the night he devastated me. It was only a single page in the spectrum of his success.

It was a debate about opportunities offered to the working classes in Britain. Medicine is a strenuous subject. You can't sit around in pubs or coffee houses or laze on the river. You can't read as many newspapers or follow the latest trends in literature. Perhaps I was not prepared. I certainly did not possess the hungry look.

There was a girl there that night. She was reading law and we had been out together a few times. We were going to have a drink after the meeting.

I got up to speak and said what I had come to say. There was a little applause and the law student beamed with pride. The stage was set for me. Things could have happened that night. You see, she used to say I was a bit of a bore. She used to say I was only interested in dissecting bodies and in medical books and knew nothing of the world.

That night, she beamed with pride. But then Derek Pritchard burst onto the scene and into my life.

He got up and began to speak. I will not repeat what he said. I will only tell you what it did to his audience. He spoke quietly, but there was charm and conviction and rhythm and power in his voice. I looked at the girl's face. It was on fire. His words formed a magic carpet for her to fly on. I ceased to exist.

The room was as quiet as a grave and they drank in all he uttered and their faces wanted more. He took every word I had said and cut it to pieces. He burned my arguments into ash and dismissed me into a corner reserved for forgotten failures. A well-lined failure. That was what he called me. What I had to say, he claimed, was of minuscule importance, of total stupidity, and best ignored and forgotten.

And then he started talking of Spain, and how she beckoned. How she needed every freedom-loving man and woman to come to her aid. How democracy must win. How it would be a crime against humanity not to go there.

The law student, like the others, was mesmerized by him. He cut flames with his soft, musical voice. I could take no more of it and walked out. I stood outside in the cold and waited for her to join me.

Later, she asked me why I had left. Did I not have the courage to face a superior argument? Was I too conceited and ill-mannered to ignore a civilized opinion contrary to my own? She saw me for what I was that night. She told me not to plead, not to crawl, not to humiliate her by begging. I did all three.

I used to see them together, Derek and her. Their affair only lasted a few months. He did not remember me at all. She introduced us one Sunday afternoon by the river. He only said, 'It's nice to meet you, Hedges', and said his name was Pritchard.

I could see she did not mean much to him. He was too deeply immersed in his own world. I did not see him again until a week before he left for Spain. I ran into him on the Strand in London.

'Hedges,' he said, 'it's you. Are you not joining us in Spain?'

I said I was doing my clinical training and added that I thought the war was stupid. He said he had to run and was gone. I was less important than a dog that day. He was with the gods on the way to Spain and I was upper-middle-class scum.

The Spanish War came and went. I did not see him or the girl again.

Then the Second World War arrived. Just after I qualified. The uniform and the rank gave me a chance of a nibble at some glory. I was doing well until I was shipped to Singapore. I was to join the regiment there, but the city had capitulated before I could catch up with it. That was where I met your father. By then he had married and had fathered you.

Over the years, I have come to disassociate him from you. You are so different. You would not have liked him much, Anna.

He did not remember me at all. He had forgotten my name. All he remembered was that I did not go to Spain.

That meeting was, for me, a disaster. The self-confidence I had managed to gain, the life I had constructed for myself were gone up the spout the minute I realized we were together for the duration.

In fact, he was, in his patronizing way, trying to make friends with me. I knew he was going to outshine me and make me a zero again.

Even there, in the bar where we sat trying to get drunk, he spent his last few pounds on buying a bloody parrot from the barman. He was intent on setting the bird free. The world was crumbling all around us. We were about to be taken prisoner, but your father was busy teaching the barman, the bird and me all about liberty.

You know most of the story by now, but what I did not tell you was that your father charmed the arse off Lieutenant Katsumata with his Spanish and his eloquence. He cornered him and monopolized him and left me out in the cold.

I suppose Katsumata was a decent chap really. He was not the cold-blooded murderer I had made him out to be. He was not much of a soldier, but his existence gave me an opportunity to build a new past for myself later on. Who was to know?

During the entire time we shared in the cell and later, on the boat and beyond, your father was condescending towards me. He played the martyr. He gave me the food he couldn't eat. He made me feel like nothing.

He said he was translating everything Katsumata said, but I know they often talked about me. That is how Katsumata came to despise me. Not as an enemy. Worse. He despised me as a man.

Even when we were supposed to enjoy ourselves, he would not let go. When Katsumata got us some women at the Oriental Hotel, he talked and talked and held us all up at the table because he knew I wanted to get back to the room. When we finally got there, he left me with the two women and stayed in the bathroom for hours. In the end I got so frustrated I made it with one while the other was watching.

We were treated well in Bang Saray. I lied about that. How could I construct Katsumata's evil character and say Bang Saray was a picnic? But it was. I had the best food I had ever tasted and German beer and French brandy and all the while Derek and Katsumata walked about and swam and played on the beach like children. You would have said they were in love.

They were inseparable.

The only blemish on that idyllic scene was the two Burmese guerrillas. That squat bastard chose his people well. Two giants, they were, who roamed about the place molesting the local women. Even the children would stop smiling when these two walked about hitting each other. They were fond of sticking their long knives into palm trunks and fishing nets and no one slept easily while they were awake. One of them took a distinct dislike to your father. He used to threaten him with his knife and seemed to take pleasure from humiliating him.

I hope you won't read this for many years yet. I hope to see you dye your hair. I hope to be needed still. I hope these pages will be burnt. Just writing it all down and then destroying it might do the trick for me.

Bang Saray.

The setting was, I suppose, very pretty. You will see for yourself. The sort of postcard view of mountains and sea and palms and wooden houses on stilts edging the water. You will see the place, but when I show it to you I shall continue to live the lie. Your father used to say the truth does not matter much. It's the end result that does.

Bang Saray. The trouble was, we did not need to be there at all. We could have been free. Your father could have talked Katsumata out of it. The man ate out of his hand.

The local man came back two days later, and all that time I was on my own. Your father did not bother to translate any of his conversation with his darling Katsumata any more. The smuggler found a local widow to distract me with. Derek always said I was only interested in enjoying myself, but I did not take the offer up. I was lonely and livid and frustrated and past human anger. Cambridge came to Bang Saray.

The man only had £450 in sovereigns. He had spent the rest on spare parts and American cigarettes or nets or something.

The smuggler was laughing about it, but the guerrillas were not. They said their leader would never believe them. They said he would accuse them of stealing the rest. There had been such misunderstandings before, they said, when they used to rob banks before the war. One coin missing and you lose your head, they said. If you want us to take you to India, you better make sure the chief believes you only had four-fifty. Otherwise he would have them shot. The smuggler said he would talk to their leader. He would go back to the rock and tell him what had happened. Maybe he would take American dollars instead. Or fishing nets. There was profit in fishing nets.

Derek was seized by an infuriating non-stop laugh. 'Fishing on the rock,' he roared. He sang it to the tune of 'Singing in the Rain'. 'I suppose they would only free one of us for that,' he said. Perhaps he meant it. Perhaps he wanted to keep me from going back, or else he did not want to be separated from Katsumata. I don't know. Your father did not have much of a sense of humour and when a man is crazed with hate the way I was he'd believe anything. I believed he was going to leave me behind.

That third night they all got drunk. Even Katsumata, who was not much of a drinker, got as high as a kite. The terrace we sat on smelt like a distillery. 'You are my responsibility,' Katsumata kept saying, and laughed. 'I will go back to Burma with you.'

'We'll all go back,' Derek said. 'The King and the Emperor and General MacArthur.' And he sang:

'We'll all go back to the rock tonight, we'll all go back to the rock.'

Believe it or not, I was the only sober man there. 'Let's go swimming now,' your father said to Katsumata, but the Japanese lieutenant could not get up. He asked the smuggler to join him, but the man could not swim. He said in his former life he had been a goat and goats do not swim. Katsumata was by now asleep and so, lastly, your father turned to me.

'Let's go swimming, Hedges,' he said. 'It may be our last chance. It's all land from here to India.'

'Don't go with Hedges,' Katsumata said. Maybe he said it in his sleep; but say it he did. For a moment I thought Derek would obey.

I got up and helped Derek to his feet. Soon we were descending the stairs and a few times he fell down, but nothing happened. 'We'll all go down to the rock today,' he sang. 'We'll all go down to the rock.'

I am not a great one for writing letters. I am writing all this down the way I would had I been talking to you.

'Why don't you stay here?' Derek asked. 'There are many needy patients here for you.' He was making fun of me, but this time it was the alcohol doing it. 'You might kill a few, but what does life mean to you, Hedges?'

Maybe that was when my subconscious took a fatal decision.

We got to the water and I took my clothes off. Derek jumped straight in, clothes and boots and all. He was a good swimmer, but he was drunk, and the water in his clothes weighed him down. I saw him stay under for almost a minute.

He surfaced, went down again and surfaced once more. He said: 'Let's all go back to the rock, Hedges. We can swim all the way there. Maybe as far as India. You'll be a hero yet.'

And then, as he was mocking me, he swallowed a mouthful of water. I heard him cough. There was a full moon above a perfectly still sea and you could see for miles around. I looked at the house. We had drifted quite a distance out. You could no longer stand. He called out to me and coughed again.

'Hedges,' he screamed, 'Hedges!' I swam out to him and expected another jibe from him because he was smiling. I got to him and put my hands on his shoulder. 'Hedges,' he said, 'don't be an ass.'

The constant, hammering, humiliating frustration I had been dealt brought about a massive emotional pressure that snapped.

'Listen, Hedges,' he said, and I heard him, but all I could think of was the rock and India and how we could have long been free. I was numb with anger. My brain was gone. I pushed his head into the water and I kept it there. He did not wriggle much. Just once did he surface again and he said 'adios'. I did not lie to your mother about that. Then he stopped moving altogether. Perhaps he had fainted. I could not think. I kept him under the water for a long time and then I pulled him towards the shore. He was as still as the sea. I looked at his face. His hair was all over his forehead. I thought his lips had curled into a sneer.

He was dead.

My daze, my anger and my momentary madness were lifted. I felt at peace.

The night was silent. You could hear the crickets and the mosquitoes and you could hear the water caress the sand.

I started calling out for help.

For a few moments no one came. Derek was lying in the shallow moonlit water and I stood over him, holding his hand. I was screaming now. There was no response. Only the village dogs barking, and I screamed, and then I saw them all coming. Katsumata ran like the devil. He was the first to reach us. He was wide awake now, and the shock had sobered him.

'Wake up, Lieutenant Pritchard,' Katsumata wailed. 'Wake up, mi amigo.'

We pulled him out onto the beach together and Katsumata looked at me. He was crying like a child. His face was drawn. I said Derek had swum too far out and I could not get to him in time because he did not call.

'He is dead now, Lieutenant Katsumata,' I said.

'Not dead,' he said, and he hit me on the chest. There was a mountain of sorrow in his eyes. 'Why did you let him die, you stupid man?' he screamed, and then he said he was sorry. He said he knew it was not my fault. It was his fault. He should have gone to the water with Lieutenant Pritchard because he had asked him to. He lifted Derek all by himself and carried him into the house. He sat by his side and he cried like a child. I think he cried all night. He mourned Derek as if he had been his brother. There was nothing anyone could do for him.

My real revenge was still to come.

CHAPTER THIRTY-FOUR

She was cold and then she was hot and then she was cold again. She opened the window to let the heat in and the air hit her face. She shut it. There was nothing but the road ahead and the back of the driver behind the fly-stained windscreen. She was hysterical. She was panting. She could not read any more. What more could he have said?

'Faster,' she whispered. 'Faster!' she screamed. 'I must get to a telephone and make a call.'

She lit another cigarette and saw she had two in her hands and she smoked them both. She put one out on her own arm and heard the hiss and felt the pain and cried.

A delayed reaction, the driver thought. He must keep calm. He had heard about the tempers *farang* women had.

'Please,' she said quietly, 'can't we go faster? Fly?'

He could have explained to her about the traffic police and their motorbikes and fast American cars and their fines. He knew it would not be of any use. He nodded, pressed the accelerator with his foot and looked ahead. The road was empty.

'Thank you, thank you,' she sobbed. Her head was lowered over her knees and her bare shoulders shook. He wanted to tell her she was young still. She would soon find another man to take her to the big hotels and the restaurants and the seaside. But he concentrated on the road and looked for the traffic police and drove as fast as he could.

'You bastard!' she screamed. 'You fat, fat bastard!'

She must tear the letter up. Lies. All lies. Tear it and burn it and throw the ashes into the wind. Liar.

'We are two different people, Yoshiro,' she said softly. 'We are someone else after all.' She was sure he could hear her because he, too, thought his father was guilty. 'I know,' he had said when she told him his father was a killer.

I know. Maybe his life had been one long pretence too. A struggle to prepare himself for Derek's daughter to come along and present him with the bill. What bill? It was all wrong. The wheel of fate was wrong. Jimmy Hedges had come clean in the end. He wrote that Katsumata had mourned Derek's death. He had taken the responsibility of it all upon himself.

It was all one big mistake. All her mother's plans. The lot. That frail, intolerant woman with nothing but hate for the wrong man. Katsumata had been her father's friend.

There were no buildings. They crossed a wide river and then there were no more rice fields. Behind her the mountains disappeared in a grey haze.

'Faster!' She hit the driver on his back. 'Faster.' He knew she was upset, but he had been concentrating on the road. Perhaps she had loved the fat *farang*? He drove some more and concentrated again and then her fist came down on his head and startled him. He lost control for a few seconds and the car swerved as he fought the steering-wheel. Close behind, a laden truck screeched on the road. It came to a halt touching the limousine. The truck driver climbed down from his cabin. He came towards them and he was shouting. He was going to hit the driver.

The driver looked at the trucker through his mirror. He was only a small man. He wouldn't dare. He opened his door, got out of the limousine and stretched. Anna jumped out.

'What the hell are you doing? Faster, I said. I did not tell you to stop.'

The chauffeur was talking to the truck driver. The menacing expressions on their faces changed into those of understanding. The two men clasped hands. Her driver came to her and gently took her hand and led her back. She sat down and she wanted to cry, but no tears came. She was not going to cry for her father. She was going to cry for the evil she had dealt Yoshiro. But she would make it all up to him. There was time.

There were two pages left to read.

You know the rest. I have often repeated it to your mother and you over the years. It is true. The guerrillas took me back to Burma and handed me to the British army at the Indian border. I told them what I told you later on. They did not know what to make of me. Was I a coward? They did not believe the story of the exchange, but in the end they decided to make me a hero and gave me a medal and sent me home.

I had thought I had forgiven myself for what I did to Derek. With time, the details of the past had sunk into oblivion. Only a little remained. I was forced to dig them all out again when I met you and your mother.

Life had just begun to settle for me. I was successful. In my way, I was happy. And then your mother contacted me out of the blue and forced me to talk of Bang Saray. The truth of what had happened there was screaming out inside me while I told her lies. Of how cruel Katsumata was. Of how Derek suffered. Of how he was murdered having just spent a night of humiliation inside a wooden crate. She was devastated, but brave.

I gave the performance of my life.

Talking about Bang Saray was torture. It still is now. I tried not to hate him then, as I was talking of his death, yet talking about it and lying about it shook me to the core. I might have begun losing my self-respect then. Perhaps I started letting myself go after that.

Do you remember our first meeting? You were very small, but I was afraid of you. Perhaps it was guilt. You made me nervous. You were a reincarnation of Derek Pritchard come to torment me from the other side.

Your mother made me tell her the story again and again and again. Not the slightest detail was too much for her. I told her things, mostly the truth, and that brought my time in this country back, but it did not bring Derek back. Not the Derek I knew.

The Derek Pritchard I had painted for your mother was mine, all mine. I could mould him any way I wanted. I could make him smile and talk and cry. The Derek I had created for you and your mother was no longer dangerous to me. I had full control over his dreams and his hopes and his words and deeds.

I omitted the humiliations he had dealt me, and Derek Pritchard became the good guy. I even got to like him in a way. Cambridge was forgotten, and the law student, and without hate I could forget what I had done to him. Without a reason there is no crime, and without a crime there is no punishment. One does not kill a friend. I thought it was all over.

I did get my revenge on Derek, though. Not by killing him. That was not enough. This may surprise you, but when I met you his investments had dwindled. He was going to come into some money the year he died, but something happened. I don't know what. I think it was all invested in some pre-war foreign bonds. Anyway, by the time your mother and you came into my life his inheritance was worthless.

So, my dear Anna, I began to subsidize Derek Pritchard's family. I got my own accountant to advise your mother on her husband's investments, but these were all my own. The money for your schooling and the renovations was always available, and your mother thought it was Derek's foresight.

That is how I got even with Derek. I had taken his family away from him by supporting it. To start with, it was revenge, and then I watched your mother grow old and you became a woman and revenge became compensation. I was paying for making you fatherless, but all the while I was getting closer to your mother and you. Oh yes, you were rude to me at times, but that was how one treats an uncle, not an enemy. I was fond of you. I was proud of your achievements. In my own way, I loved you. You had become the closest thing to a daughter.

Derek's family had become mine.

During the last few years, I was looking for ways to ease your mother's life. It is hard to give her anything, but I succeeded. It was hard enough, I assure you, to get her to spend what I was paying her.

We are going into the future now. When my time comes, I hope you do not judge me too harshly. I have mellowed. I did not have to tell you all this, but I am a human being, and being human I made errors. Where I am going they make you pay for murder. Never fear.

Do not tell your mother all this, Anna. Do not ruin what is left. Let her go and face whatever there is on the other side in peace. If we do meet again over there, I shall tell her myself. I do not think we shall, however.

So don't tell her about this letter if you ever receive it. Derek was a special man to her. So am I, or should I say so was I? Don't destroy her innocence, Anna. Don't destroy her love, her memories or her hopes.

Just destroy this letter.

That is all. I said I thought I had forgiven myself for killing Derek, but on the road down here I found I had not. I cannot plead insanity. I cannot ask you to forget. I shall not ask you to forgive.

I am asking you to understand.

I love you both and have done for years, Jimmy.

The car was labouring. It was crawling along Nana Road. It was lunchtime. The driver said they were coming close. Ten minutes more. Fifteen, maybe. She would think about it. She had time. She would burn the letter and never think of it again because it was not important. What was important was her own life and her own plans and decisions. But first she must call Yoshiro. She would speak to him. He was the real victim of it all.

It was early still. She was bound to get him at the office. Japan was two hours ahead. She could speak to him, apologize to him, go to him if he only asked. Look into his sad eyes and hug him like she would a baby.

He had been wronged, but she would wipe it all clean. He would never have to plead with her again. She would scrub his house for him and wash his shirts and polish his shoes. He was in the office right now. He was thinking of her, surely. And when she called he would smile. His face would light up like a million lanterns and his white teeth would show. 'The wheel of fortune is smiling on us again,' he would say.

Would she spend the rest of her life apologizing? No. He would not ask her to do that. 'I am sorry, Yoshiro,' she sobbed. 'I shall make it up to you.' Had she ever called him 'darling'? Had she used any term of endearment? She felt old, but not tired.

Any minute now, she would be there. The porter and the bellboy would smile. The telephone operator would tell her to wait a few minutes and then she would talk to him. She would tell him all was well.

His father was not a killer.

Her father was not his victim.

They were two other people all the while.

Had been, from the start. He would understand that. It was his idea.

He had said it first.

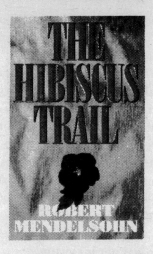

The Hibiscus Trail

The Hibiscus Trail takes you on a journey that spans the globe. It follows the lives of three men and women interwoven by chance. Their destiny forms a gripping story of adventure, love and betrayal that builds to an unexpected climax.

"At long last an exciting thriller complete with unpredictable relationships among fascinating characters."
Patricia Miller, reviewer, Bestseller Magazine

"It is an utterly compulsive read from the very first sentence."
Jan Shure, Impressions

"This is Mendelsohn at his sweaty, steamy best."
Val Hennessy, reviewer, National Press

Paperback   ISBN 1 85375 110 3   £4.99
Hardback   ISBN 1 85375 111 1   £12.95

The Red Pagoda

Take a disaffected US Air pilot in search of an identity, a French-Vietnamese beauty in thrall to the Vietcong, the undeviating passion of a guerilla/poet, and the tireless sleuthing of an ex-Hong Kong policeman ... and you have some of the ingredients of this tautly written love story within a love story in which ideology is repeatedly over-turned by deeper human drives.

"It is about time a novel of this quality came out. It is a sophisticated vision of the other Vietnam ... beneath a fast-moving mystery ... he writes about a handful of characters forever changed ... touched by inevitable tenderness, it celebrates the stubborn spirit of a beautiful and abused land ... His best story to date."

Toronto Sun

Paperback   ISBN 1 85375 094 8   £4.99
Hardback   ISBN 1 85375 069 7   £12.95

Footsteps on a Drum

A British officer deserts the army for love, and his travels away from judgement take him to central America and the Caribbean. Many years later, he returns to England in his quest for a quiet life. This is a tale as moral and fatalistic as any by Graham Greene. It is full of fast action, rich characterisation and passion. These and the pungent themes that run through it — seduction, sedition, slavery and voodoo — give the book a cinematic quality which is wonderfully disturbing.

Published in hardback ISBN 1 85375 028 X   £12.95